KU-778-271

Home to Big Stone Gap

Adriana Trigiani

W F HOWES LTD

This large print edition published in 2006 by
W F Howes Ltd
Unit 4, Rearsby Business Park, Gaddesby Lane,
Rearsby, Leicester LE7 4YH

1 3 5 7 9 10 8 6 4 2

First published in the United Kingdom in 2006
by Simon & Schuster UK Ltd

A CIP catalogue record for this book is available
from the British Library

ISBN 1 84505 830 5

Typeset by Palimpsest Book Production Limited,
Grangemouth, Stirlingshire
Printed and bound in Great Britain
by Antony Rowe Ltd, Chippenham, Wilts.

In memory of Gregory D. Cantrell

CONTENTS

CHAPTER 1

CRACKER'S NECK HOLLER

1998

As the wind blows through our bedroom window, it sounds like a whistling teakettle. As I wake, for a split second, I forget where I am. As soon as I see our suitcases piled next to the closet door, in the exact place where we dropped them, I remember. Etta's wedding, though it was just one week ago, already seems like a faraway dream.

When we drove up the road last night, our home in Cracker's Neck Holler looked like a castle in the mist. The first days of autumn always bring the cold fog, which makes every twist and turn on these mountain roads treacherous. Etta used to call the September fog the Murky Murk. She told me, 'I don't like it when I can't see the mountains, Mama.'

This morning they're in plain view again. Since we've been gone, the mossy field out back has turned to brown velvet, and the woods beyond have a silver patina from the first frost. I take a deep breath.

1

In a way, it's good to be home, where everything is in its place. The same beam of sunlight that comes over the mountain at dawn splits our house in two, one half drenched in brightness and the other in dark shadow. Shoo the Cat sleeps on the same embroidered pillow on the old rocker, as he has every night since he came to stay. Small, familiar comforts matter when everything is changing.

I pull on my robe. Before I leave the room, I tuck the quilt around my husband. He's not waking up anytime soon; his breath is rhythmic and deep. I make my way through the stone house, and it feels so empty – as it did before there were children. I don't know if there is a sound lonelier than the silence of everybody gone.

The first thing I do is measure the coffee into the old two-part pot Papa gave me from a shop in Schilpario. I put the pot on the stove, and blue gas flames shoot up when I turn the dial. It's chilly, so I take a long, thin match from the box on the mantel and light the fire in the hearth. One of the things I love best about my husband is that he never leaves a fireplace barren. No matter what time of year, there's a crisscross of dry logs on a bed of kindling and a neat newspaper bundle good to go. The paper crackles, and soon the logs catch and the flames leap up like laughter from a school yard.

There's a note on the fridge from my friend Iva Lou: *Welcome home. How was it? Call me.* When I look inside, she's stocked us for breakfast: a few of Faye Pobst's rolls (I can tell by the shape of the tinfoil package), a jar of fresh jam, a crock of country butter, and a glass carafe of fresh cream, no doubt from her aunt's farm down in Rose Hill. What would I do without Iva Lou? I really don't like to think about it, but I do; in fact, I've been obsessed with loss lately. The past year brought my happy circus to an abrupt close – Spec died, Pearl moved to Boston, and I lost Etta to her new life in Italy. I don't like change. I said that so much, Jack Mac finally said, 'Get used to it.' Doesn't make it one bit easier, though, not one bit.

There's a deep stack of mail waiting for me on the table. Bills. Flyers. A letter from Saint Mary's College requesting alumnae donations. An envelope for Jack from the United Mine Workers of America – another cut in benefits, no doubt. A puffy envelope from the home shopping channel containing a pair of earrings I bought for Fleeta's birthday on back-order (took long enough). Underneath is a postcard from Schilpario, Italy, the town we'd just left a day ago. I flip it over quickly and read:

Dear Ave Maria,
By the time you get this, Etta will be married, you'll be home, and I'll be back in New York. This is a reminder. Start living your life for YOU. Got it? Love, Theodore.

I put the postcard from my best pal under a magnet on the door of the fridge. I'll take any free advice I can get. Noticing the clutter on the door – all reminders of my daughter and her senior year of high school – I begin to take things down. Etta's high school graduation schedule from last June is taped to a ribbon of photos she took in a booth at the Fort Henry Mall. She looks like a girl in the pictures. Her coppery hair in long braids makes her seem even younger. She *is* young, too young to be married, and too young to be so far from home. I close my eyes. Is it ever really possible for a mother to let go?

The coffee churns up into the cap of the pot, signaling it's ready to be poured. I grab an oven mitt off its hook and pour the coffee into the mug. The delicious scent of a hickory fire and fresh-roasted coffee is the perfect welcome home.

I kick the screen door open and go out on the porch to watch the sun take its place in the sky over Big Stone Gap. Autumn is my favorite time of year; it seems to say 'Let go' with every leaf that turns and falls to the ground and every dingy cloud that rolls by overhead. Let go. (So hard to do when your nature tells you to hang on.)

At the edge of the woods, a spindly dead branch high in a treetop crackles under the weight of a blackbird, which flies off into the charcoal sky until it's a speck in the distance. I have to remind Jack that the property line needs some attention. He's always so busy fixing other people's houses

4

that our needs are last on the list. The wild raspberry bushes have taken over the far side of the field, a tangled mess of wires and vines. Pruning, composting, raking – all those chores will occupy us until the winter comes.

I hear more snapping coming from the woods, so I squint at the treetops, expecting more blackbirds, but there is no movement. The sound seems to be coming from the ground. I lean forward as I sit and study the woods. I hear more crackling. What is it? I wonder. Then something strange happens: I have a moment of fear. I know there's nothing to be afraid of – the sun is up, Jack is inside, and there's a working phone in the kitchen – but for some reason, I shudder.

As I stand to go back into the house, I see a figure in the woods. It looks like a man. A young man. With curly brown hair. I can see that much from my place on the porch, but not much else – his face is obscured behind the thick branches. I raise my hand to wave to him, and open my mouth to shout to him, but as soon as I do, he is gone. I close my eyes and listen for more footsteps. There is nothing but silence.

'What are you doing out here?' Jack says from the door. 'It's cold. Come inside.'

I follow him into the house. Once we're in the kitchen, I throw my arms around him. 'Honey, I saw something. Someone.'

'Where?'

'In the woods.'

'When?'

'Right now. This second. He was walking along the property line. I saw him.'

'Well, it's hunting season.'

'He wasn't a hunter.'

'Maybe he's hiking.'

'No.'

'What, then?'

'It was Joe.'

'Joe?' Jack Mac is confused – so confused, he sits. 'Our Joe?'

I nod.

'Jesus, Ave Maria. You know that's impossible.'

'I know.' My eyes fill with tears. 'But I think I'd know my son when I see him.'

Without hesitating, Jack takes his work jacket off the hook, pulls it on, and goes outside. I watch him as he walks across the field and into the woods. He surveys our property line, looking for the young man. Sometimes he takes a few steps into the woods and disappears. I don't know why, but I'm relieved each time he re-emerges. I stand at the window waiting as he checks the side yard and his wood shop. I half expect him to return with someone. With Joe. I hear the bang of the screen door.

'There's no one there. It was a long trip. You're tired. You're imagining things. Really.' Jack takes off his jacket. 'I didn't see any footprints in the mud. Nothing.'

'I'm not making it up.'

6

Jack sits and pulls me onto his lap. 'What did he look like?'

'He wasn't four years old, like when he died, but older. Like twenty.'

'You know that can't be.'

'I know.' I stand up. I go to the stove and pour a cup of coffee into a mug and hand it to him. I pull the rolls from the tinfoil and put them on a baking sheet. I slide them into the oven to warm them.

'It was someone else,' Jack says practically as he sorts the mail.

'Or it wasn't anybody. My eyes played a trick on me. I hadn't even had my coffee, and I'm half asleep here in my big fat empty nest. I miss Etta, and that always makes me miss Joe.' I pull the rolls from the oven and peel back the tinfoil.

'You're not going to lose it on me, are you?'

'I'm not crazy.'

'Good.' Jack Mac smiles at me. 'I can handle just about anything but a crazy woman.' He tosses the junk mail into the fire.

I slather the rolls with butter and jam. Jack studies a bill from the mail, so I feed him the roll. He takes a bite; I turn to get a plate. Jack grabs my hand and licks the jam off my finger. I look into his eyes and see the exact color of the morning sky. He looks at me in that way he never looks at anyone else. With all we've been through, that look still delights me. 'What are you doing?' I ask him, but after nineteen years of marriage, I have a pretty good idea.

He doesn't answer; instead, he kisses my neck and loosens the belt on my robe, which conveniently drops to the floor – I say 'conveniently' because I'm still holding the roll, which I lob into the sink like a fly ball. As Jack kisses me, my mind begins to race, never a good idea when you're making love – the whole point is to stay in the moment – but I'm in my memory bank, trying to recall if we've ever made love in the kitchen. Pale blue ribbons of smoke are curling up from plastic windows on the junk mail; I watch until flames engulf the envelopes entirely and turn them to black flakes that float up the flue. I sit on the kitchen table and pull my husband close. The very idea of this makes me feel like laughing, but I don't. I feel his heart racing with mine, and I think, This is what's good about being married – knowing everything about someone and yet still being surprised before breakfast.

I hold Jack's face, then I slide my hands down his neck and outline his broad shoulders, down his arms, muscular from all that construction work. He is drenched in sweat, so I pull him away from the fire. He smiles and takes in deep gulps of air. I listen to his heart, which beats loud and clear and true and, in an instant, too fast.

'I have to sit,' Jack whispers. I help him to the rocker by the hearth. He sits down and leans back in it, closing his eyes.

'Are you okay?' I go to the sink and run a glass of water and take it to him.

'I'm old.'

'No, you're not. If you're old then I'm old, and I'm not old.'

'Dream on.' He smiles.

I put my head to his chest. 'Wait here,' I tell him.

I go to the hall closet and reach up to the high shelf and pull down Spec's emergency kit from the Rescue Squad. Leola, Spec's widow, gave it to me when he died. I've never opened it. Every time I go into the closet, it glares at me from the shelf, hand-painted by Spec in Day-Glo prison orange. I even remember the day he painted it. I was in his office, and he sat at his desk, which was covered in newspaper, and painted the tin box with a tiny brush like it was a Monet. I take it into the kitchen.

Jack is standing by the sink. 'What are you doing?'

'Sit down. I'm going to take your blood pressure.'

Jack sits down in the chair. I open Spec's emergency kit reverently. He always took such good care of the Rescue Squad equipment – the ambulance always gleamed, the sheets for the stretcher were always bleached a pristine white, his own vest was always pressed; he was very particular. The blood pressure gauge and cuff are nestled neatly among boxes of bandages, iodine, small bottles of tinctures, and tins of salves. I lift it out.

'Give me your arm,' I say. I strap the band around

9

his arm. I pump until the numbers spin around like a betting wheel: 170/110. 'Honey, you need to go to the doctor.' I loosen the band and try not to panic.

'What for?'

'You're off the charts.'

'I feel fine.' He pulls me close. 'You're so good you almost killed me.'

'Not funny. How's your vision? Blurry?'

'It's normal,' Jack promises.

'I knew something was different. It sounds like an arrhythmia.' I put my ear to his chest again. My days on the Rescue Squad taught me a few things – Spec and I dealt with plenty of heart patients – and numbers like Jack's are a pretty good sign that something is very wrong.

'Yoo-hoo!' Iva Lou calls from the front door.

'Just a second,' I holler back. I grab my robe and hand Jack his clothes. Jack makes a beeline for the downstairs bedroom and closes the door behind him. I sit down at the breakfast table. 'Come on in!'

Iva Lou comes into the kitchen and puts her navy blue patent-leather purse down on the bench. She wears a navy blue suit with a slim skirt and peplum jacket, nipped at the waist by a matching belt with ruby-red grommets. Her high-heeled pumps are navy-and-white striped with flat red patent-leather bows. Her blond hair is blown straight to her shoulders. If you didn't know Iva Lou by her voice, you'd know her by her perfume.

It's not just one perfume either. It's a grab bag – always strong but never too loud. Today she smells like vanilla and peaches with a whoosh of amber.

'Thank you for the breakfast treats.' I give her a kiss. 'You look so pretty. So professional.'

'I hope so. I have a meeting up in Wise at the li-burry. And then I'm having lunch at Bonterra's with the girls.' Iva Lou surveys the empty kitchen table. The mail and newspapers are on the floor, exactly where they went when I cleared the table. 'From the looks of things round here, there's been a rockin' robin in the empty nest.'

I'm all set to deny it, but I've been friends with Iva Lou too long. 'How can you tell?' I say softly as I pick the mail up off the floor.

'Nobody ever wastes one of Faye's rolls.' She points to the sink. 'You must've had a sweeter offer.' Iva Lou winks.

'It's like you're a psychic or something.'

'Honey-o, I'm what you call a Detective for Love. Some people have a nose for business, others for crafts and sewing, and then there's me – I specialize in the Call of the Wild.'

Jack comes out of the downstairs bedroom, waving to Iva Lou before he goes up the stairs.

'Good to have ya back,' she says gaily, then she turns to me. 'We got big news around here. You won't believe it. Fleeta and Otto are getting murried.'

'You're kidding. She won't even acknowledge that she's dating him.'

11

'Let me tell you something about your friend Fleeta. Deep down, she's a true romantic. All that crust on her is an act.'

'Whatever you say.' I think Iva Lou's observation is nuts, but I'm not about to argue. Fleeta Mullins is far from romantic. One time we went to the mall in Kingsport, and a man and woman were singing a duet with each other on 'Play Our Organ Day' at Witt's Instruments, and Fleeta turned in the opposite direction and walked the long way around the mall to avoid them. 'I hate PDAs,' she told me at the time.

I look at Iva Lou. 'Why would they get married?'

'I asked her that.' Iva Lou cuts one of Faye's rolls in half and spoons some jam onto it. She stands over the sink, holding the roll away from her suit. She leans forward and takes a bite. 'She said it was for the insurance.'

'She *has* insurance.'

'Right, but he doesn't. Fleeta is a-feared of Medicare not holding up to cover Otto's various conditions, and she don't want to get caught holding the bag if Otto gets sick.'

'So it's sort of an act of charity on Fleeta's part.'

'A little. But there's also the fear of God.'

'Fleeta thinks churchgoers are a bunch of hypocrites. Believe me, God is more afraid of Fleeta than the other way around.'

'Not for nothin', Preacher and Mrs Mutter made a stop over there one day when they was collecting cans for the food bank. And they got to talking.

12

Fleeta ain't been in church since she was a girl, and Otto never went at all. Evidently, the singing convention and revivals don't count as church-going. Who knew? Anyhow, as they was loading cans into the truck, some sort of conversion took place, and Preacher Mutter convinced them that they should honor their love with a proper cere-mony, set a decent example for their children, and simultaneously become members of the United Methodist Church.'

'So Fleeta had an epiphany.'

'Truth be told, she was humiliated. She couldn't believe a preacher would actually have the guts to say anything to her about her private life. For the record, Otto's the one who's afraid of hell.'

'Is he gonna be baptized?'

'Oh yeah. I'm buying front-row seats to that shindig. Wait till you see old Otto dunked in the Powell River like an old tire. That right there is reason number one I leave my donated cans on the porch when the Methodists come collection'. I don't need to be saved, I have no interest in it. Here's a tip for you: never get into a conversation with a preacher on a weekday. It starts out as idle chitchat, then next thing you know, they got you volunteering to do God knows what and agreeing to things you're dead set against.'

'When's the wedding?'

'Soon. You're in charge of the decorations, and I'm doing the food.'

'What is Fleeta doing?'

Iva Lou dabs the last bit of jam from the corner of her mouth with a napkin. 'She's gonna show up.'

When Jack and I head up to the hospital later in the day, the road to Norton is slick in spots from the frost. Jack drives as though it's the middle of summer, taking the truck around the curves like he's Dale Earnhardt. I hold on to the handle over the window. 'Slow down, would you, please? I want to live.'

'I don't have time for this.'

'You have to make the time. It's your health.' What is it with men, anyway? Why do they hate going to the doctor? As a pharmacist, I've seen it all – I even knew a wife who mashed up pills and put them in a pie to get her husband to take his meds. When a husband comes to the Mutual's to pick up a prescription, he carries the sack out of the store like he's holding a dead rat. I don't get it.

'I don't need a lecture.'

'I'm not lecturing.'

'The last thing I need is to take a morning off to run up to Saint Mary's. The trip to Italy really messed me up. We were gone for three weeks, and I'm backed up through the new year now.'

'That's enough, Jack. It's not like I posted your name on the online Baptist prayer wheel. It's a checkup. That's all. Let's not argue. It's not good for you to get upset.'

'Why? Because I'll have a heart attack?'

'Now you're just sniping. Knock it off,' I tell him.

We pull into the parking lot at Saint Mary's Hospital in Norton. I reach over and pat my husband on the leg and then climb out of the cab. 'Well, come on,' I tell him. He sits staring straight ahead. 'We'll be late,' I say. He doesn't move, so I climb back into the cab. 'Please. They squeezed you in. I begged. Let's go.' I look at my husband's profile; it's every bit as strong as the day I married him. The set of his jaw is still like stone, his nose as regal and straight. Most of the light brown hair is gone, but he's not one bit less handsome without it. Sometimes I feel I know everything about him, and other times I think I'll never crack him. I put my hand on his face. When I do, he breaks his faraway stare and looks at me. When I look into his eyes, I know. 'You're scared.'

'Wouldn't you be?'

'I guess I would,' I answer. 'You know, Jack, Theodore always says, when we're afraid and questioning everything, that deep down we know the truth. We just don't want to face our feelings sometimes. What does your gut tell you? What do you know?'

Jack exhales and looks away. 'I think there's something wrong with me.'

It's as if I've been stabbed. I try not to show any panic. 'What?' I hear the squeak in my voice and cough to try and hide it.

15

Jack looks at me. 'I haven't felt right in a while.'

'How long?'

'A few months. I get foggy in the afternoon, and I don't have the energy I used to. Sometimes I can't catch my breath. Now, part of that is being fifty-four, and part of it isn't right.'

'Let's go in and see Dr Stemple. She'll get to the bottom of things. Okay?' I give him a quick kiss. We climb out of the truck, and I take his hand as we go up the steps into the hospital.

We sign in at the desk and take a seat outside the glass partition and wait. I put my arm around my husband. We don't talk. What is there to say?

I must be the worst wife in the world. He hasn't felt right for several months, and I didn't even notice. Of course, there were other things on my mind. My daughter decided to drop college and get married in a foreign country, for starters. The truth is, I wouldn't have noticed anything about Jack unless he keeled over in front of me. I was wrapped up in my own feelings and worries about our daughter's future. I promise myself that from this moment forward, I will stay alert to his needs. He deserves that.

The nurse calls his name.

'You want me to come?' I ask him. He shrugs, so I follow him into the examining room, a sunny, small space painted pale pink. 'This is the tough-guy room,' I joke.

'I'm not feeling very tough,' Jack says as he goes behind the changing screen to undress. He throws his sweater over the top. Instinctively, I pull it down, shake it out, and fold it neatly over my arm.

Dr Stemple pushes the door open. 'How are we today?' Jack emerges from behind the screen. Dr Stemple extends her hand to him. 'You look pretty good.'

'You think?'

I take a seat on the chair near the door and watch as Jack is examined and answers the doctor's questions like Gary Cooper in *High Noon*: he yups and nopes and occasionally gives a silent shrug. When she asks about dizziness and indigestion and shooting pains down his arms, Jack says nope each time with conviction. I'm relieved. Maybe it's not Jack's heart. Maybe it's some small problem, easily fixed.

'I'm going to send you over to Kingsport for a stress test,' she tells him. She tears a sheet off her clipboard and hands it to Jack. 'You check out fine, except that blood pressure. It's on the high side.'

'Too high?' I chirp.

'I don't like it,' she says simply. 'I want them to do a tissue sample on your lungs too.'

'Why?' Jack's voice breaks.

'You worked in the mines for almost thirty years, Jack. It's important to stay on top of any changes in your lungs. You have some congestion.' She makes a note on her clipboard. 'Look, it could be nothing. You just took a transatlantic flight – that's a regular germ bath. Don't worry.' She pats his hand and smiles at me. 'I'm glad you came to see me,' she says as she leaves the room.

I look at my husband. 'See, it's good news.'

'Now I gotta go get poked and prodded in Kingsport. Great.'

CHAPTER 2

ROARING BRANCH

I f you didn't know it was September by watching the mountains fade from the bright, saturated tones of a Technicolor movie to the soft gray shades of a black-and-white one, you'd know it for sure as you drove through town. It's football season, and the signs are everywhere. Literally. Long runners of white butcher paper (donated by Bob's Market out in the southern section of town) have been hand-painted by the cheerleaders with aphorisms to inspire the Powell Valley Vikings to victory. My favorite: A LOSER IS JUST A WINNER WHO'S HAD A BAD DAY.

Fleeta, getting a jump on holiday sales ('Honey, we can't fool around. We gots to compete with the Wal-Mart for tradin', and they's playin' for keeps'), has decorated the Pharmacy windows for Halloween. She has dressed two skeletons as a bride and groom, inspired, I'm sure, by her subconscious disdain for traditional unions. In the foreground of the window she placed a small fan that blows the long white ribbons on the bouquet of the bride like kite strings; the bony hand rattles a bit from the breeze. Over the happy

19

couple is a sign in Old English script and glitter: GHOUL LOVE.

'I'm back!' I call out. The first thing I notice is that Fleeta moved the perfume carousel to the front of the store, so a barrage of sweet lavender, crisp cedar, and wild freesia greets me as I step inside.

Fleeta, in electric blue leggings and a red-and-white Powell Valley band booster jacket, appears in the office door with an unlit cigarette dangling from her hot-pink lips. 'It's about time you showed your face. How was the trip?'

'Etta was beautiful.' I fish through my purse for pictures and give them to Fleeta.

'Well, we knew that.' Fleeta flips through the photos like playing cards. She holds up a picture of Etta and whistles low. 'Now, is that a MacChesney or what?'

'Oh, she's a MacChesney all right. Hey, I'm very excited about your own news. You went and got *fiancéd* while I was gone.'

'We live in perilous times.' Fleeta shrugs. 'It had to be done.'

'You're not having your bunions removed, you're getting married. It's a joyful thing. Usually.'

'Otto is around all the time anyhow, we might as well make it legal.'

'Did you turn Methodist?'

'Just Otto.'

'Are you sure you want to get married?'

'Why don't you just congratulate me and git it over with?' Fleeta extends her right hand and new

20

engagement ring toward me. It's a simple round stone set in pink gold.

'Congratulations,' I say with more concern than jubilation.

'You sound like I feel.' Fleeta sits down on a packing crate. 'Law me. I never thought I'd git murried again. And here I am, right back in it to win it. I'm up to my left knee in a bear trap. Can't run. Can't hide. You know, Portly and I were young loves – and once you had that, you sort of sour on anything else.'

'You had a fine husband. And he was a good father.'

'Yes, he was. When he died, I didn't fit nowheres. I had been in a couple since I could remember. 'There ain't no place in the world for a widder woman,' my mama used to say, and boy, she was right. People thought I was pitiful. I hated that. Plus, I got lonely, I'll be honest with ye. I missed the companionship of a man. Otto was always hangin' around, and it just sort of became natural – I started missin' him when he'd go, and it turns out he got attached to me too. At first I thought it was crazy – and then I thought, What the hell, what good is life when you're alone? It weren't the same, going over to Kingsport for the wrestling matches all by myself. Bowling over at Shug's got to be sad too. One ball. One lane. One scorecard. I got sick of my own company.'

'You know what you need. That's good.' I aim for upbeat.

'Uh-huh. I learnt a lot, being on the market at my age. Most men want a younger wife. And let's face it, I am many things, but I ain't young. What men is left at my age would make you weep. They're like used cars. They look good on the lot, and you get 'em home and they fall apart. Piece by piece. What ain't rusted out on 'em is rotted out. Otto was about the sturdiest of the bunch. So I settled, I guess.'

'Otto is a good man; I don't think that's settling.'

'The best part is, he's older than me.' Fleeta takes a drag off her unlit cigarette and lifts her right eyebrow. 'I get to be the younger woman. Trust me – nobody wants to make love to a grandmaw, exceptin' maybe a great-grandpaw.' She chuckles. 'You know men. No matter how old they is, they like 'em younger.'

The bells on the front door jingle, and another sure sign of autumn walks through the door. Nellie Goodloe wears a black sweater with rows of orange felt jack-o'-lanterns embroidered across it. The collar is gold-sequined, and the buttons are small plastic ghosts with black eyes. Her hair, arranged in an updo of lacquered red curls, really brings out the orange of the pumpkins.

'That's some sweater.' Fleeta looks Nellie up and down, taking in her ensemble. 'Ain't it early for Halloween?'

Nellie smoothes down the placket of the sweater neatly. 'I don't get a lot of wear out of it if I wait for the actual day.'

'That's the problem with holiday sweaters. Short shelf life.' Fleeta goes to the café kitchen. 'I'm gonna get lunch prepped. Here.' She gives Nellie the wedding pictures. 'Feast your eyes on these.'

Nellie looks through the pictures, oohing and aahing almost too much, which makes me wonder why she's here. But Nellie's a cut-to-the-chase girl, so I needn't have worried.

'Ave Maria, the Music Study Club has a favor to ask of you.' Nellie smiles. 'We'd love to get you back into the theater. The officers took a vote, and we'd like you to direct the winter musical.'

'That's sweet of you to think of me, but—'

'I'll be honest. You weren't the first choice. Our director, Boyd Blondell from the drama department up at the college, fell out. He has to go north to help his mother with her hip replacement next month, so he's unavailable.'

'Well, it's still sweet,' I say wryly. 'But I'm really woefully out of practice when it comes to the theater.' It's true. It's been years since I directed the Outdoor Drama.

'Oh, it'll come right back to you. We've practically cast the show already.'

'Really.' This is what I was afraid of. 'What's the show?'

'*The Sound of Music*. We thought if there was a way for you to work tap into the show, that would be nice.'

'Tap dancing?'

'Yes, Miss Angie says she'll provide the manpower from her Tops in Taps school.'

Under normal circumstances, I would take a pass on this offer. But, looking ahead, I may wish I had something to do on long winter evenings when Jack's working late. 'I'll do it.'

Nellie claps her hands together. 'Great! Rehearsals begin November first.'

As Fleeta writes the lunch specials on the blackboard propped in the entryway (soup beans and com bread, collard greens, and stewed apples), I check the pharmacy desk, where Eddie Carleton has left a few notes for me. Eddie's a good guy; I can always count on him to cover for me if I'm away. I check my e-mails and open one from Etta immediately.

> *Dear Ma, I hope you had a good flight home. Stefano and I love Rimini. It's too cold for the beach, but we walk it anyway. The Adriatic Sea reminds me of our trips to the ocean in North Carolina. I miss you both. xoxoxo Etta (Stefano says hi)*

I write back to her, and though each word I type makes me feel worse, I send a happy message. After all, that's a mother's job, to be cheerful.

'Ave, what say you?' Otto holds out his arms and walks over to my counter. He already looks the part of groom. His white hair is neatly combed, his khaki work pants are pressed, and he smells like Aqua

Velva. Fleeta is particular about grooming. I climb down from the counter and give him a hug. His son, Worley, in denim coveralls, stands back.

'I can't believe you're getting married, Otto!'

'Plus I found the Lord.'

'I heard. It's almost too much.'

Before Otto can speak, Worley says, 'It is indeed.' Worley removes his baseball cap and heads for the café.

'Worley's got an attitude. Thinks it's crazy for me to get murried. But I want to.'

'He'll come around.'

Fleeta waves a spoon. 'Otto, you need to get over here. I only got so many soup beans and so much corn bread.'

'See there? Bossing me around already.' Otto smiles.

FLEETA'S SOUP BEANS AND CORN BREAD

Serves 2 hungry mountain men or 4 regular people

SOUP BEANS
1 pound pinto or mixed beans
⅓ cup corn oil
Salt

Soak beans in water overnight. Wash beans and bring to a boil in a fresh pot of water, stirring occasionally. Season with corn oil.

Salt to taste. Lower heat; add more water if necessary. Cook slowly until beans are done and soup is thick.

CORN BREAD
2 cups self-rising cornmeal
1¼ to 1½ cup buttermilk
1 egg

Preheat oven to 425 degrees. Grease a heavy 8- to 10-inch skillet or 8-by-8-inch baking pan. Mix all ingredients and pour into skillet or pan.
Bake for 25 to 30 minutes, or until golden-brown.

Over the years, more and more of my working day is spent in the Jeep, making deliveries. When I started working in the Pharmacy, I had two or three drop-offs a day. Now that folks are older and less mobile, there are well over ten deliveries each day. We have to compete with the big chains, and they have no problem driving pills forty miles to make a sale. It's not possible for me to drive those distances and still fill prescriptions in the Pharmacy, so I limit my deliveries to town and the hollers just above Big Stone Gap.

I don't know if the changes in these hills come from the outside world pushing through, or just the aging process, but we've become a bedroom community. Most of the stores on Main Street have closed, though we still have the Tri-State Carpet Rug & Books, Ball's TV & Record Shop, Sue's Hallmark, and Horton's Florists. Seems most of the businesses that remain cater to getting married or buried. Or to history. The Southwest Virginia Museum gets lots of visitors, so it spawned tours at local points of interest like the John Fox, Jr., house. Over at the Outdoor Drama, the Tolliver House is open to the public year-round. Besides tours of the theater, there's a school memorabilia room spearheaded by Garnett Gilliam, and a gift shop that sells a collection of antique quilts, fine art, and sundries – a real plus for any tourists who come through.

As I drive through Cracker's Neck Holler at twilight and pass the school, I remember picking Etta up from band practice on nights like this. I'd swing by after work, and there she'd be on the school steps, waiting for me. She'd climb in and start with the news of the day. That was our time, and I remember wishing the ride up the mountain would never end.

Tonight the Murky Murk has lifted; our house is bathed in the last pale orange beams of daylight, before the sun disappears behind the mountain. Jack beat me home. The first thing he does, before he looks at the mail, is light the fire in the hearth. I can see the tufts of smoke from the chimney.

There is an unfamiliar truck parked outside the

house, as well as that of Jack's partner, Mousey. I wasn't expecting company, but it's not unusual for Jack to have the guys in for a beer after work. I climb the steps with a foil package of corn bread from Fleeta, hoping there's enough if Jack invites his guests to stay for supper. I have mastered many dishes over the years, but I can't top Fleeta's corn bread, so I don't even try (the secret is in the buttermilk and the iron skillet she inherited from her mamaw). I hear voices as I push the screen door open and enter the house.

My husband stands next to the mantel listening carefully to a man in a suit, a man I've never seen before. He's in his mid-thirties and doesn't look like he's from around here. His pin-striped suit is fine wool, and his tie, bright blue silk, seems expensive.

'Ave Maria.' My husband looks up and smiles. 'I'd like you to meet Tyler Hutchinson from Pittsburgh.'

I extend my hand to the young man. 'Good to meet you.'

'And you too, Mrs MacChesney.' Tyler smiles. His high forehead and ears tell me that he's bright, and the strong jawline says he's persistent, if not stubborn. The tilt of his mouth, with deep indentations on either side, tells me he's not to be trusted. He's one of those men with a big head and tiny teeth, which means he's a man with big ideas and a matching ego. I wish Jack would have taken my beloved Ancient Art of

28

Chinese Face-Reading seriously, but alas, it's one arena that I could never get my husband interested in.

'What brings you to Cracker's Neck?' I ask him.

'Your husband.'

'Good reason.' I stand beside Jack and put my arm around his shoulders.

'His years of service to Westmoreland Coal Company are legendary.'

'Thirty years of dedication,' I boast, sounding like a proud Nancy Reagan standin' by her man. Jack looks at me out of the corner of his eye like I'm insane.

'The mining business has changed quite a bit since Jack was in,' Tyler begins. 'I'm here to try and convince him to join us in a new way of doing things.'

'Mountaintop removal,' Mousey chimes in.

'We know all about that,' I tell Tyler.

'We're aware that folks aren't too thrilled with it. But we've come up with ways to reclaim the mountainside after we've mined.'

'It's hard to reclaim a mountain when it's gone,' I say pleasantly. I'm sure my husband is only being polite by entertaining this gentleman in our home. We don't believe in mountaintop removal – in fact, the stories out of eastern Kentucky are frightening. Instead of using traditional techniques where miners go into the earth to extract coal, now they mine from the outside in. The Blue Ridge Mountains are scarred, at the least, and at the worst, rerouting the terrain causes dangerous mudslides and pollution to streams and lakes. The floods caused by this style of butchering have destroyed communities. The plant life lost is unforgivable. There's more involved in reclamation than throwing seeds around to create ground cover.

'We're working on that. We care about the environment too. We're trying to figure out ways to provide jobs and respect the land at the same time,' Tyler says.

'Okay.' I look at my husband.

'Mr MacChesney . . .' Tyler rises and extends his hand. 'I hope you'll consider our offer to you.'

'I will.' Jack smiles and walks Tyler to the door. 'Thank you for stopping by.'

The screen door is barely shut when I turn to Mousey. 'Now they go door-to-door like the Mormons.'

'Honey, don't start.' Jack gives me a look.

'The last thing these mountains need is some opportunist coal company coming in and ruining the land. Do they think we're idiots? Reclamation? How? It's a joke.'

'Well, y'all, I'm gonna shove off.' Mousey stands and puts on his baseball cap.

'See there, Ave, you're scaring Mousey.'

'No, no, I ain't skeered. I got one just like her at home.'

'Give Nancy my best.'

'Yes, ma'am.' Mousey nods at Jack and goes.

'You're tough. You cleared the room,' my husband says as he goes to the kitchen.

I follow him. 'I thought I was polite.'

'This fellow has some new ways of going about it that don't sound so bad.' Jack lifts the lid off the pot of beef stew and stirs. 'I think it's important to consider all our options.'

'You don't want to work with this guy, do you?'

'Tyler's a graduate of Virginia Tech. He comes from a family of coal miners in Pennsylvania. I liked him.'

'Great. Play cards with him, but you don't have to work with him.'

'Ave, don't start.'

'Start what? Sometimes you're gullible. I'm trying to protect you.'

'I can take care of myself.'

I set the table in silence. Jack hands me the salad to toss. 'At my age, I have to think seriously when a young man comes to the door and offers me a job. It doesn't happen every day.'

'You have a job. A nice construction outfit. A company that turns a profit.'

'We could do better.'

'You do fine. With my salary—'

'This is not about you, it's about me,' Jack says firmly. 'Maybe I want to contribute more.'

He unwraps the corn bread from Fleeta and puts it in a basket. I sit down at the table as he ladles the stew into bowls and brings it to the table.

There's at least one ongoing argument in every marriage, and ours has always been about money. My husband believes in the system: put your years in, and at the end of the rainbow is a good pension and union protection. When I point out how the coal companies have reneged on their promises and the union has depleted the pension fund, he gets angry with me, as if I'm pointing out a personal defect in him. He's proud of his tenure in the mines, and he should be. But he isn't savvy enough to see how these companies have taken advantage of him. It's a blind spot in Jack MacChesney.

'I'm not sold on mountaintop removal. But this guy seems to think there's a way to do it that won't ruin the terrain. Someone local needs to get involved, if only to protect what we've got here.'

'Oh, I see. Join 'em and infiltrate.'

Jack puts down his spoon. 'Do you have to do this?'

'What?'

'Do you have to fight me?'

'You worked for Westmoreland for thirty years. They cut your benefits to nothing. Your union is in bad shape. All the promises those people made to you, they've broken them one by one. You can't trust these guys. They're not on your side.'

'And you are?'

'Always.'

'Doesn't sound like it.' Jack puts down his

napkin and pushes his chair away from the table. He stands. 'I've lost my appetite.'

I hear the screen door snap shut as he goes outside. I eat a bite of stew and remember something my mother used to say: 'When you argue while you eat, the food turns to poison in your body.' So I put down my napkin and follow Jack out the back door. I can't find him, so I turn on the back porch light and wait. Then I see him walking through the woods beyond the field out back. He's really angry, but so am I. No matter what I do or say, he's too trusting. From time to time, he's put his faith in people I don't approve of. We almost split up when he befriended Karen Bell, who wanted to sell him more than lumber from her Coeburn store.

There was a time when I would have run across the field and made a joke to diffuse his anger. I'd apologize, and he'd be terse for a while, and then he'd come around and we'd be back on track. For some reason, I don't move. I just watch him as he goes, pushing branches out of his way with a stick. I turn around and go back in the house. I'm not giving an inch on this one; he should have thrown that fresh-scrubbed Hokie out of our house.

I guess I'm getting more stubborn as the years go by. Sometimes I want to be right more than I want peace. I've earned that, haven't I?

The Slemp Memorial Library is my favorite building in Big Stone Gap. It's nestled in the rolling landscape of Poplar Hill beneath the museum. It's a lovely brick building with a grand entrance, decorated (by Iva Lou) with sheafs of wheat and Indian corn. When it was built back in the late 1970s, it became an instant gathering place for kids to do their homework, and for adults to find the latest best sellers. I mourned the loss of the Bookmobile, but when Iva Lou was made head librarian, she traded her wheels for her own branch. Iva Lou blossomed when she was put in charge. With a modern facility, she was able to make the library a viable part of the community. She started story time for the kids and invited local clubs, from the Lions to the Junior League, to have their monthly meetings there. It's a bit of an unofficial community center, but you can't beat it when you want a quiet place to browse. Iva Lou took a corner of the main room and turned it into a living area with sofas, coffee tables, and racks of national newspapers on large wooden spindles. Where else in Wise County can a girl read *The Washington Post?*

I pull in to the parking lot and climb out with a thermos of hot coffee and a few of Fleeta's sticky buns. Iva Lou has called a breakfast meeting in her office to plan for Fleeta's wedding. Fall leaves dance in the gutter, and the pungent smell of pine fills the air. Iva Lou and Nancy Kilgore-Hall are chatting when I join them.

'Nancy told me you called her straightway when

I assigned you the decorations,' Iva Lou says to me.

'Yes, ma'am.' I'm no fool. The first thing I did when I heard I was in charge of the decorations for Fleeta's wedding was call Nancy to enlist the expertise of the Intermont Garden Club. They've got the creativity to come up with a solid theme, and the rank and file to do the actual work. You can ask Nancy to do just about anything when it comes to making something pretty. She cannot resist an event in need of style and flair.

The Methodist Church Fellowship Hall is a challenge – it's a basement, after all, with large pillars sectioning off the space, low ceilings, and very little light. The Garden Club has decorated the space over the years with great success. They've transported guests from downtown Big Stone to exotic ports of call using paint, chicken wire, crepe paper, fresh flowers, and a lot of elbow grease. It's always a treat to see them work their magic on those pesky pillars. They've done it all; in a rondelet of historical time periods, the pillars became Roman columns or tropical palm trees and, once, a garden of giant sunflowers. Fleeta is more low-key when it comes to themes, so this time the Garden Club will keep it simple: Autumn in the Mountains Means Love Is in the Air. It'll look good on the napkins.

'Nancy, honey, I'm gonna need your recipe for the wedding mints. I'm thinking of making orange wedding bells and red fall leaves, and I'll place 'em on gold-leaf doilies. I love me an autumnal theme.' Iva Lou leans so far back in her office chair, she has to use her tippy toes for balance. 'Your mints are a classic, and that's what we're going for with this here wedding.'

'"Classic" is a fancy word for old,' I tell them.

'When the bride's over sixty and the groom's over seventy, what the hell else you gonna call it?'

'A miracle.' Nancy's brown eyes squeeze into half-moons as she smiles. A decorating guru as well as a local maven of fashion, Nancy always has her light brown hair cut and highlighted in the current style. Lately, she's been sporting a chin-length bob, straightened via blowout, with blond tips and a thick fringe of bangs. She's a girl's girl, but she has also developed a hard shell from working in insurance. Everybody knows that adjusters have the toughest hides in the county. From a corporate viewpoint, the last thing you want in an insurance rep is Mother Teresa. Somebody once said Nancy Kilgore-Hall had permanent lockjaw from saying no. They say it's harder to get her to cut a check than it is for Fleeta to pay a compliment. 'You need my molds, don't you?' she asks Iva Lou.

'The only molds I got are for Christmas,' Iva Lou tells her. 'I checked.'

'No problem, I'll loan you mine. You need leaves and bells.' Nancy jots down the candy recipe and hands it to Iva Lou.

NANCY KILGORE-HALL'S
WEDDING MINTS

*Makes 120 mints if molds are used, less if you
hand-cut them from the log.*

COURTESY OF MARGIE MABE
2 boxes plus 2 cups powdered sugar
¾ cup butter or margarine
4–5 tablespoons cold water
2 capfuls peppermint oil

Blend ingredients with a mixer until doughy
consistency forms.
Roll out on wax paper coated with powdered
sugar.

Cut with small cookie cutters or use molds.
To use molds, break the mixture into small
balls, coat in finely granulated sugar, and
press in molds. Let sit for two days, then
pop out.

Can be frozen.
*You can add food coloring of choice.

'All right, girls, I gotta scoot,' says Nancy.
'What are you adjusting?' Iva Lou asks as she
tucks the recipe into her date book.
'There was a wreck in Appalachia by the train
trestle.'

'People think Appy Strait is a speedway.'

'They do indeed.' Nancy snaps her purse shut. 'That curve right under the Roaring Branch always gets them.'

'It's from people leaning to see the waterfall. You know, lookieloos and rubberneckers.' Iva Lou shrugs.

'I guess so. Y'all call me if you need anything else.' Nancy takes her assignment and goes.

Iva Lou checks off her list. 'I'm making the orange sherbet punch, one bowl with vodka and one without. Wedding cake is gonna be carrot. Janine wants to make it for her mama. The Tuckett twins said they'd make the Chex mix. So that leaves me with the salted pea-nits and the candy mints.'

'You got off easy.'

'What about you? Farming your job out to that overachiever Nancy Kilgore-Hall.'

'Guilty.'

'I don't blame you – them Garden Clubbers are semiprofessionals, as it were. Let 'em do what they do, 'cause they do it better than anybody else.'

'Mrs MacChesney?' The library aid, Emma Morrissey, a delicate blonde with blue eyes, appears in the doorway. I can never tell her apart from her sister, Charlotte, who is her dead ringer.

Iva Lou smiles. 'That there is Emma, in case you were wondering.'

'There's a call for you on line one,' Emma says to me.

38

Iva Lou shoves the phone toward me. 'Something the matter?' She glances at Emma, who looks concerned.

I pick up the phone and say hello.

'Ave? It's Mousey. We need you to come over to Holston Valley right away.'

'What's wrong?'

'It's Jack Mac, ma'am. He's in intensive care.'

'What happened?' I feel faint.

'He passed out on us, and we brought him here. The doctor says it's serious. You need to hurry.'

Iva Lou puts down the extension that she picked up when I asked what was wrong. 'Let's go,' she says. 'I'll drive.'

CHAPTER 3

KINGSPORT

Iva Lou doesn't say a word as we drive to Holston Valley Hospital in Kingsport. I'm numb as my thoughts tumble over one another; my feelings come and go in waves of panic. Iva Lou pumps the gas pedal, lifting it off to take each curve with precision. She barrels out of town and into Wildcat Holler at a clip. The stone walls, where they blasted through the mountain to put in the highway, are charcoal blurs on either side as we go. It seems that time has stopped entirely, and yet we're speeding through it. Soon we're outside Hiltons and the Carter Family Fold. When the road straightens into Gate City, Iva Lou deftly passes cars two at a time to get me there. To Jack.

I feel sick. Jack and I went to bed angry at each other last night, even though my inner voice told me to apologize. This morning I didn't even bring him his coffee. I just hollered up the stairs that I'd be home at six, and left for work early, without waiting for his reply. This is what makes me the saddest, that I didn't wait to hear his answer. I beg God to let him live just so I can hear his voice again.

40

Iva Lou pulls in to the parking lot outside the hospital. 'He'll be in Building A,' she says quietly. She knows this hospital well – it's where she had her surgery – so there's no confusion about where to go or what to do. We jump out of the car and run into the hospital. Mousey is waiting for us inside.

'What happened?' I ask.

'We were hanging Sheetrock, nothin' strenuous, and we was talking, and then he passed out. He didn't say nothing. He just hit the floor.'

My stomach turns at the thought of my husband falling to the ground.

'Me and Rick tried to revive him, then we called the Rescue Squad. And since we was over in Blackwater workin', we was closer to here than home, so we brought him here.'

'You did the right thing. Thank you.' I give Mousey a hug, and he seems relieved.

Iva Lou has been talking to a nurse and motions for me to join her. 'Come on.'

I follow Iva Lou and the nurse through the doors to intensive care, a large ward filled with patients in their beds. I look around the beds, searching for my husband. When I see him, tubes coming out of his nose and mouth, I almost collapse. Iva Lou whispers, 'Buck up,' and sashays to my husband's bedside, motioning for me to join her.

'You look good, Jack,' she says to him. 'I like you in hospital green.'

41

I look at Jack's face and force a smile. I try to act as though nothing is wrong. 'Okay, okay, you win. I was wrong and you were right,' I whisper into his ear, apologizing for our argument the night before. I take his hands and squeeze them. 'I'm sorry.'

He rolls his eyes.

'He can't talk right now.' The nurse makes a motion to the tube. 'If you'll come with me, the doctor would like to talk to you.'

I don't want to let go of my husband's hands. Ever. I kiss him ten times too many before leaving his side. Again he rolls his eyes. As I step away, he closes them.

The nurse shows Iva Lou and me to a small, bare office outside the intensive-care unit. Dr Smiddy, who is lanky and droll, motions for me to sit. I feel small next to him, like a kid, and in a situation like this, that's a good thing. I want the doctor to be an all-knowing father, an expert. I want to believe Dr Smiddy can fix anything.

'What's wrong with my husband?' I ask.

'He's a very lucky man. He hasn't had a heart attack. But he does have a blockage in his carotid artery.' Dr Smiddy shows me a drawing of the head and neck. He points to the neck on the left side. 'I'm afraid of the blockage splintering off and causing further problems. We need to operate immediately.'

'When?'

'Right away.'

'Today?'

'Yes, ma'am.'

'Why so soon?'

'I explained everything to your husband.'

I feel such anger. My husband passed out and fell; explaining anything to him is a ridiculous concept. Jack's in no condition to say yes or no to any of this medical menu. They're rushing me, us, and I need time to think. I start to speak, but the doctor stops me.

'Let me finish,' he continues. 'We're going to go in and clean out the artery and put in a stint to keep the blood flowing.'

Keep the blood flowing? What is he talking about? It sounds like Jack is dying. Is he dying?

'Hopefully, this is the only blockage. Then we'll do a PET scan—'

'What's that?'

'A head-to-toe scan. We'll do it as soon as Jack recovers.'

Recovers? How did we go from 'hopefully' to 'blockage' to 'recovers' so quickly? Maybe Jack is fine; maybe they'll operate and see that it's not a big deal. Or maybe they'll take a scan and see that the problem is worse.

The doctor explains the options, but I barely hear him. I'm in a daze of disbelief. How did this happen? Why didn't we catch it sooner? I wasn't persistent enough with Jack; I'd let doctor appointments slide because I was tired of begging him to go. Somehow I feel that even this is my fault. I wasn't diligent enough, so now my husband has to pay.

The nurse leads me back to Jack, who is about to be transported to the operating room. I tell him that I love him, and he smiles. I tell him that everything is going to be all right, and try not to cry, but I can't help it. I cry. I'm afraid of the feelings I have, the depth of them in this moment. I really love my husband, though I don't always show it. I wish there was something I could say that would express to him the deep meaning he has brought to my life. So I lean down and say, 'Thank you.'

The orderlies wheel him away, and I watch until he is through the doors at the end of the long hallway. I think of the hundreds of times in nineteen years that I've watched Jack go, when he'd back down the hill onto Cracker's Neck Road in his truck, or drive away after dropping me at the airport, or how I'd wait until he disappeared from sight after taking me to Iva Lou's trailer for girls' poker night. Jack says that I'm hooked on good-byes. I savor them. I count them. I get lost in them. Does he know how much I treasure him? I wonder. Is that enough to sustain him now?

There's something in the way the sheer pale blue curtains surrounding this bed are draped that reminds me of the day Jack's mother died in the hospital. I always loved Mrs Mac; she had good old-fashioned common sense. She was a direct person – some would say brutally honest – but was never hurtful. She was a mountain girl who lived by a naturalist code: she grew her own vegetables, made her own fires, and quilted her own blankets. She could make do in any situation. I remember how Jack held her when she was dying. He didn't let go for a long time. I stood back and watched him through the blue curtain. Finally, the nurse gently touched his shoulder, and he knew that he had to leave her. I was waiting on the other side of the curtain.

I think about dying and all those I loved who are now gone. I feel as though I am falling in line behind them, my mother, my father, Fred, my beloved Spec, and Joe. I had my mother to talk to when Fred died, and when she died, I had Iva Lou to help me. When Spec died, it seemed I had the whole county to mourn with me, so I never felt alone. When our son died, it was the worst thing that could happen to us, but it was happening to our family, and there was much consolation in Etta's love, and a lot to learn from a little girl as she grieved. Somehow, to share the very worst of life with Jack made it bearable. He showed me how to live with pain, live through it to get beyond it. I wouldn't have known how to do it without him.

But there is no one to share this with, and it's terrifying.

I smooth the sheets on his bed. Then I decide

to make the bed. Maybe, if I tuck the corners neatly and fluff the pillow, the surgeons will take the same care with my husband. If I'm very quiet and very neat, maybe the doctors will go that extra mile, and he'll be all right.

There's a linen pocket on the side of the mattress for personal effects, since there are no side tables in the ICU. I reach inside and collect Jack's watch, his chain and medal of the Blessed Lady that I bought for him in Florence, and his wallet. A small notepad with a tiny golf pencil is attached to his wallet with a rubber band.

Jack always carries this small pad and pencil. I special-order them from the same stationer in Richmond who provides me with the blue airmail envelopes and paper for letters to Italy. Jack and I always joke about the tiny notepads. What would he do if they ever stopped making them? The scraps of paper from these pads have been a bone of contention with me for years. All around the house, I find tiny pieces of paper with numbers jotted on them, the measurements and numbers meaningless to everyone but Jack. He keeps these scraps in his pants pockets, on windowsills, and in his truck. He leaves them anywhere and every-where, and it drives me nuts. I flip the notepad open and see a list.

At first it doesn't look like Jack's handwriting at all. Then I see a familiar 'E' shaped like a backward 3, which gives me pause. It is my husband's handwriting, but the effects of the fall are apparent. The print is wobbly. He must've written it lying in this bed moments *ago*. The note says:

STILL TO DO
1. *build a bridge*
2. *hold my first grandchild*
3. *see Scotland*
4. *Annie*

I study the list. The thought of my husband dying without having held his grandchildren makes me cry again; worse, to think that he wouldn't be around to be an influence on them. I don't want to be a grandparent if he's not here. I don't want to be anything if he's not here. So many memories come rushing back, just moments, small pictures, jumbled, out of order. Jack and Etta when she was three, high on her papa's shoulders, walking across the field out back. He looked like a giant, and she so small. Jack, when Joe was born; he held our son before I did. It just seemed natural; after all, it was the son he had dreamed of and for so long. Jack at Joe's grave when we buried him. He could not stop his tears. Jack on our wedding day in Italy, when he toasted my father and looked at him with such respect. Jack helping his mother down the steps at church so she wouldn't fall on the ice. He treats all women like fine china.

Scotland: we always said we'd go, but we never

found the time. How many hints did I need to know his true heart's desire and *do* something about it? The signs were everywhere. He checked out books from the library on Scottish clan battles, even chose a shade of red paint for our living room from a book called *The Best of Highland Castles*. I didn't take his dream seriously enough. I made vacation plans, and he went along with them. We were always going to Italy, it seemed, whenever we went anywhere. Maybe Jack was helping me to make up for all the years I didn't know my father in Schilpario. Maybe he felt he had to put aside his dreams for mine. I should have insisted he go! Why didn't I? After all, Britain is close to Italy – just an hour flight. I always joke that Italy is the Florida of the UK. We could have done it – we should have.

Build a bridge? Jack never mentioned a bridge to me. Not once, not ever. This one is a complete mystery to me.

Annie? I never heard him mention an Annie. For a second I feel betrayed – where am I on his list? I didn't even make it. It doesn't matter. I don't deserve to be one of his last concerns – I haven't earned that. He's been the good one all these years. The righteous one. The one with the big heart. All the sweetness, all the light, all the gentle strength, all the things he is. It's all ending. I can't believe it. I would give everything I have for more time. Please give me more time. It's all

48

happening so fast, too fast. I want to slow everything down, buy time. If time stops, that means no harm will come to him.

I stay next to the bed for a long while, as long as the nurses will let me. I can still picture my husband lying there, and maybe they understand that this is as close as I can get to him for now. The idea of him has to do. After a while, I pick up my purse and Jack's things and go out into the empty waiting area. Iva Lou is off somewhere, so I sit down and hold Jack's watch. I trace the numbers with my finger, wishing I could stop the movement of the hands, turn them back to a week ago, when Jack was fine and his artery was clear. I put his watch on my wrist, remembering that it was ticking on his arm just a few minutes ago.

Iva Lou gives me a cup of coffee. 'Here, drink this.'

'No, thanks.'

'Now, don't do this. Don't go to that place.' Iva Lou sits down next to me.

'I'm going to lose him, Iva Lou. I know it. I'm being punished. I wasn't grateful enough. I wasn't good enough to him. I made him work too hard to love me.'

'You're being silly. You're human. You're not some perfect thing that does everything right all the time. None of us are. He's gonna pull through this because he's strong. And because he wants to.'

49

I look at Iva Lou, hoping that I will see on her face a validation of all she says. I would like to believe it. But I'm afraid she's wrong. I hand her the list I found.

'What's this?' she asks.

'It's from Jack's notepad.'

'Jack wrote this?' Iva Lou sits down and reads it. '"Still to Do." Told ya. He's making lists of things – ole Jack Mac ain't going anywhere. Who the hell is Annie?'

'I have no idea.'

'I'm sure it's nothing.' A worry crease appears between Iva Lou's eyes.

'For Godsakes, Iva Lou, I don't care about that.'

'I would. I don't care how sick Lyle gits, he better not write some mystery woman's name on a pad for me to find. I'd rip his wig off.' Iva Lou pokes me. I manage a smile. 'Jack's in good hands. Got the best surgeon here.'

'How do you know?' I ask.

'What?'

'How do you know he's not going to die?'

'He didn't have the look.' Iva Lou exhales.

'What look?'

'Surrender.'

'He seemed so sad.' I open my purse, looking for a tissue.

'That's just Jack Mac not wanting to be any trouble. He was lying on that gurney wondering if the surgeon'd had his lunch. He doesn't want to bother people. You know how he is.'

I nod.

'Your husband is and will forever be a giver and not a taker. I never saw him take nothin' – and I know men.'

'You're right.'

'When I had my cancer . . .'

I nod that I remember.

'Well, I knew I wasn't a goner. I just knew it. And Jack knows he ain't a goner. You should pray for peace of mind, not anything else. He's gonna be around a long time.'

I take Iva Lou's hand. 'What if he isn't? What will I do?'

'Don't go there.'

'I can't help it. I'm scared.'

'Of course you are. He's irreplaceable. I know they say that anybody can be replaced. Well, there's two places that's not true: right here, in Jack Mac, and at the county library. Ever since Mrs Home died, the main branch has been a mess.'

'I've got to call Etta!' I stand.

'You'll do no such thing!' Iva Lou pulls me back down to the chair. 'She's all the way over in It-lee. There's nothing she can do.'

'If it were me in there, Jack would call right away.'

'And I'd stop him the same as I'm stoppin' you. You ain't thinkin' clearly. Call her when you got good news from the surgery, and not before.'

If there was ever a daughter with a deep affinity for her father, it's Etta and he, Jack, for her. There were times when I felt they were closer than Etta

51

and I were, but I never minded. I'd spent most of my life craving that connection to Fred Mulligan, and then once I'd met my real father, I had waves of it. Etta and Jack's relationship has an edge over me and my dad, of course, because they've had a connection since the day she was born, while I had to wait thirty-five years for mine. Iva Lou is right, though. What good would it do to burden her at this point?

'I meant to tell you something. When you stopped by the house the other morning,' I say.

'What's that?' Iva Lou looks at me.

'I thought I saw my son in the woods.'

'What do you mean?'

'I saw a young man walking in the woods, and he looked like Joe, if Joe had lived.'

'Honey-o, now you're scaring me.'

'I was scared. I must've looked a fright, because Jack went out in the woods and looked for him.'

'Bless his heart.'

'I know. He'd do anything for me. Even when I'm crazy, he tries to make sense of it.'

'Why do you think you saw Joe after so long?'

'I don't know.'

'Maybe he was trying to tell you something. Sometimes angels do that, you know. They try and guide us in small ways.'

'Maybe he was coming to get Jack.'

'Don't let your imagination run wild.'

'Too late for that.'

★　　★　　★

52

A few hours later, I wake up to the persistent sound of a ringing phone. I fell asleep in the chair next to Jack's bed after hearing that the surgery went well and Jack would be under the anesthesia for a few more hours. I must've been so relieved, I went right to sleep. I sit up and grab the phone. Jack is still asleep in the hospital bed. I have a dull headache, my back is sore, and the heat that has kicked in makes the air so dry, it's hard to breathe.

'Hello?'

'Ma, it's Etta. I got your message.'

'Hi, honey.'

'What's wrong? Why are you at the hospital?'

'It's Daddy.' I start to cry.

'What happened?' she says evenly.

'He fell at work, and it turns out he had a blockage in his artery. He had surgery this morning, and he's doing really well.'

'Why didn't you call right away?'

'The time difference,' I lie. 'There was nothing you could do.'

'I could worry for you! I'm coming home.'

'No, no. He's going to be fine.'

'Can I talk to him?'

'He's sleeping.'

'Mom, you're not lying to me, are you? Is it worse than you're saying?'

I go into a long explanation of the surgery, repeating everything the doctor told me. I give her the good news; there was plenty of that. I recount that Jack's heart is strong, he just had a buildup of plaque in the arteries, and now he's on blood thinners and he will heal.

'I'm coming home.'

'Etta. I would tell you if it was bad.'

'I want to talk to Dad.'

The nurse comes in and checks Jack. I watch as she takes his blood pressure and checks the dressing on his bandages. Jack stirs a little when she touches him.

'Can we call you later? When he wakes up?' I ask.

'Okay.' Etta begins to cry. 'Is he going to be all right?'

'Yes. Yes. I promise.'

'Mom?'

'Yes?'

'I don't know what I'd do if something happened to Daddy.'

My heart breaks for her, but I don't cry. 'Listen to me, Etta. Your father loves you, and he's proud of you. Your happiness makes him strong. He wants you to be happy.'

'How can I do that when he's suffering?'

'Because you have to.'

'I want to come home and take care of him.'

'Don't worry. I'm waiting on him like he's a duke.'

'I shouldn't be here. I should be home with you.'

I had prayed for Etta to come to this realization before she moved abroad, got married, and decided to go to college in Italy. I knew there would be a moment when she wished she was nearer to home, closer to us. This is one time when I wish I hadn't been right.

'Don't be silly,' I tell her. 'Your life is there, with your husband who loves you. Don't worry.'

CHAPTER 4

MOUNTAIN VIEW

The thunder is so loud over Cracker's Neck Holler, it sounds like the mountains are splitting open. The occasional bolt of white lightning in the dark, followed by deafening claps, sends Shoo the Cat under the sofa. I place some chunks of black coal on the fire. The flames from the logs engulf the coal; it crackles with small pops of silver where the dust hits the fire.

'You done good with that farr, honey.' Jack puts his arms around me.

He's been home a few weeks now, and the truth is, I'm getting pretty good at building fires myself, because I won't let him lift a thing. 'You banked it, I just added the coal.'

'Some storm.'

'Terrible.'

'We'll wake up to butterscotch mountains in the morning.'

'You think so?'

Jack and Etta used to name the mountains by season. In late November, when the rains came in, the last of the changing leaves' shimmering colors would go; ruby and gold and orange would give way to bare fingers of deep blue branches as far as the eye could see. Even the pine would lose some of its green luster, turning to a dusty purple as the cold set in. The earth below would turn the color of butterscotch.

'Today is the first day I feel like myself.' Jack sits in the chair and puts his feet up.

'The doctor said it would take six weeks.'

'I didn't believe him.'

'Do you need anything?' I kneel next to Jack's chair. 'How about a cup of tea?'

'I sort of like you waiting on me hand and foot.'

'This is what it was like in the pioneer days, before women had careers.'

'I like it.'

I kiss Jack on the cheek. 'Why wouldn't you?' He pulls me onto his lap. I put my arms around his neck. 'Did you e-mail Etta?'

'I sure did. I don't like that instant-message feature at all.'

I laugh. 'I know. It's annoying.'

'Do you ever think all the romance has gone out of the world?'

'What do you mean?'

'I miss paper and ink and the thought it took to write a letter. To really figure out what you wanted to say.'

'What do you want to say?'

Jack looks at me. 'Thank you for taking such good care of me.'

'I'm happy to.'

'You've been great.'

'I'm relieved,' I say.

'Why?'

'I thought it was the end. Iva Lou told me to never, ever say that to you. But I was really scared. I actually thought, Oh, this is how it ends.' I tear up as I say this.

'That's funny. I wasn't one bit scared.'

'Not at all?'

'No. I'm not afraid to die. I thought about it every single day when I went into the mines. First thing at the beginning of a shift as I prepped my gear, I thought about what could go wrong. Then once I was inside, I'd get to work, and I wouldn't think about it again.'

'I wouldn't have stopped thinking about it for a moment.'

'Eventually, you do. My dad did forty years in there.'

'And he died of black lung.'

'Complications of it, they said. And he smoked, so we'll never know exactly what took him. When he died, I remember thinking, Well, at least wherever we go after this life, it'll be ready for us with Pop getting there first. He was a fixer, he could build anything. I just figured he went ahead to make a way for the rest of us. When Ma died, I knew he was waiting for her, so I didn't worry. Ever since Joe died, I knew that when my time came, I'd see him again. It's not that I want to die, but I don't think it's so terrible, because I know he'll be there. I'm looking forward to seeing him.'

'I didn't know you felt this way.' As I say this, my voice breaks.

'Really? I figure you know me pretty well. It's been almost twenty years.'

Sometimes these twenty years seem like twenty minutes. I think I know my husband, and then something happens, he reacts a certain way, and I'm utterly surprised. There are certain aspects to his character that I can count on, and his habits are as ingrained as his ideals – it's hard to separate the behavior from the man. But when it's life or death, all bets are off. We make that walk alone, and no amount of love or wishing will change the outcome.

This time Jack wasn't ready to go, so he didn't.

I am haunted by small details the doctor has shared. If Jack hadn't been close to the hospital, if this had happened in his sleep, he might have had a massive stroke. If the clot had formed an inch from where it was, it would have meant sudden and certain death. All these ifs, there's a pile of them, one scenario more frightening than the next. We are lucky. We know it.

'Stand still, Ma.' Janine crouches on the floor pinning the hem on Fleeta's wedding gown. I flip the closing sign on the entrance door of Mutual's while Fleeta stands on a packing crate playing supermodel.

'How weird is this? A daughter sewing a mother's wedding gown? I'm ashamed.' Fleeta puffs on her unlit cigarette. (I miss the actual smoke rings Fleeta used to blow, but when she gave up smoking, she gave up lighting them.)

'You sewed mine,' Janine says.

'That were different. This here is backwards to how it's supposed to be. I'm too old for this nonsense.'

'You need to get over your prejudices,' I tell Fleeta pleasantly.

'Look who's talking. You're the one who asked why didn't I just live with Otto instead of gettin' murried?'

'I hope you didn't tell Reverend Mutter I said that.'

'I done told him everything.'

'Great. They already think Catholics are a bunch of hypocrites—'

'And now he's got proof.' Fleeta chuckles.

'Stay still, Ma. I mean it,' Janine barks. Janine is a no-nonsense mountain girl with a purpose. She's focused, college-educated, ambitious, and driven. Now in her late thirties, looking far younger, she is an exact replica of her mother. We call her 'Fleeta Part Two.' She's petite and has a slight build but makes up for it with moxie. Her black hair is cut in a shag, and she inherited her mother's clothes sense: she likes bright sweaters and leggings and ankle boots. Janine took over the management of the Mutual Pharmacy when Pearl left to go to Boston. We don't see a lot of Janine – she stays at the Mutual branch down in Lee County – but she's sharp and a managerial whiz. She has us turning a profit, and these days that's not easy.

'Pavis ain't comin to the wedding,' Fleeta says, and shrugs.

'He said he was gonna try,' Janine says.

'That new wife of his said the trip is too long and they can't make it.'

'What wife is this for Pavis?' I ask.

'Third,' Fleeta says.

'Fourth,' Janine corrects her. 'You never count that first one that Pavis married in high school.'

'He was sixteen, she was twenty. Betty Jane Cline. How could I forget her? I had to sign permission to let him get murried. He threatened me with a grandbaby, so I had to sign him away. Jane weren't so bad for him, though. She whipped Pavis into shape, made him git a job, lease a trailer. Grown-up stuff. When she left him – and I knew she would – he fell to pieces, then we was stuck putting him back together again. Took us about four years till he stopped crying about her. I don't like older womens and young men together. Something ain't right about that. And that right there was proof.'

'I think older women and younger men make sense. Do the math. Men die about eight years sooner than women,' I say.

'Maybe that's a gift.'

61

'Fleeta!'

'My God, Ma, with all Ave Maria's been through, that's a terrible thing to say.'

'She knows what I mean.'

'Never mind me. What about Otto? Don't you wish him many years of health and happiness with you?' I say.

'What will be, will be, and what ain't will have to do.'

'You got that right,' I tell her.

'Ma, you need not say everything you're thinkin'.'

'Why not?' asks Fleeta.

'Your mother has never been subtle,' I say.

'What's the point? Are you almost done, Janine? I'm bored stiff standin' here. And I want to get to the ballpark. You know it don't set right with me to miss kickoff. I'd rather not go at all if I miss it.'

'Okay, Ma. I'm done. Ave, can you help me get her out of this?'

I unbutton the back of the dress and undo the zipper. The dress is shell-pink silk, with long sleeves and a sweeping peplum of matching chiffon. It's tasteful and understated. It's the last gown I would have expected Fleeta to pick. 'I love this dress,' I say.

'Thank Janine. She's got an eye for formal wear. Remember those Nadine gowns you wore to the prom?' Fleeta says to Janine, and steps out of the dress. Janine folds it carefully. 'I loved the white eyelet with the pale green velvet-ribbon trim. Now, that there was a classic.'

'I still have it, Ma.'

'You'd better. Ten months of layaway at Dave's department store in Appalachia. Layaway – can you imagine? Now everything's on the Visa.'

'What a world.' I help Janine put the gown in the dress box.

'What are you doing with your hair? A veil?' I ask Fleeta.

'Hell, no. A veil at my age, I'd look like a beekeeper. No, I'ma doin' baby's breath. I just love me some baby's breath. It's elegant.' Fleeta fishes in her purse for her cigarettes. She puts one in her mouth. It dangles dangerously from her lower lip. 'Ave, you coming to the game?'

'I wouldn't miss it.'

'Janine?'

'Nope, I have to git home.'

'There was a time when you wouldn't miss a football game.'

'I have work to do, Ma. This hem will take me all night.' Janine kisses Fleeta and goes.

'Come on.' Fleeta puts on her Vikings jacket. 'We don't want to be late.' She grabs her purse. 'The band is doing a special salute to Harley Stallard. You remember him, don't you?'

'How could I forget him? He was my high school principal. He was beloved.'

'Yeah, well, they're doing the salute up right. They's makin' a big 'H.S.' on the field, and the

63

majorettes are gonna twirl fire at the tips of the letters. You know I love me a halftime show.'

I pull on my red velvet swing coat and stop by the lipstick display, quickly applying a coat of Revlon's Burgundy Mocha from the sample tubes. Fleeta leans in and looks at the mirror. 'That's a good color on you.'

'You think so?'

'Take the tube. What the hell.'

I put the tube in my pocket. The idea that I'm shoplifting from my own pharmacy makes me smile.

Every parking spot is filled to the edge of town, including our lot. Bullitt Park is just a few blocks from the Pharmacy, so we hoof it quickly. Fleeta is serious about her high school football, and the long-standing rivalry between the hometown Powell Valley Vikings and the Appalachia Bulldogs is the game of the year. She won't miss a single play, and she'll stay to the final whistle.

As we turn the corner on to Gilley Avenue, we hear the kids cheering in the stands. We quicken our pace and follow the line through the ticket booth. Fleeta and I hand the ticket-taker (Mr Bates, the biology teacher) our five-dollar bills. The stands are full to overflowing, home and visitors. 'Everybody in the damn county turned out,' Fleeta grouses. We make our way to the field, pushing through the crowd. 'Otto said he'd be in the end zone with your husband,' Fleeta shouts over the din.

This is Jack's first night out since his surgery. It's been two months, and the doctor said it would be a good idea for him to 'take a field trip.' I'm having my doubts as I scan the standing-room-only stadium. What if something happened? How would we get him out of here? And there's a real chill in the air; this can't be good for him.

'There they is!' Fleeta points to Jack, Otto, Worley, Mousey, Rick, and a group of guys standing in the end zone. Jack looks robust – thinner, but his color is good. I'm so happy to see him out with his friends; instantly, my worries lift like the red streamers unfurled by the Booster Club in the student section. It's like old times, old times with new hope.

The teams aren't on the field yet. The cheerleaders are doing a pyramid formation on the fifty-yard line. They look like an upside-down red, white, and Carolina-blue ice-cream cone. The Viking band's rhythm section provides an up-tempo beat. The student section claps along. The highest cheerleader dives off the top and is caught by two girls at the base. The crowd cheers.

I lose Fleeta in the sea of fans, but knowing her, she went for a chili dog and a Coke. I am shoved and push back as I make my way through. I hear the sound of my husband's laughter and follow it. Finally, I wedge through a group of onlookers to join Jack. I can see his face, so I move toward him. The crowd pushes me, and I almost topple someone. I look to apologize to the person I've landed on, and it's a woman. I pull back. My heart races when I look at her bronzed face, kohl-rimmed eyes, and coral lip gloss. Nothing understated in the details. It's Karen Bell.

'Excuse me,' I say loudly, forcing a smile.

'Oh, hi,' she says. She wears a blue baseball cap over her blond shoulder-length hair, and she's as tanned as she would be in July. She's dressed in a white windbreaker and jeans.

Jack looks away from me quickly. 'Honey, you remember Karen.'

'I do.'

'Well, Jack – fellas – I'll see you around.' She disappears into the crowd.

Rick and Mousey look away. Those two. They're just scared of me right now. Otto chatters nervously about the odds of the game. Jack puts his arm around me. I'm not so sure I want his arm around me. I bury my hands in my pockets as kickoff is announced, and feel the tube of Burgundy Mocha. At least I met the enemy wearing a new lipstick.

The next day, the Big Stone Gap *Post* has a picture of Fleeta and Otto and an announcement of their open church wedding. The headline reads: MULLINS AND OLINGER BANNS OF MARRIAGE. In the picture, they're standing in front of the Ruby Falls (one of the Seven Wonders of the World) sign on the road to Gatlinburg. Otto has his arm around her shoulder. They're wearing matching Vikings State Champ football jerseys. It's the only smiling photo of Fleeta I have ever seen. Otto is beaming.

Fleeta Mullins and Otto Olinger
invite you to an open church wedding
on November 30, 1998, at the United Methodist
Church. Friends and family are welcome. Reception
to follow in the Fellowship Hall. No gifts—
your presence is our present.

'What do you think?' Fleeta folds the paper neatly in half. 'Classy?'

'Oh, yes,' I tell her.

'Look at us. They stuck us next to the Coughlins' announcement. They's celebrating forty-five years of marriage, and they's younger than we are. It's awful.'

'Who cares what other people think?'

'I do. 'Cause I care what other people do.'

'Your relationship is nothing to be ashamed of,' I remind her.

'You know, it just ain't fittin' . . .'

'What?'

'You know.'

'No, I don't.'

'I don't like public displays and feelings. You know what I mean. Hand-holding, eye-rolling, and squeeze-as-you-please antics in public. Makes me feel cheap.'

Nevertheless, Fleeta takes the picture and puts it on the community announcement board next to the cash register. It's a big move for Fleeta – it's the first sign that she's genuinely happy about getting married. 'You know, you roll the dice when you have an open church wedding. You can't control the riffraff. Some of my second cousins from Scott County, those carpetbaggers, the bunch of 'em, are sure to show up just for the free eats. And when they see they don't have to give no gift, hell, they'll load up a bus of folks and bring 'em.'

'You can't blame them. The eats are gonna be magnificent.' I get on the computer and e-mail Theodore the picture from the online edition of our hometown paper. He loves the stories of local politics (VOTERS BRIBED WITH PROMISE OF PORK RINDS), beauty and diet tips (JELL-O CAN WHITTLE YOUR WAISTLINE) and crime (MAMAW, AGE 90, PRINTS MONEY IN KEOKEE BASEMENT). An instant message pops up from Theodore: 'I'm calling you right now.'

Within seconds, the phone rings.

'Hello, Theodore.'

'How are you?'

'I'm holding up. I have a nervous bride-to-be here.'

'I ain't nervous!' Fleeta hollers from the café.

'She's a wreck.'

Theodore laughs. 'How's your husband?'

'He's getting better all the time. Slowly, slowly, he's getting his strength back.'

'Good. And how about you?'

'I stay overwhelmed. I'm having a hard time adjusting to Etta being gone. I'm almost ashamed, it's so hard for me.'

'When can you go and see her?'

'I don't know. I don't want to be a nuisance. Besides, I'm trying to get Jack to Scotland.'

'What for?'

'He's always wanted to go. He made a list in the hospital of things he wanted to do before he died, and that was on it. By the way, he doesn't know I found the list, so don't say anything.'

'Up to your old sneaky ways.'

'Uh-huh.'

'I have news. They've asked me to be on the board of UVA-Wise.'

'Congratulations! That means you'll visit more often.' I'm so happy to hear this news. The University of Virginia at Wise is our local arm of the Charlottesville main campus. It's a good college in our county seat. Many proud sons and daughters of coal miners have graduated from there.

'I said I'd do it. They're trying to get the arts department up and running. You know, they have a private jet.'

'You're kidding.'

'No, and it comes to New York City on a regular basis, when it's not hauling death-row inmates to your prison from out of state. I said I'd take the position if they could fly me in and out. Get your spare room ready.'

69

'I really need you here.'

'I miss you too, Ave.'

'How's Max?'

'Well, everything my mother taught me about relationships has come to pass. Especially her final warning before she went to meet her maker. She looked at me and said, "Familiarity breeds contempt." Max and I are taking a little break. Evidently, I have bred some contempt.'

'I'm sorry. He's such a great guy. And he can cook.'

'I know. On a gastronomic level, he is irreplaceable. But on an emotional level, he is distant and reserved and in need of counseling.'

'I know all about that.'

'Still prying feelings out of Jack Mac?'

'With tongs.'

'That must make for some scintillating conversation.'

'Oh, you have no idea. I'm longing for connection so badly, I told Nellie Goodloe I'd direct *The Sound of Music*. We open Christmas week.'

'How awful.'

'The casting is multicultural. I have a Baptist Melungeon from Esserville playing Mother Superior, an Indian playing Rolfe, and several Filipinos in the chorus. Should be interesting.'

'I'd love to see it.'

'Why don't you come for Christmas?'

'I thought you'd never ask!'

'Are you serious? You're really going to come?'

'Max kicked me to the curb for Hanukkah, so I'm all yours.'

I hang up the phone and immediately start making a holiday to-do list. I hadn't been planning to put up a tree this year – what's the point, Etta's not going to be home – but now I'm going to drag every plastic elf and string of lights and glass ball out of the attic and do up the house like the main floor of Belk's.

Fleeta puts a slice of pie down on my counter. 'What are you so happy about?'

'Theodore's coming for Christmas.'

'He's gonna miss my wedding, but he's got the ducats to fly down here for Christmas? Where are the man's priorities?'

'Fleeta, you didn't even want *me* at your wedding.'

'I know. But I'm getting the fever now. I can't hardly help it. It's the biggest party I'll ever be at, thanks to you and Iva Lou.'

'Finally, you're happy!'

'Only thing I have a broken heart about is Pavis. Me and him never got along too good. He was a good baby, but when he growed up, he just walked on the wrong side. I tried everything to help him. I give him money, bailed him out several times – oh, and the women he brought home, if you can call 'em that. Pack of flappers – party girls without the means to support the habit, you know what I mean. And they done took him for all he was worth, four times and counting.'

'Why don't you call him?'

'He told Janine that Portly wouldn't approve of me gittin' murried again.'

'How does he know that? Portly's in heaven.'

'I don't have no guilt about Portly, not one drop! I took good care of him all the days of our murried life, and I gave him my youth, my middle age, and a good portion of whatever stage you call this dead end that I'm in right here and now. I don't have a single regret.'

'Portly wants you to be happy.'

'He better would.' Fleeta pushes the pie toward me. 'Can I tell you something?'

'Sure.'

'It gits better at my age.' Fleeta winks.

'What?'

'It.' Fleeta wipes her hands on a dish towel and then looks at her long fingernail tips, painted in small tasteful stripes in the high school colors of red, white, and blue.

'Come on.' I'm a little stunned.

She leans across the counter and lowers her voice. 'And we don't need no help in that urr-ea neither.'

'Really.'

'In fact, old Otto told me that he's gonna get me some of that Vi-*nag*-ra.'

'It's *Viagra*, and you don't take it. He does.'

'No, it's Vi-*nag*-ra. That's what Otto calls it, 'cause I'm always nagging him for some personal attention.' Fleeta blushes for the first time in all the years I've known her.

CHAPTER 5

DANBERRY HEIGHTS

Thanksgiving Day was always a MacChesney family favorite, so for years I'd turn it into a big party and invite half the town. If you didn't know I was Italian by birth, you'd have guessed it by my style of entertaining: more is more. I dragged the family into my holiday madness. I'd bake a few weeks in advance, freezing pies and cookies and a Texas sheet cake (Etta's request). We'd set the table the night before. Jack would make cider, Etta would print the place cards, and Shoo the Cat would stay out of the way.

We'd put out a buffet of roasted turkey, fresh ham, buttery mashed potatoes, cranberry sauce, green-bean casserole, and pumpkin pie. Etta was in charge of decorations. We would gather branches of bitter-sweet berries and put them on the mantelpiece. We'd make a centerpiece of fresh pumpkins and gourds, carving out the tiny pumpkins and putting votive candles in them. We'd have games in the yard in the afternoon (croquet is more fun on fallen leaves), and as the sun was setting, we'd come inside to eat. We'd laugh and talk through dinner, then play poker until somebody went bankrupt and ran out of pennies. The kids would roast marshmallows in the fireplace as we played cards. Midnight would come way too soon, and everyone would go home with leftovers.

This year will be different. I miss Etta so much that it seems almost like a betrayal to have a big party. People seem to understand. Since Jack's been sick, we've received more invitations to dinner than we can count. So we decided to go to Iva Lou's trailer. She's a great cook, and Jack likes Lyle, so it will be a quiet day with football on TV and good food among friends. It won't be like it used to be, but it will be fun.

As I slide out of Jack's truck, I juggle a blackberry pie and a bottle of champagne. He grabs a six-pack of beer from the truck bed. Iva Lou has festooned her front door with an autumn wreath of cranberries nestled in green velvet leaves and a shock of Indian corn where the bow usually goes. I can hear the football game on television from the back of the trailer. Iva Lou pushes the door open, giving each of us a hug. 'Jack, go on back, Lyle has your chair ready.'

I follow Iva Lou into the kitchen, which she has redecorated about four times since she's owned this trailer. 'Wallpapering is good for the soul,' she always says. The current look is lovely. The wallpaper has a white background with tiny bright yellow lemons on it – sort of a dotted-Swiss look. The wallpaper is offset by china-blue cabinets and place mats on the glass-topped table. She carries the crisp blue and yellow theme down to the teacups, which dangle on small gold hooks from her white curio shelf. The café curtains are yellow-and-white-striped with rows of hot-pink rickrack on the hems. Over the sink she has a series of miniature Degas ballerina prints that pick up the pink details of the curtains.

Iva Lou oohs and aahs over the pie and puts the champagne in the refrigerator. She lowers her voice. 'Don't worry. At the football game, I was watching Jack Mac and Karen Bell the whole time through my bi-knocks. It was platonic.'

'I'm not worried.'

'You look worried. What the hell is he doing talking to her anyhow?' Iva Lou fiddles with the temperature dials on the stove. The question sounds more like a judgment.

'I don't know. I never asked him.'

'Are you serious?'

'Couldn't.'

'Why, I'd have taken Lyle by the hair of the head and dragged him out of that stadium and let him know that I am not about to put up with that kind of behavior.'

'I thought you said it looked platonic through your binoculars.'

'On Jack's part. Not hers. I don't trust her. Word is, she broke up with her current boyfriend. You don't want a woman like that on the loose around a man who isn't. You should say something to

Jack. Tell him he doesn't have any business chatting with man-eaters in Bullitt Park.'

'I'm not going to say a word.'

'Mistake.'

'And you wouldn't either. The most important thing I have learned as a married woman is to say a quarter of what I'm thinking and leave the rest in my head, where it belongs. I might wind up in the nuthouse, but I'll stay married.'

'Them's your choices?'

'Jack's only seven weeks out of the hospital. I don't want to upset him.' Saying the name Karen Bell would be like lighting a cherry bomb in my house. I won't do it.

'Okay. I just hope you ain't keeping everything bottled up inside yourself. That ain't good.'

'I can tell you my troubles, can't I?'

'Of course, honey. That's what I'm here fer. Spill.'

'I'm tiptoeing around about everything, and to be honest, I think Jack likes it better.'

'He's never been chatty.'

'No, he hasn't. I've pulled his feelings out of him for twenty years. And I have the carpal tunnel syndrome to prove it.'

'All men are that way.'

'Maybe.'

'How are you feeling? You know, since that morning you saw Joe.' Iva Lou pours me a glass of wine and motions for me to sit.

'I can't shake this feeling of doom. I dream of him a lot.'

'Honey-o, that's normal. You lost him during the winter. I don't know if you've ever noticed, but you always get blue about now. I'm not one bit surprised you thought you saw him in the woods. You're looking for him.'

It's true. When it turns to winter, I begin to feel unnerved. I have bad dreams and I feel desperate. The weather doesn't help. Winter is dreary in our mountains. The rusty slopes close in on you, and the drab sky overhead makes the mountain walls almost prisonlike.

I've been waiting for that magical day when time will finally heal all my wounds. I've always heard that it can (that has certainly been said enough at the funerals I've attended). There are days when it feels like no time has passed at all. Time can do a lot of things – it can make memories sweet and it can dull pain – but it doesn't take away pain entirely.

I replay every day of Joe's illness over and over again in my mind, and sometimes I allow different endings to the terrible story. Sometimes there's a cure for him, other times I die instead of him, and there's even a scenario where he tells me why he has to die. I've tried to make sense of it all these years, and I can't. 'Do you think he's trying to tell me something?'

'I think you've been through a lot in the last six months. Etta's leaving did not help one bit. You thought you had four more years with her around. Nearby. Even if she went away to college, she'd still have been close enough to see every once in a while. That's what all this missing Joe is about. Your feelings are raw. That's all.'

There's a knock at the door. 'Is there more company coming?'

'Nope. Just the four of us.' Iva Lou shrugs, checks her lipstick in the toaster, and goes to the door. I can hear the Notre Dame/Army game from the den. Notre Dame must have scored. The fight song plays through.

Iva Lou opens the door. Whoever's there seems to be going into a long-winded explanation of something. Iva Lou puts her hands on her hips. She's leaning in, listening intently. I get up and look around the corner to see who it is. There's a woman standing on the deck. She might be forty. She has long blond hair pushed back off her face by her sunglasses, which are perched on her head like a tortoiseshell tiara. She's pretty. Small features, perfect rosebud lips. She's exactly Iva Lou's height. She wears a khaki barn jacket with navy blue velvet trim. Her hands are shoved deeply into her pockets. I've never seen her before. I don't know why, but I go to the door.

'Hi!' I say brightly.

Iva Lou looks at me, and I see that the color has drained from her face. My interruption causes the woman to look away. Iva Lou doesn't say anything either.

'Are you okay?' I ask Iva Lou, then I turn to the woman. 'I'm Ave Maria MacChesney.'

'I'm sorry. I didn't know you had company,' the

woman says to Iva Lou. She extends her hand. 'My name is Lovely Carter.'

'What a beautiful name.' I look at Iva Lou and smile, but she isn't looking at me. She studies Lovely's face as though it's a map.

'Thank you,' Lovely says. 'I could come back another time.'

'Well, it's just that I have company today. Tomorrow is good. I have to work, but I could figure something out.' Iva Lou seems unnerved.

'Would you like my number?'

'Sure, sure.' Iva Lou goes to the kitchen. She opens and closes drawers, looking for a paper and pencil. There's something odd about the way she's doing it. She doesn't seem to really look at what's inside the drawer – it's as if she's going through the motions but doesn't really want to find the pencil and paper.

'I have a pen in my purse.' I reach over the room divider to the bookshelf, pick up my purse, and dig out the pen. 'Here.' I give it to Lovely.

'Thanks.' Lovely writes her phone number on the back of a grocery receipt from her pocket. 'Here.' She gives it to Iva Lou.

'I'll walk you to your car.' Iva Lou grabs her coat and follows Lovely out the door.

'Happy Thanksgiving!' I call after the woman. The energy between Iva Lou and Lovely was so strange that I feel I have to make up for it by being warm. Why do I always have to try and fix things? What business is it of mine?

After a few minutes, Iva Lou comes back into the trailer. She takes off her coat and hangs it on the hook.

'Who was that?'

'She's from Johnson City.'

'What's she doing here?'

'Oh, she heard about me from up in the county li-burry and stopped in to introduce herself.'

'She's a librarian?'

'No, no.'

'Then what's the connection?'

'Connection?'

'Yeah. Why did she come to see you?'

'She wanted to see where I lived.' Iva Lou begins taking casseroles and pans out of the oven.

'Why would she want to see where you live?'

'Are you some sort of a detective?' Iva Lou snaps.

'I'm sorry,' I tell her.

'Look. I don't know how to answer any of your questions, so I'd appreciate it if you wouldn't ask them.'

'What's the matter?'

'Nothing.'

Iva Lou puts out the plates and silverware, wrapped in cloth napkins and tied with a ribbon. We don't talk as Iva Lou sets the table. I break the silence. 'Did Lovely say something to offend you?'

'No, no. I just wasn't expecting her. That's all.'

Her tone of voice tells me not to pursue it further.

Iva Lou makes the gravy on the stovetop. She stirs the broth from the turkey pan, slowly adding in the flour; as she whisks, she makes small talk about goings-on at the library. It's odd. She's acting as though the stranger never showed up at the door unannounced. I wonder who Lovely is. Maybe she wanted money or wanted to sell Iva Lou something, but why would she do that on a holiday? Or maybe she's Iva Lou's Karen Bell, and Lyle got friendly with her at work. Who knows? Iva Lou doesn't want to say. But I have a feeling this isn't the last we've seen of Lovely Carter.

The Saturday after Thanksgiving turns out to be a glorious wedding day for Fleeta and Otto. The sun burns high and bright orange in a pale white sky, casting a glow on our town, bathing the bare tree branches and caramel fields in warmth. It's cold enough to see your breath, but that doesn't matter. The United Methodist Church just got a new boiler, so the service and reception will be downright toasty.

It's always a treat for me when Jack puts on a suit, because it's so rare for him. His blue jeans, work shirt, and boots are his uniform. Jack calls them 'his workingman ensemble.' What with Etta's graduation and wedding, and now Fleeta's big day, he's worn a suit more times this year than he has in the last ten. If only he knew how handsome he looked. (Maybe it's better if he doesn't!) My papa and Giacomina gave Jack an elegant green silk tie when we were over in Italy. I watch as he makes the loop in the mirror.

'You're pretty good at that,' I compliment him.

'If I go slow, I get it right.'

I fix the cuffs on the sleeves of my dress. My mother's dress. It's a pale green sheath of ruched silk with long sleeves and a boat neck. I remember when Mama did the ruching on the dress. It took days to get the folds in the fabric to lie correctly.

'You look beautiful.' Jack puts his arms around me.

'We match.'

He smiles.

We have to park a couple blocks away, in front of Doc Polly's house, because every space around the church is taken. Fleeta was right: this will be a standing-room-only situation. Iva Lou estimates she made fifteen batches of mints, so there will be plenty of those. Jean Hendrick volunteered to make tea and sandwiches, while Barbara Polly made Kentucky truffles, chocolate balls soaked in bourbon. Connie Polly, Barbara's daughter-in-law, whipped up a monster batch of cheese straws that she transported from Roanoke like fine china.

Jack takes my hand as we walk up the church steps. I tell him to save me a seat; I want to check the Fellowship Hall.

I push the basement door open. The Garden Club has done an exquisite job. Bare branches twisted with burgundy berries adorn the ceiling, making a canopy. The pillars are covered in tapestry fabric and trimmed in cloth leaves. The cake has six tiers, white swirly buttercream icing, and a bride and groom on top – just like Fleeta wanted. Janine did a good job. The punch tables are covered in crisp white linens. Nancy Kilgore-Hall made sure the silver was polished. Members of the Intermont Garden Clubbers' Junior Division bustle around, placing napkins and bowls of salted nuts here and there. They will be the waitstaff for the reception.

'Lordy, did you see the cars?' Iva Lou says from the service kitchen. 'You'd think it was the Division D football championship.'

'It's packed wall-to-wall upstairs.'

'Thank God we have enough food. I panicked yesterday and started making calls. I had Evadean Church make a batch of her famous sand-dollar cookies, even though she's a Pentecost. She was so sweet. Just made the cookies regardless of church affiliation. Dropped 'em off on trays here this morning. You gotta love that.'

'It's gorgeous. Not that I lifted a finger, but it's perfect.'

'You got the right idea. Delegate. Maybe I'll figure that out next time.'

'You coming up?'

'In a minute. I gotta start the coffee. I didn't borrey Barbara Horton's silver urns for nothing. She went to the trouble to dig 'em out and polish 'em, so I gotta use 'em. I'll catch Fleets and Otto before they kiss. Never fear.'

I sneak up the back stairs and into the church.

I spot my husband at the end of a pew. He turns, looking for me, and motions for me to come and sit. The organist starts to play 'Islands in the Stream,' and the procession begins. Janine looks lovely in a ballet-length pink skirt and a white blouse. She carries a bouquet of miniature pink roses and baby's breath. Next comes Preacher Mutter and his wife, wearing dark blue robes with bright yellow sashes. As they pass, they greet the congregation on either side of the aisle. Then Fleeta and Otto enter, arm in arm. Otto looks sharp in a navy blue suit and a pink plaid silk bow tie. Fleeta looks stunning. Her hair is licorice black (L'Oréal #147, 'Deeply Ebony,' Aisle 3 at the Mutual's), slicked back in a French braid with a long shiny corkscrew curl in front of each ear. The curls are inlaid with bunches of baby's breath studded with small pink jewels that glitter as the flashbulbs pop.

I pull a camera out of my purse and start clicking away, along with the rest of the guests. Methodist services are short, so I snap as many pictures as I can, and quickly. Preacher Mutter's introductions are practically drowned out by the sound of cameras rewinding. I scan the front rows and see some of Fleeta's cousins from Scott County. They wear gloves and hats. Fleeta calls them 'fancies.'

Worley is the best man, and he's smiling (good sign). Fleeta said that Worley has slowly come to accept the inevitable. When the vows begin, Janine takes her mother's bouquet and gives her a kiss.

Fleeta takes her daughter's hand and pulls her close. Then Fleeta does something I've never seen: she makes the groom and best man join hands also. Worley is a little uncomfortable with that but complies. Fleeta turns and motions to the front pew. The crowd signs as Pavis joins them at the altar. Reverend Mutter smiles.

'Preacher must've had an intervention,' Jack whispers. Clerics love a family affair, that's for sure.

When Preacher Mutter pronounces them man and wife, Fleeta and Otto kiss, and the guests whoop and holler so loudly, it sounds like we're at a professional wrestling match. The organ music swells (this time it's an arrangement of Charlie Rich's 'Behind Closed Doors,' leading me to believe that no one checked the musical selections with the preacher). Otto and Fleeta lock arms and recess, followed by the wedding party. As Fleeta passes me, she grabs my hand for a second and says, 'Whoo.' I look to the back of the church, where Iva Lou is wiping away a tear of joy.

The congregation takes a detour downstairs to the Fellowship Hall, directly to the punch bowls, instead of going outside for an official receiving line. I've never seen a crowd this big in the church basement. I remember one time years ago, Spec cleared the hall during the Cub Scouts Pinewood Derby due to 'unaccounted-for overflow.' I'll bet we have twice as many people here tonight.

While Fleeta and Otto are outside 'meetin' and

greetin" and taking photos, the Garden Club kids hand out bottles of bubbles in net bags, which the guests commence blowing. Iva Lou fills the punch bowls as the Reedy Creek band plays a jazzy rendition of 'Here Comes the Bride.'

Fleeta and Otto enter the reception to another loud ovation, this one punctuated by earsplitting wolf whistles. Otto takes Fleeta in his arms. They dance in a dreamland of silver bubbles, as though they're in a snow globe where the glitter's been shaken. The rest of us form a deep circle around the dance floor and sway. Janine reaches over and squeezes my hand. Her brother, Pavis, joins us.

'Pavis, it means the world to your mother that you came,' I tell him.

Pavis wears a navy blue pin-striped suit and a tie printed with rows of tiny hot-pink champagne bottles. His black hair is sprayed into a clean tailfin sweep with a side part (they have a thing about hair in the Mullins family – they're particular and partial to definitive shapes).

'I'm glad I could make it.' Pavis smiles. 'Janine said she'd haul off and kill me if I didn't show up.'

'You'll do right to listen to your sister.'

'You got that right. I been skeered of her all my life.' Pavis winks one eye slowly. 'Don't mess with the Boss.'

Jack pulls me onto the dance floor. I exhale a huge sigh of relief. No matter what, weddings are stressful, and I've been on the front lines of this one since we returned from Italy. Jack and I do more shifting than dancing on the crowded floor, but I don't care. I'm in the arms of my true love, we're dressed up, he smells like fresh cedar and lemon, and the music is wonderful. 'Remember when you weren't allowed to dance at weddings?' Jack whispers in my ear.

'And we lived in a dry country?' I point to Iva Lou, pouring vodka into a punch bowl.

'Progress.' Jack laughs.

Eddie Carleton was kind enough to cover for me at the Mutual's, so I have the rest of Fleeta's wedding day off. There are so many things I want to do in the house before Theodore arrives. I've been meaning to clean out closets, flip mattresses, and repaint the spare bedroom, and now I have a reason to actually get some of these chores done. There's nothing like a deadline to force me to reorganize.

Jack is out back, working on a project. He won't tell me what it is; he wants to surprise me. I watch out the kitchen window as he lifts a small plank of wood and carries it into the forest. A few moments later, he returns for his toolbox on the porch.

Mousey and Rick came over and split logs for us, and Jack helped them stack, though not much more than that. The doctor wants him to exercise but avoid overexertion. The phone rings. As I answer it, I don't take my eyes off the path to the forest. Since Jack had his surgery, I watch after him a lot, like I did the children when they were small – where they are and what they're doing is always on my mind.

'Hi, Mom. It's Etta.'

She sounds terrible. 'How are you, honey?' I ask.

'Okay. How was Aunt Fleeta's wedding?'

'A sellout. The whole county turned out.'

'Good for them. Mom, I'm in Schilpario.'

'Did you go to Grandpop's for the weekend?'

'Not exactly. He called me to come up last night. Stefano is with me.'

'Is Papa all right?' I feel my stomach turn.

'He's fine. It's Nonna. Ma, she passed away early this morning.'

'No!' I sit down.

'She went very peacefully. We were all with her. She woke up this morning, had her coffee and hot milk, took a bite of a roll, and said she was tired. So we took her back to bed, and she died.'

I begin to cry. All the things she meant to me come flooding back. I remember when Nonna came to Big Stone Gap twenty years ago with Papa – how she kept a bright red cotton handkerchief, starched and pressed, tucked in her sleeve at all times; how she made fried eggs in a hearty marinara sauce in a skillet and then tossed them through fresh greens, and I thought it was the most delicious thing I'd ever tasted. She didn't make an ordinary tossed salad. Her wild greens were spiked with color, flower petals tossed through to add pizzazz. She taught me which flowers were edible (sweet woodruff, rose of

Sharon, African marigolds) and which weren't (calla lilies and crocus). My grandmother taught me how to make fresh gnocchi when I stayed for the summer in Schilpario. Nonna even tried to teach me how to make lace, but I couldn't get it right. I never tired of watching her dip the threads in sugar water and weave them over a ceramic plate until the strands became an ornate pattern, each an original. Every doily in her house was homemade. In fact, everything she touched was beautiful. On a hot summer day, she'd dip grapes in ice water and roll them in sugar, and they'd look like they were drenched in diamonds. She knew how to make the ordinary seem magical.

'I'm sorry, Ma,' Etta says.

'How's Grandpop?'

'He's very sad. But death isn't scary here. People don't seem to dread it; they sort of expect it. I don't know how to explain it.'

'In America, we think we're going to live forever.' As soon as I say it, I wish I hadn't. After all, I have a husband whom I wish would live forever.

'Here, they celebrate a long life for the gift it is.'

'I'm so glad you were there.'

'It was amazing, Ma. Really. It's like she went to sleep. Very sweet. So peaceful. I gave her a kiss from you and Dad. She smiled when I did it.'

'Thanks, honey.'

'The last thing she said to all of us was 'Don't cry.' And then she made a fist. We all laughed, but she meant it. And then she was gone.'

My daughter has such a good heart. No matter how frustrated I can be with her decisions, she instinctively knows the loving thing to do. She knows what people around her need and how to comfort them, and that's more important to me than the so-called big stuff. Etta possesses the kind of wealth we value: a generous spirit, first and always.

'Do you want to talk to Grandpop?' Etta asks.

'Ave Maria?' I hear my father's voice, and I try not to cry, but I can't help it.

'I'm so sorry, Papa.'

'She told me she was going to die before the end of the year. And she did. She was ninety-seven years old.'

'We should be so grateful for her long life.'

'We are. We are.'

'Papa, do you want me to come home?'

'There's no need. She was so happy that she could go to Etta's wedding. She really liked Stefano. So she felt like she had been given a gift.'

Papa talks about the townspeople stopping by to visit, and how bereft they are; after all, Nonna witnessed three generations come and go in their village.

I pull on my jacket and go out to find Jack and tell him the news. Since he's been sick, I've tried to avoid any discussion of death and dying. If we're watching something on TV and someone dies, I change the channel. If I see a story in the news-paper about a fatal accident, I pull out the page.

If I hear a story about someone suffering, I tend not to repeat it to him. He probably thinks about health and mortality enough; I certainly don't need to pile it on. I wish I didn't have to tell him about Nonna.

As I make my way to the woods, the field crunches underneath my feet. I see a scythe, a rake, and an ax at the fence line, which means Jack was planning on clearing some brush. I see his footprints at the edge of the field and take the path into the woods. I hear the sound of a hammer against wood, so I follow the sound. The afternoon sun makes pink ribbons of light through the gray trees.

'Jack?' I call out.

'Over here.'

I follow the sound of his voice over the hill toward the flats where the creek runs from Big Cherry Lake down the mountain. The path is muddy where the creek gets wide in the spring, so I hold on to the tree trunks to get to my husband. I see Jack take the hammer and put it back in his tool belt, like James Stewart with a Smith & Wesson in *The Man Who Shot Liberty Valance*. When I get to him, he steps aside and says, 'What do you think?'

Jack points to a small bridge over the creek. It's about five feet long and three feet high. It's made of mottled old barn wood. A perfectly shaped crescent, the small bridge fits over the creek at a narrow pass. Clear water pulses over the shiny black rocks underneath. The bridge is so beautiful, in scale and placement, it looks like it has been there a hundred years.

'Is this the surprise?'

'Yep.'

'It's gorgeous. I love it.'

'Thanks, hon. It always bothered me. We've needed a footbridge over this creek for a long time. I used to have to carry Etta and Joe over the rushing water when the spring rains would come. Now, if we want to get to the blackberry path, we have a bridge.' Jack looks at me. 'Are you sure you like it?'

'No, no, it's wonderful.'

'I had Mousey and Rick do the heavy stuff. They cut the wood and sized it.'

'I'm sure you didn't overdo it.' I put my arms around him.

'I'm trying to follow doctor's orders.'

'I know you are.'

'I hate asking the guys to do things for me. I can't wait till Doc gives me the go-ahead to work like I used to.'

'He will. You just have to be patient.'

Jack holds me a long time.

'I have sad news,' I finally say. 'Etta called. Nonna died.'

'I'm sorry to hear that. Are you okay?'

'I feel like everything is ending.'

'She was very old.'

'But it's still ending. It doesn't matter how old she was, she's gone. Why did we do it, Jack?'

'Do what?'

'Why did we have children when we knew how sad the world could be?'

'Well, that's a philosophical question.'

'Uh-huh.'

'And I'm not a philosopher.'

'I know that.'

'But I know why we had children.'

'You do?'

'Because most of it is really good. And if grief is the price you pay for what's really good, it is well worth it. Now, try ole Blackberry Bridge.' Jack takes my hand and helps me across. 'What do you think?'

'You built a bridge.'

Jack smiles. 'I always wanted to.'

Iva Lou calls and invites us for wedding leftovers, but I just don't feel up to it. She's sad to hear about Nonna. Though no one is surprised because of Nonna's age, nobody can believe such a life force has gone.

I'm reluctant to let go of any of the members of my Italian family, because no matter how much time I have with them, it will never be enough. I began this race with time when I met my father. I had missed thirty-five years of connection and was desperate to make up for it. My Italian family never knew me as a baby, or a girl, or a young woman. We missed so much, so many holidays, graduations, and birthdays; special times that should have been rich with celebration were hollow for me. I didn't know why, of course. I was just aware that something was missing.

I try not to think about how I behaved when Nonna saw me last. I didn't hide my feelings of disapproval about Etta and Stefano's wedding. I was so opposed to the marriage, for reasons practical and emotional, and now I find out that the very thing that brought me angst gave my grandmother joy. I was so wrapped up in my own drama that I didn't take time to be comforted by her wisdom and support. She did what family should do: she stood with Etta and trusted her. Whether Nonna agreed with the marriage or not, she did not say.

Papa told me that Nonna had made many cakes for the brides in Schilpario over the years. She considered the wedding cakes works of art. At the time I thought she'd stayed in the kitchen, baking Etta's cake, because she needed something to do. The truth is, she wanted to make the cake for her great-granddaughter because she wanted Etta to have a perfect day.

Maybe Nonna knew at her advanced age that life can be long, but true love doesn't come as a guarantee, if it comes at all. She saw something wonderful in Etta and Stefano together that I, as Etta's mother, was blind to. Or maybe I didn't want to see how happy my daughter was because then I would have had to support her decision. Nonna knew it was Etta's moment, and she wanted her to have it, to hold it, to own it. Nonna knew it might not come again.

It took Nonna days to make the marzipan cherubs for the cake. She carved them herself out of white-sugar paste with a small paring knife. They looked like putti you find hovering in Renaissance murals, some smiling with full faces, resting on wings without bodies (those were secured into the frosting, as if in relief), and others with chubby bodies and delicate spun-sugar wings doing the heavy lifting, holding up the layers between the tiers.

For every moment that I have wished Etta to be home, near me, I now begin to see some wisdom in her decision to marry Stefano and live in Italy. There are things she needs to experience in order to grow beyond the world we created in our home. Of course, I wanted her to be a single woman experiencing those things, savoring her glorious solitude and building her own life without worrying about a husband's needs. But, as with most decisions your children make, you can be sure of them only when time has passed and there's a context for their choices.

I want my daughter to be happy; all good mothers who ever were and ever will be have the same dream for their children. When I saw Etta take an enormous risk for her future at the expense of her youth, I couldn't accept it. There are still days when I question it. When Etta married so young, I could not think of a single good thing to come of it. Now I see one. She is there, in Italy. Her young marriage gave my daughter the opportunity to be with her great-grandmother when she died. There is a great gift in being with those you love as they're dying. When you've said all you can say, when you've done everything you can to make your loved one comfortable, when there is at last nothing left to *do*, all that remains is the mystical moment of surrender. Why should anyone face that alone? Maybe there *is* some master plan at work; maybe Etta knows something I don't. How could one so young see things so clearly? Was it her fate to be there? Maybe fate is the footwork of decisions made with loving intentions.

Someday, if I've done my job, Etta will lead this family after I'm gone, after Jack is gone, and after her children have grown up and left her. We don't stop being mothers when our children leave us; we continue to teach them in everything we say and do. I still marvel at how much I count on my mother's love and advice, even though she has been gone over twenty years. I close my eyes and can still hear her voice, and there's never any question in my mind what her advice would be. Mama is still my most important model in all things.

Taking care of my mother when she was sick prepared me to look after my son and then my husband when he fell ill. I couldn't see it at the time, but my mother, even as she was dying, was still teaching me how to be a good person right up to the moment I lost her. 'There is no such thing as too much generosity,' she used to say. She wasn't talking about dropping off soup for someone sick (though that's important) or running errands for someone homebound (though that's kind). She was talking about a generosity of spirit, about being present when a person is afraid. She taught me not to run but to stay and listen. When people are sick, they crave reassurance and care, and when they're dying, they need to feel treasured. They need to know that you loved them, and that you always will. I'm sure Etta gave that to Nonna. There couldn't have been a better emissary for my heart's desire than my daughter.

CHAPTER 6

SALZBURG

The cast of *The Sound of Music* gathers on the stage of the Powell Valley High School auditorium with anticipation. They greet one another, chatting and laughing, as they take their seats in folding chairs, which I have placed in a wide circle. The work lights are on, the coffee is brewing, highlighters are out and at the ready. It's time to do the first read-through of the script.

I'm about to call roll when Nellie Goodloe runs down the aisle waving a letter. 'It's here! The letter from Mr Ted Chapin of the Rodgers and Hammerstein Organization in New York City! We are cleared to do *The Sound of Music*!'

The cast whistles and applauds. This is good news indeed. We thought there was a chance that they wouldn't allow us to mount a production at all. You see, we fell into disfavor with the Rodgers & Hammerstein folks over nonpayment of royalties for a production of *The King and I* that we did in 1987. Nellie didn't pay because she had scripts and scores from a production they had done back in 1969, so she didn't see any need for our town to pay twice. Mr Chapin set her straight with a letter embargoing the production. We had to have a bake sale, a car wash, and a seed sale to make the nut and go on with the show. It did go on, after we paid our back royalties and fees.

Nellie gives me the letter. 'Fantastic,' I tell her as I scan the page and wonder if we can import Mr Chapin to direct the dang thing. Nellie has precast the musical, so directing this show is like being the general of an all-volunteer army without guns.

Nellie has a flair for lots of things – her talents range from horticulture to home decorating. She is forever coming up with ideas to turn Big Stone Gap from a coal mining town into an elegant tourist attraction for those who might want to experience the natural beauty of our mountains. She was in charge of the refurbishment of the downtown area. It was her idea to place hanging baskets of blooming flowers on the streetlights and electrical poles down Main Street. I wish she had the same vision when it comes to casting. Alas, she mistakes exuberance for skill. She says yes to everyone who wants to be in a play, instead of finding the right person for the role. Our chorus of *Mame* was so enormous, we could have restaged *Ben-Hur*, and we almost did during the fox-hunt scene.

The surplus of bodies begins with my chorus. I have an overstock of nuns (members of the Lonesome Pine Hospital Auxiliary, the Methodist Sewing Circle, the Dogwood, Intermont, and Green Thumb garden clubs, and Liz Ann Noel's bridge club all thought it would be 'fun' to be in the production, so I've got the nuns outnumbering the bad guys two to one), age-inappropriate children (my Gretl is thirteen, with a figure like Ava Gardner's, when in reality she should be five), and my Captain Von Trapp (Gregory Kress), while attractive and a terrific baritone (thank you, First Baptist Church Revival Choir), is on the sunny side of seventy.

Maria will be played by Tayloe Slagle Lassiter, who we are convinced, without her teenage marriage and responsibilities at home, could have made it on the Great White Way, outdazzling any New York klieg lights with her beauty and talent. Tayloe is thirty-six years old, but her figure is better than ever, and her face is as porcelain-perfect as the day she debuted in the Outdoor Drama as June Tolliver at the age of sixteen. Still, we are asking a lot of our audience to accept a novice nearing forty in a convent. After all, Tayloe is no Dolores Hart. As I survey the cast gathered onstage, I realize this is surely the least of my problems.

Tayloe's daughter, Misty, who is around Etta's age, moved to Kingsport and became a roving reporter for WCYB-TV while attending East Tennessee State. She's got her mother's beauty and her father's brains, which makes for good camera work and short interviews.

'Where's my script?' Iva Lou enters from stage right. With one hand, she unbuttons her black velvet trench coat with leopard trim, and with the other, she pulls her leopard reading glasses out of her décolletage. 'I watched the movie about seven times,' she admits. 'I think I got the Baroness down.'

'Take your seat, please, Iva Lou,' I tell her. 'Welcome to our first rehearsal. I think it would be in our best interest *not* to watch the movie; rather, let's focus on our own interpretation of the story. The music rehearsals will be conducted by Virginia Meador, and I'm asking – let me say, begging – you all to be on time and take your work seriously.'

Virginia, petite in plaid, waves from the piano in the pit. She's been a steady force in all our productions since 1970, even though she was heard telling folks at the Post Office that she didn't have platinum streaks in her chestnut-brown hair until she started accompanying our musicals on the piano. Let's face it, it's stressful.

Iva Lou pulls a thermos of hot coffee out of her tote bag. 'I'll tell you one thing. We need to rewrite the ending of this old chestnut right here and now. Tayloe, you might be a singer and a dancer and a nun, but make no mistake, I'm the femme fatale of this here piece, and I want the Captain. You need to know that I'm not going down without a fight.'

'Now, ladies.' Greg rises from his seat and holds his arms out as if to stop a fistfight between the two women.

Tayloe laughs. 'See you in the Abbey.'

Louise Camblos raises her hand. 'Hey, Madame Director, when do we get fitted for our costumes? I've waited my whole life to be a nun. None in the morning and none at night.' The cast chuckles.

'Carolyn Beech is in charge of costumes again this year.' I motion for Carolyn to stand.

Cranky Carolyn stands up and raises a finger of warning. Her slender pointer finger is as bony as her body. She's had the same Dorothy Hamill wedge haircut since 1976, but it's a good choice because it balances her pronounced chin. Carolyn is good-looking but has the sloped shoulders of a woman who has spent most of her life bent over a Singer sewing machine and isn't one bit happy about it. 'I want to ask everybody to stay within a two-to-five-pound weight range after measurements. I didn't appreciate it last year when the chorus of *Oklahoma!* decided to go on Jenny Craig after I measured them. I had to pull all-nighters for a week, taking in those sundresses. My fingers ain't been right since. In fact, there's days when I have no feeling at all in my right pinky. Please be aware that we are not creating the town musical in a vacuum. Unless you get a bad disease and can't help it, I don't want see a substantial weight loss before opening night. Thank you.'

Iva Lou raises her hand. 'As a cancer survivor, I don't need to hear that.'

Carolyn stands. 'Sorry, but you know what I mean.' She sits.

'Anyone else?' I ask.

'Eddie Shankle can't play Rolfe,' Nellie pipes up. 'He was called in for weekend duty in Knoxville with the National Guard.' She bites her lip nervously.

'So who have we got?'

Ravi Balu raises his hand. 'Me, ma'am.' Ravi is the twenty-year-old son of one of our doctors at Lonesome Pine Hospital. He is handsome, with jet-black hair and luminous coffee-colored skin. His family moved to Southwest Virginia from India when Ravi was a boy.

'How on earth can Ravi play Rolfe? Rolfe is supposed to be a blond,' Louise Camblos wonders aloud. 'And German.'

'Let me know now if you want me to wig him,' Carolyn barks.

'I don't know about a wig,' I tell her diplomatically.

'Whew.' Ravi dramatically wipes his brow. The cast cracks up.

'Well, just let me know one way or the other. I don't need to be tracking down special hairpieces and all kinds of makeup at the last minute,' Carolyn says.

'I think we'll skip the wig,' I tell her. 'And the makeup.'

'Fine.' Carolyn waves me off like she's cheating a hot flash. I wonder if she's even read the play.

The cast begins to read the script aloud, and waves of futility peel through me as they struggle with the words. I'm not the only one who's nervous. The smell of Greg Kress's Wild Country cologne wafts over us as he sweats (I recognize the Avon aftershave because Worley Olinger wears it, or it wears him, however you want to look at it). This is Greg's first leading role, and he's feeling the pressure. It's a long way from the choir loft of the Free Will Baptist Church to the bright lights of the Powell Valley High School auditorium.

As we read, some actors actually attempt Austrian accents; they fail miserably, falling into the Vivien Leigh Four-Door Ford problem. The story goes that when England's Vivien Leigh auditioned for the role of Scarlett O'Hara in *Gone with the Wind*, they brought in a dialogue coach to help take her accent from British highbrow to Southern fried. She'd say 'four-door Ford' as 'fo-ah do-ah fo-ah,' over and over again, hoping to capture our twang. Evidently, I'm not the only one familiar with the *GWTW* dialogue-coach story. Iva Lou is playing the Baroness like Belle Watling. She goes up on the ends of sentences as though all the lines are written with a question mark (they're not).

The only thing European about this production will be the German chocolate cake Fleeta makes for the opening-night party. Ravi Balu as Rolfe? Local newsman Bill Hendrick as Uncle Max? We'll just have to take that leap of faith and hope the audience goes along for the ride.

'"Oh, George . . ."' Iva Lou reads from the script.

I can't take it another second, so I correct her. 'It's *GAY-org. GAY-org.*'

'Honey, I don't care if he's gay or hetero, I'm the Baroness Von Love Interest, and the Captain's gonna know it before the final curtain.'

Slick patches of gray ice cover the curves of the road as I drive up to church. I slip the Jeep into a low gear to keep from sliding. My mind keeps wandering back to the disastrous read-through. I will light every candle in the sacristy this morning in hopes that some showmanship will grip my motley cast as rehearsals continue.

Sacred Heart Church sits on top of the hill in the southern section of Big Stone Gap, above the train tracks ('the southern line'; hence the name) and the WLSD radio station. WLSD doesn't stand for dropping acid; rather, the letters represent the counties (Wise, Lee, Scott, and Dickenson) that can hear the programming from the radio tower that blinks above Big Stone Gap like the Eiffel Tower.

I've bought radio ads for the Mutual Pharmacy since I can remember. They run them during the afternoon music-marathon programs, which are called Pop Corn, since the DJs play pop and country music.

There was a little bit of controversy when Sacred Heart Catholic Church moved from Appalachia to Big Stone Gap. The church in Appalachia was a small, sweet blue clapboard building next to the railroad tracks on the edge of the Powell River. Roman Catholics in these parts have always been a very small but diverse group. You had sons and daughters of immigrant coal miners who came to make their living: Polish, Czech, Italian (who returned to Italy as soon as they saved enough money), and then the converts who, for whatever reason, decided to become Catholic despite the low cachet of such a move in these mountains. You could count the converts on one hand. When our ranks grew to a hundred or so in the 1970s, the church hierarchy decided to build a mod new church and rectory in Big Stone Gap (respectful of their Appalachian roots, they saved the bell tower, which now adorns the roof). Today the bells are ringing for a memorial mass held in honor of Nonna.

There are lots of cars parked outside Sacred Heart. I'm surprised, but Fleeta reminded me that lots of folks remember my grandmother from her visit to Big Stone Gap. The cars of some prominent Protestants are parked alongside those of our members. There was a time when a God-fearing Baptist wouldn't set foot in a Catholic church. Those days are over. People around here are generally happy if anyone goes to church regularly at all – wherever you go is fine with them.

I pull in to a parking space. My husband is waiting for me outside the church. I left home early this morning to make an emergency delivery up on Skeen's Ridge. Jack waves to me. Once again he's wearing a suit – this is a world record. It's the fourth time this year, and I'm counting because I like it.

Papa is having a memorial mass said in Italy today, so Nonna will get a double boost on her journey to heaven (not that she'll need it – but to be on the safe side, it's better to have two masses than one or none). The one thing the Catholics get right is praying for the dead. When we pray for them, we honor their lives while helping them move up the afterlife's angelic food chain. For example, if loved ones are stuck in purgatory, a few prayers may give them the pass out of there and into heaven.

Father Drake, our serene pastor who delivers meaningful homilies with a gentle countenance, has placed a picture of Nonna on the lectern (Jack must have brought it – I didn't think of it). As we begin the mass, I am swept into the words and ritual that have meant so much to me through the years. I would never say I'm a religious person, but I am a person of tradition and habit. So when I hear prayers I learned in childhood, I am still moved by them.

Jack gets up and reads the story of Ruth from the Old Testament, which always gets to me because it's about a woman who leads her family, which is what Nonna did for us. Iva Lou reads the second scripture and cries all the way through it. It's the passage about Mary the mother giving her son over to die. (Father Drake must have chosen the weepies for this service.) Nellie Goodloe, a Presbyterian, muffles her sobs with a handkerchief, though I can't be sure if she's missing my grandmother or crying about the disastrous first reading of *The Sound of Music*. We'll never know.

Father Drake keeps the mass mercifully short – the less kneeling/standing/sitting combos the Protestants have to endure, the better. Father says the final prayer and recesses, stopping to embrace Jack and me. The congregation follow him out. They make their way downstairs to the meeting room, where we said mass for years before the top of the building was added to form an actual church.

I take a moment alone at the altar with Nonna's picture. There's a bouquet of flowers: delicate white roses and yellow daisies in a crystal vase. The card says, 'All our love and sympathy, the Bakagese family.' Pearl Grimes was just a girl when she met Nonna twenty years ago, but she didn't forget Nonna, and she never forgets me, and that makes me cry a few more tears.

'Come on, honey,' Jack says from the back of the church. He holds my hand as we go downstairs. The meeting room is fragrant with rich coffee and sweet butterscotch pie. Our friends gather around us and express their sympathies.

FLEETA'S BUTTERSCOTCH PIE

Makes 8 servings

CRUST
2 cups all-purpose flour
1 teaspoon salt
⅔ cup Crisco
6–7 tablespoons cold water

PIE FILLING AND MERINGUE
½ to ¾ cup brown sugar
2½ tablespoons cornstarch
A pinch of salt
1 cup milk
1 cup cream
3 egg yolks (save egg whites for meringue)
2 tablespoons butter or margarine
1 teaspoon vanilla
⅓ cup sugar

For crust: Sift together flour and salt. Cut in Crisco with a pastry blender or blending fork until pieces are the size of small peas. To make pastry extra tender and flaky, divide Crisco in half. Cut in first half until mixture looks like cornmeal. Then cut in remaining half until pieces are the size of peas.
OR
Put all crust ingredients in a food processor and blend until mixed. Place in oven at 450

degrees for 12–15 minutes. Makes 2 pie crusts and can be frozen for later use.

For the filling and meringue: Mix brown sugar, cornstarch, and salt together until well blended. Add milk and cream, stirring constantly over medium heat. Add egg yolks and cook until thickened. Add butter and vanilla, stir in, and pour into baked pie crust. Beat egg whites until almost stiff. Add ⅓ cup sugar and beat until stiff. Spread on pie and bake in oven at 325 degrees for 10–15 minutes until meringue is browned.

The buffet is loaded with more of Fleeta's blue-ribbon dishes. There are trays of delicate 'ham and biscuits' (tiny sandwiches made with thin-sliced ham, mustard, and flaky, fresh biscuits), hot serving dishes of scalloped-potato squares, crystal bowls of fresh fruit salad, individual Jell-O molds with whipped cream, peanut-butter cookies, and a wire basket overflowing with Catherine Rumschlag's butter rolls from the Bread and Chicken House. I don't know how Fleeta does it – when it comes to events, she has almost a psychic ability about how much food to make and whom to call to fill in the holes. Jack and I get in line for the buffet behind Father Drake.

'Here.' Fleeta gives me a cup of hot coffee in a Styrofoam cup. 'That there was a sad service, and we didn't even have the body here.'

'What can you do?'

'Not a goddamn thing.' Fleeta shakes her head. 'Can I get you a cup of coffee, Father?'

'You don't have to wait on me, Fleeta.'

'You got that right, Padre. Self-serve is easier on everybody.'

Father Drake smiles. Fleeta goes back into the service kitchen, where she barks orders at Otto and Worley, who are prepping more platters.

'Sorry about Fleeta's cursing,' I say.

Father shrugs. 'What can you do?'

Iva Lou has her coat and sunglasses on and her car keys in hand. She gives me a quick kiss on the cheek. 'Honey-o, I gotta get to work. We're doing our annual inventory. Last time I missed, the volunteers took all my Jackie Collins books and put them in the discard bin. It was traumatic.'

'You like Jackie Collins?' Father Drake asks.

'Love her. She's my hero. She has her finger on the pulse and her thighs in fishnet. You can't beat that. Do you read her?'

'*Dangerous Kiss* was my favorite.'

'Father!' Iva Lou covers her mouth. 'I swan!'

Father winks. 'The Old Testament gets a little dry sometimes.'

'I'll say.' Iva Lou gives Father a thumbs-up and goes.

My time is stretched to the limit with work and *The Sound of Music* rehearsals. I want to have the house ready for Theodore's arrival. I convinced him to come down for a couple of weeks and have a nice, long visit. This is our first Christmas without Etta, and I need total diversion. Jack doesn't say it, but I know he's also sad that she won't be here. But I guess he still feels he needs to be totally supportive of Etta and Stefano's marriage, because I wasn't.

Theodore is not one to sit around by the fire, so we plan to go spelunking in the sand caves (just like the old days!), to the South-west Virginia Museum for the Dogwood Garden Club Christmas show (the festival of trees is *not* to be missed) and to catch the Big Stone and Appalachia holiday parades. Theodore is used to those glamorous Fifth Avenue parades now, but there's nothing like our hometown ones, complete with Santa throwing candy into the crowd.

I still haven't said a word to Jack about the list I found when he was in the hospital. Neither of us keeps a diary, but I'm sure if we did, we wouldn't want each other to read it. So, unless he brings it up, I'll keep mum on the subject. He has rebounded from his surgery beautifully, and every day I thank God that it wasn't worse. There won't be a day when I don't worry about his heart, but at least I didn't lose him. I'll never forget what it felt like when I didn't know.

It's odd to bring the ornaments down from the attic without Etta. When she was little, she'd start asking about Christmas around September, and I'd spend the next three months promising her that the holidays were coming; she'd say, 'When?' and I'd say, 'Soon, soon.' When she got older, she did more and more of the decorating. Last Christmas she and Jack put the tree up when I was at work, and by the time I got home, she had it decorated.

'I guess I better go and get a tree,' Jack says when he sees the piles of crates in the hallway.

'Good idea. And can you make me a holly wreath for the front door? I like the leaves with the red berries. Oh, and let's put Santa and the reindeer on the roof. Make sure you get the guys to help you. The kids loved it. They could see it from the road below.'

'I thought we were keeping it simple.'

'I'll feel better if we're lit up.'

'Okay.'

'Maybe you can put a string of lights on your new bridge.'

'For who? The squirrels?'

'You never know who'll traipse through our woods.'

There's a knock at the door. Jack and I look at each other. We didn't hear anyone drive up – but who would? I'm playing the Firestone Christmas CDs at top volume through the house.

I open the front door.

'Hello, Ave Maria,' Lovely Carter says and smiles.

'Why, hello,' I say. We met only once, but there's something familiar about her that puts me at ease, so I open the door and invite her in. 'Jack, this is Lovely Carter.'

'Nice to meet you. Great name.'

'Thanks. I can't take any credit for it. My mother found it in a yearbook.'

'I met Lovely down at Iva Lou's on Thanksgiving Day. You were watching football,' I say.

Jack smiles. 'I'll put on a pot of coffee.'

'That would be nice,' Lovely says, looking around our house. 'This is a beautiful home.'

'Thank you. It's been my husband's family home for three generations. Can you believe it? I'm lighting fires in hearths that are over a hundred years old.'

Lovely follows me into the living room and sits on the sofa. I take a seat in the old armchair across from her.

'So, what can I do for you?'

'Well, it's a long story.'

'The best ones are.'

'I don't know if Iva Lou said anything to you about me.'

'She didn't.' I won't share that Iva Lou seemed rattled after Lovely's visit; something tells me that would be a breach of our friendship.

'I guess I should start at the beginning. I contacted Iva Lou's aunt down in Lee County in August of last year.'

'Why?'

'I was trying to find Iva Lou.'

'Everybody knows Iva Lou.'

'I found that to be very true.'

'She's basically a legend. She's been driving the Bookmobile since I was in high school. And that's a long time ago.'

'Did you know much about her?'

'What do you mean?'

'Where she came from.'

'London, Kentucky,' I say.

'Right.'

'And then she moved here,' I go on. 'She had kin here and there in the area. And she was a workingwoman, a single workingwoman until she met Lyle Makin.' Why am I telling Lovely so many details? I feel like I'm defending my friend. There's something in Lovely's tone that makes me feel I have to. 'Oh, sorry. I don't mean to ramble.'

'I don't mind. Anything you tell me helps.' Lovely's clear blue eyes fill with tears.

'Is there a problem?'

Lovely snaps open her purse and pulls out a Kleenex. 'I'm sorry.'

'Is there some reason you came to talk to me?'

'Yes, ma'am.'

'Whatever it is, you can say it.'

Jack comes in with a tray of coffee and a few leftover cookies from Fleeta's memorial spread. He puts the tray down on the coffee table. 'I'll leave you ladies alone.'

'Thanks, honey.'

Jack goes, giving me a quizzical look, as Lovely dries her tears.

'I didn't want to have to do this, but I need your help. I just turned forty. I was born in 1958, and I'm adopted. For many years I wondered who my parents were, and they finally unsealed the records in Kentucky, and I was able, with the help of an adoptee group, to start the process of finding my biological mother. In fact, I have found her. But she doesn't want to talk about it.'

'Lovely, who is your mother?'

'Iva Lou Wade Makin.'

I've taken in all sorts of information in my life, and even when the news was surprising, I would take it in stride. But at this I gasp aloud.

Lovely looks at me, surprised. 'She never told you?'

'No.' So many thoughts swirl through my head at once. I'm close to Iva Lou, as close as friends get without being family. She's been a part of my life through all the good times and the terrible moments too. She was an honorary aunt to both my children. She got me through my romantic travails with Theodore, my fate with Jack, Joe's death, and Etta's marriage – I can't imagine why she wouldn't have told me this. It's inconceivable. I blurt, 'Are you sure?'

Lovely is put off. 'Yes, I'm sure.'

'I'm sorry. It's just – I'm so close to her, I can't believe she wouldn't have told me.'

'I believe she put the whole event out of her mind.' For the first time, I hear anger in Lovely's voice.

'That doesn't sound like Iva Lou.'

'I don't know what her reasons are –' Lovely begins.

'I can't imagine.'

'Maybe she's ashamed of what happened.'

'How do you know that?'

'She told me that she was sorry she had to give me up, but she believed she did the best thing for me.'

'When did she tell you that?'

'After I came over on Thanksgiving, I realized that was awfully rude of me. I just assumed she'd be gone that day and I'd leave a note with my phone number. I found her address, so I thought, I'll just leave my information under her door. That way, if she wanted to see me, she could call, and if she didn't want to, well, I had my answer. But when she opened the door, I had to say something, so I sort of blurted it out – and she was stunned. But she took my number and called. We met again for lunch in Norton today.'

'Today?' Iva Lou had said she had inventory.

'Yes, ma'am. And we talked everything through. It was very emotional for her and for me.'

'Of course it was.'

'We both did a lot of crying. I felt terrible. I didn't want to hurt her. Eventually, we came to a place where we both were feeling a little more in control of our feelings. And then I asked her who my father was, and it was like a wall went up. She didn't want to tell me – and she wouldn't.'

'Why not?'

'I don't know. That's why I'm here.'

'But I don't know who your father is.'

'Everyone said you and Iva Lou were the closest of friends. I want you to find out who my father is for me.' Lovely implores me with her eyes. She looks so sad, I might promise her anything to see that sadness go.

'Lovely, I'm . . . Well, I'm so stunned by your news, I'll have to think about that. I'm not sure she'll tell me – I mean, she never told me about you. Iva Lou came to work here around 1958. I didn't really know anything about her before that.'

'But she would tell you if you asked her.'

'I don't know why she would. She never told me about you, why would she open up about your father?'

'Mrs MacChesney, I'm worried I will run out of time. For years and years, I swore I'd never, ever try to find my biological parents. My mom and dad are the best – well, my mom was the best. She died this year. She always encouraged me to find my biological parents; she never set up a single obstacle. And as clear as I was about not trying to find them, one day my feelings changed. Maybe it's my age, or the fact that I have children, or maybe I was just tired of wondering. But now I won't rest until I meet him. I can't tell you how devastating it is to know my mother – for her to admit that, yes, she's my mother, and she'd like a relationship, but only if she can keep the identity of my father a secret. I don't know if you can understand that.'

I should set Lovely Carter straight here and now. I found out who my *real* father was after my mother's death, in a letter she left behind with a photograph of him. Lovely has no idea how many times since that day I have read that letter. Just a few weeks ago, I read it again. It's the only proof I have that my mother wanted me to live in truth. Thank God Mario Barbari was alive, and is still alive, and somehow, with time and care, we've built a beautiful father/daughter relationship. This relationship, in many ways, saved me and held me together as I dealt with the death of my son, a crisis in my marriage, and Etta's marriage. In fact, if my father weren't in Italy, close to Etta, I couldn't cope with her decision at all. At the outset, the only saving grace of her marriage for me was my father's close proximity to them. I don't know Lovely, and I don't want to bury her with our similarities when she is so clearly in pain. I don't know if it would help. I lean toward her. She settles back in the chair. I say, 'I completely understand how you feel. I was raised by a father who wasn't my biological father, and it was kept secret from me.'

'So you know!'

'Yes, I do. And I can tell you that you have to come to this with a loving heart – without judgment.'

'I don't judge Iva Lou!'

'But you have. You sort of gave her terms for a

relationship with you – and made the identity of your father the deal breaker.'

'But I'm in pain about this!' she cries.

'I understand that pain. I know it well. But I also know that you have to trust Iva Lou. She is a thoughtful, contemplative, bright woman.'

'I have a right to know!'

Lovely is emotional, so I lower my voice to a soothing level to comfort her. 'Iva Lou doesn't make decisions in a rash way. I've never seen her buckle under pressure, or snap at anyone. She's a rock. If you want to have a friendship with her now, you should know that she never would have made a flip decision when it came to your best interests.'

'I understand that. She explained that to me today.'

'It was different back then too.'

'I'm sure it was.' Lovely stands abruptly. I find myself standing as well.

'If you think you can help me, here's my number.' Lovely gives me her phone number on a scrap of paper.

Her body language has changed: her spine has stiffened, and she pulls her purse close to her waist as though she has locked a gate. It's as if a wall of clear ice has formed around her. I can see her, but she's removed – certainly she is different than the woman who came to my door to seek some information.

Instead of finding her behavior odd, I realize it's

familiar. It's what I used to do before Mario Barbari came to meet me. I'd find myself at a party, or in a large group, or even in a quiet conversation, and then suddenly I'd have to leave. It was as if someone were cutting off my oxygen. I'd get up, despite pleas to stay from whomever I was talking to; I couldn't take another second of chatter, of conversation, of noise. I was living my life, but *it* always intruded. The *it* would not go away; it was my center. It was confusion from my lack of resolution about who I was. I kept shoving it down, and it would stay down for long periods of time, and then something would bring those feelings to the surface again. Silly, innocuous things like a passing comment or a look on someone's face. I'd feel that anger rise, and I'd have to leave.

After I found out my mother's secret, I remember thinking that if my own father didn't care about me or want to know me, who would? Why did my mother, who loved me completely, keep the truth from me for so long? If I was too weak or fragile to know the truth, then what was I? Had my mother been keeping the truth from me so I wouldn't get angry with her? Maybe she was afraid she'd lose me. I will never know. I did know that the only way to keep safe was to be alone. No one would ever see how lonely I was or know my rage. That was *my* secret. I pretended I wanted love, but I never experienced it, because I didn't think I deserved it. What would I bring to a relationship? Who would love me? Who could, when I had no way to know who I really was?

There is no romantic love, no husband, no friend, no relationship on earth that can fill the void of a mother's love lost or a father's rejection. We need our parents, and we need them as long as they are alive. When they're gone, we must go about shoring up our memory banks with the wisdom they imparted while letting go of the secrets and the hurts, which do us no good when we're moving forward. I remember the feeling in my body when I was trapped in anger – it was like being buried in wet cement. I couldn't look to the past, because it was riddled with half-truths, and I couldn't move forward because I couldn't let go of my anger at the lies told to protect me.

I learned bitterness is the most destructive emotional force there is. Bitterness is anger with a few years on it (and I'd had thirty-five long years). Bitterness prevents us from loving, and without love, we are without sun and water and sustenance – without love, our bodies wither and our souls long to die. I remember thinking, Well, I'm thirty-five years old now. It won't be that long until I'm old and death will come. I'll just keep busy until then. I'll fill up the years with work and trips and hobbies. Time will fly; I'll hardly notice it passing. I'll keep a garden and my job. That will get me through.

I look at Lovely and wish I could say, I understand. I get it! But I can't say any of these things, because she won't hear them. She can't hear them.

She found the road to truth, and she's been denied it again. I want to say all these things so she won't feel so alone. Instead, I hold the piece of paper with her number on it. 'I will call you. I promise.'

Lovely goes to the door. I follow and open it for her.

'Thank you, Mrs MacChesney.' Lovely's eyes fill with tears again. 'I just want peace.'

'I know you do.' I reach to embrace her, but she steps away and goes down the steps quickly and into her car. I watch her as she drives away, until her red brake lights disappear into the black like rubies at midnight.

'What was that all about?' Jack asks from the kitchen.

'You won't believe it,' I tell him. And I can't believe it. I can't.

CHAPTER 7

STONE MOUNTAIN

High in the hills, a layer of white clouds settles on the horizon like cotton padding in a gold-foil jewelry box.

'Snow,' my husband says as he drops me at the Pharmacy. 'I'm gonna run some errands. Then I have a lunch date at the Mutual's.'

'Don't make it sound so casual. You're meeting the enemy.'

'Tyler Hutchinson is not the enemy. He may love these mountains as much as you do.'

'We'll see.' I give Jack a quick kiss on the cheek and climb out.

Fleeta is in the café serving lunch. I see a RESERVED sign on the corner table (or should I say, Jack's meeting site with the enemy). She waves to me.

'Need me?' I ask her.

'Hell, no. People's clearing out early 'cause of the weather.'

'Is it really going to snow?'

Fleeta looks at me like I'm an idiot. 'It smells like snow.'

'You and Jack are like hunting dogs.'

'Serves us well. There is a particular smell when it's gonna snow. It's a sort of a frosty, smoky smell. You have to be open to it.' Fleeta gives me an order form for the café. 'E-mail this list to Cover Girl for me, will ye?'

'Okay, but just this one last time. You have to learn how to e-mail our distributors yourself.'

'I hate modern times! Hate it. Why should I, at my age, have to learn anything new? My head is already full of a bunch of useless information that will just cloud me up as I get older. I'm trying to learn less, not more.'

'I'll show you again later,' I say, trying not to snap at her. 'You should be placing your own orders.'

'I got a favor to ask of ye.'

'What is it?'

'You know, when I die, do me like your granny. Just do a picture up there on the pulpit. A good picture. Caskets always skeered me.'

I hate to disappoint Fleeta, but there was a casket in Italy, and I know because Giacomina took pictures of Nonna in the casket – it's a tradition over there. 'I'll do as you say, Fleets.'

'I want to be cremated and put in a pot. Now, the way me and Otto got it figgered is when he dies, he goes to Holding Funeral Home, and when I die, I go down to Gilliam's. This way both funeral homes in town get a piece of our business. It's only right. Car Wash Gilliam always did right by me, and you know I got a special place in my heart for his wife, Want Wax.'

'I know you do.'

'I'll get ole Lew Eisenberg to write it in a will.'

'Good idea.'

Iva Lou pushes through the front door in full snow gear: a hot-pink faux shearling coat with a white fake-fur-lined hood, beige knee boots with zippers up the calf, and a matching Cossack hat.

'Look who's ready for the snow.' Fleeta wipes off the counter.

'What you got to go that's fast?' Iva Lou asks her.

'I'll make you a hammy sammy. Got fresh biscuits and some ham in the back.'

'Perfect. I gotta get up to Wise before it freezes.'

I've seen Iva Lou at rehearsals since Lovely came to see me, but I haven't had a chance to talk to her about it. I've tried to pick up the phone, and I can't. Jack says I should go over and see her in person, but that's even more upsetting to me than talking about it over the phone. Outside of rehearsals, I avoid her. I wonder if she notices.

'Hey, Ave.' Iva Lou slides onto a stool at the counter. 'How'm I doing with the Baroness part?'

'I think you're a total original.'

'I know that.' Iva Lou fluffs her fur hood. 'I mean, on an acting level.'

'You fit in with the rest of the cast perfectly.'

'Thank you. You know I'm a-tryin'.'

'It'll be great by opening night. Theodore can't wait to see it.'

'It'll be good to see him. The three of us back together again.'

'Yep.'

Iva Lou looks at her hands. She reaches over the counter and pumps some of Fleeta's hand cream into her palm. 'Everything all right with you?'

I nod that I'm fine.

'I'm glad. 'Cause you seem a little distant.'

How can I tell Iva Lou I'm feeling preoccupied because she's failed to tell me that she has a daughter? It's almost as if I'm testing her, waiting for her to tell me. I don't understand why she'd keep it from me. But she has, and for all the years I've known her. Am I trying to respect her privacy? I think I am. 'Oh, I'm just up to my ears. And I'm missing Etta.'

Iva Lou pats my hand. 'I know, honey-o. We always had so much fun with her at Christmastime.'

'So much fun,' I agree. 'Well, girls, I've got to get to work. Be careful driving up to Wise.'

'I will. Don't worry. Lyle put the chains on my tires, so I won't wind up over Powell Mountain.'

Obviously, Lovely didn't tell Iva Lou that she came to see me. This makes it even worse. How do I bring it up?

The doorbells jingle as Iva Lou goes. Fleeta leans over my counter. 'What's going on with you two?'

'What do you mean?' I don't look up from my work.

'You're acting as cold as a cuke to old Iva Lou.'

'I don't mean to.'

'Now, lookee here, Ave. I've been around too

127

long for you to tell me a story. What's on your mind?'

'Do you really want to know?'

Fleeta nods.

'A woman came to see me at the house the other night. And she said some shocking things to me.'

'Who was she?'

'Her name is Lovely Carter.'

Fleeta's face turns the color of Pond's cold cream. 'Oh.'

'You know her?'

'Not personally. I know the name Carter.'

'But you know *about* her.'

'Uh-huh. That's the baby that Iva Lou done gave away.'

'*You* knew about that?'

Fleeta nods. 'For yars and yars.'

'Years? And you didn't tell me?'

'What fer?'

'It's a huge thing.'

'That's Iva Lou's business.'

'Yes, it is. I feel she should have told me.'

'Why?'

'Because we're – we have been – very close.'

'Maybe that's why she didn't tell you.'

'I don't understand.'

'Maybe y'all is too close. And it's too much for her.'

'Do people around here know about Lovely? Besides you?'

'Most of 'em's dead now. Spec knew.'

'He did?'

'Oh, yeah. But that old rascal knew pert near everything that went on in this four-county area.'

'I need a cup of coffee.' I get up from my counter and go to the café. Fleeta follows close behind me. 'Where did you hear about it?' I ask.

Fleeta sits down on a stool. 'Iva Lou told me herself,' she says.

'What?'

'Shortly after she moved here.'

'You can keep a secret – I'll give you that.'

'I'm known fer it.' Fleeta throws her shoulders back. 'It was odd how I found out though. Back in the day, we made up Christmas baskets for the poor. We didn't just put food in them things neither. There was toys and warm socks and even underwear. They was more like boxes instead of baskets. Anyhow, Iva Lou was only workin' at the library a few weeks when she volunteered to help us. She was a fresh import at that time – do you remember when she got here?'

'Yes, I do.' I remember all the women trying to look like her and smell like her and move like her. She was very beautiful and blond. Funny and friendly. Very warm and mountain-gracious.

Fleeta chuckles. 'Iva Lou drove the Bookmobile like a Sherman tank. She'd take those curves on holler roads on two wheels, skiddin' all over the damn place, then she'd barrel into town here and plow over trash cans and street signs if they were in the way when she went to park. I remember when she took out Ida Holyfield's mailbox after she threw the Bookmobile into reverse out on Valley Road. More than once Chief Bentoski would chide her for her reckless driving. She'd work her charms on him, and instead of writing a ticket, he'd smile and send her on her way.'

'I remember her wardrobe.'

'Who could forget it?'

Iva Lou was known countywide for her fashion sense. She wore co-ordinated ensembles – I remember a certain pair of lime-green cotton gloves, with buttons in the shape of tiny plastic lemons on the wrist, that she used to wear in the early 1960s with a bright yellow suit. She'd match head to toe and then throw on a hat in a contrasting color. Then there was the jewelry. Lots of shine. She won a trip to Hawaii for selling the most Sarah Coventry jewelry back in the 1970s. Despite her glamour IQ, she knew books. She gave me lots of things to read that I might not have ever selected on my own. When she drove her circuit, she'd make sure to stop the Bookmobile in Big Stone Gap first, so we'd get the best picks from the county library. 'Where would I be if she hadn't given me *The Ancient Art of Chinese Face-Reading*?'

'You were obsessed with that book.' Fleeta need not remind me.

'It changed my life. It was like I was a carpenter and somebody finally handed me a hammer and nails and wood. Everything clicked.'

'Yeah, that book done changed you. You was able to look at people in the face finally. Your shyness left you.'

When I was a teenager, Iva Lou gave me classics. The first book she insisted I read was *The House of Mirth*. I don't know what she saw in me that made her think I would connect with Edith Wharton, but I did. How was I to relate to a woman struggling to climb the impossibly elegant social ladder in New York City in the last century? Looking back, I realize she often gave me books about women who didn't fit into society. She wanted me to know that I wasn't alone. Iva Lou knew that books, filled with insight, language, and relationships, could save an Eye-talian girl marooned in loneliness in a place she didn't belong.

I used to take long walks in town with my mother. Everybody drives in Big Stone Gap, so Mama and I were a couple of oddballs, walking the few blocks from our house down to the Pharmacy or for a run to the Post Office or to meet the Bookmobile. I thought we walked everywhere because Fred Mulligan didn't want my mother to spend money on gas; he was frugal to a fault. But I loved those walks; they gave me a chance to talk to my mother, and they bonded me to her. When I was a girl, Iva Lou called me Lizzie, because, like Elizabeth Bennet in *Pride and Prejudice* (another book she recommended), I savored long walks to sort things out.

I remember when she gave me *Good Morning,*

Miss Dove. The gift of that book was a warning that I should live my life for me, but it didn't matter; like Miss Dove, I eventually became the woman known as the Town Spinster.

When I returned from college, Iva Lou figured I had gotten worldly, so she gave me contemporary novels, like *Valley of the Dolls* and *The Prime of Miss Jean Brodie*. Iva Lou looked at novels like sex manuals, in a way. Those racy subplots gave us something to talk about on the Bookmobile, and boy, she loved to talk about wild goings-on in places like Hollywood and Europe. Iva Lou thought if I read about sex and love, I might find the courage to express myself romantically and to own my own heart. She believed romance was a birthright, that the search for true love was mandatory and that, ultimately, life was downright sad without it. I always looked at romance as though it were an extra, and only if a woman was lucky would she find her happiness. It was as if Iva Lou was emptying the shelves of the county library, trying desperately to find proof in the pages of books that I too could be happy and spin my own tale of daring and seduction. 'Don't be a Melanie, be a Scarlett!' she said when she gave me *Gone with the Wind*. I was no Scarlett, but I wasn't Melanie either, as I hadn't yet found my Ashley Wilkes.

Iva Lou would try to help me feel part of a greater universe with popular Italian-American titles too, which was so funny to me because I didn't know any other Italian-Americans, growing up. I was stunned by *The Godfather*. I was working full-time in the Pharmacy by then. I remember the black-and-white jacket, covered carefully in Mylar by Iva Lou. The book made me understand that family loyalty was something missing in my life. I didn't have the myriad of siblings, cousins, aunts, and uncles to rescue me or to celebrate with me. I didn't have a family name I would die for, or a code to live by; right or wrong, it didn't matter. I was adrift always. The only anchor I had was Mama. The Mulligans were always feuding, and later, I found out why I didn't respond to their dynamic. I couldn't because I wasn't a Mulligan.

Mario Puzo wrote of the Corleones with passion, and while they weren't gentle people, they were a family, something I hadn't known as an Italian. I longed to celebrate my mother's heritage, which was why I planned the trip to Italy, the one that Mama and I never took. She didn't like that I read *The Godfather*; she believed it was immoral. I reasoned with her: 'Mama, it's just a novel.'

When I look back, though, I see that the books Iva Lou recommended were, for the most part, stories about strong women at a crossroads. She liked plots wherein a female protagonist struggles to learn how to stand up for herself, until, with newfound strength, she finally takes charge of her destiny and finds happiness. I remember she said, 'There ain't nothing like a woman-in-peril story.'

I didn't count on the fact that Iva Lou had one of her own.

'You shouldn't be surprised by anything about Iva Lou,' says Fleeta as she pours herself a cup of coffee. 'Iva Lou's a character. She's a had a life. A full life.'

'I know.'

'Anyhow, them Christmas baskets. We drove way up in the hills, almost to the top of Stone Mountain. Back then it nearly always rained on Christmas Eve. It was awful dreary up there. We went so far up the ridge, I thought we'd get to the top and fall off the other side. We didn't, though. There's a house in a holler up there, and me and her got out of the truck and brought a basket to a family. They opened the door, and there was kids everywhere – seemed like a hundred of 'em – though it was probably ten or so. They had nothin' up there. Nothin'. The mama was holding a baby around ten months old. She was a pretty blond baby, with those big pink cheeks that look like two bubblegum bubbles. Iva Lou took that woman's baby and held her tight. The baby cooed, and that's when Iva Lou started crying. So I quick made an excuse, handing the baby back to its mama, and me and Iva Lou went outside. And that's when she told me that holding that baby reminded her of her own. Said she had a baby once and she gave the baby to a good family named Carter out of Hazard, Kentucky.'

'And you never told anyone.'

'Not even Portly. And I never brought it up to Iva Lou again neither. What good would come of that?'

'You didn't?' I feel guilty now – I shouldn't have told Jack. But he's good with a secret; it will go no further.

'And I still think you ought not say a word to her.'

'I have to.'

'No, you don't.'

'What if Lovely tells Iva Lou she talked to me?'

'Then it's her sayin' it. Look, it wasn't easy for girls back then. If they got pregnant, well, a lot of times there was nowhere to turn – hell, most times. You knew girls that left school and went off to live with relatives for the duration and then would come back, and everybody knew they went off and had a baby and then had to give it away. And you's younger than me; it was even worse when I was a girl. I didn't even know how exactly a girl got pregnant. Not too easy to dodge something you ain't sure of. Best way to keep yourself safe was to go on and get murried, then when you had the babies, you had some help. Of course, getting murried was a crapshoot too. My mama and daddy couldn't help me and Portly much. They didn't have nothin'. My own mama was sixteen when she had me, so there was still youngins at home when I left. I saw how hard it was to have a baby when you're a young mama like that. And if you were alone, it made for some desperate decisions sometimes. Women have always kept secrets because we had to. There wasn't no place to turn. And I'll bet you that's how Iva Lou felt.'

'But she's met with her daughter and talked to her. It's 1998, for Godsakes. It's different now. Even here, in the land that time forgot.'

'It don't matter. That's a deep wound right there. It's best to leave it alone.'

The snowflakes Jack and Fleeta promised are starting to come down in lazy spirals over Big Stone Gap. Main Street is getting a light dusting of the white powder, looking like one of Cab's doughnuts rolled in confectioners' sugar. I hope Iva Lou takes it easy on the road.

The bells on the front door jingle. Jack comes in with Tyler Hutchinson; they're laughing.

'Hi, honey.' Jack marches in place on the mat to get the snow off his shoes.

'Hello, Mrs MacChesney.' Tyler flashes me a big, wide Virginia Tech smile.

'Hello, Tyler.'

'Well, come on, you two. Everybody's done gone. I got beef tips on toast fer ye.'

'Sounds great, Fleeta.'

Tyler sits at the reserved table, which, in our empty café, looks silly. Jack folds Fleeta's handwritten sign neatly and places it on the counter. He joins Tyler at the table. Jack is so animated with this man; it's as if he's found a brother.

I stand back and watch them from my counter and wonder how many businessmen came to these parts and had these kinds of meetings with men like my husband. Tyler doesn't know that this sort of deal almost never works out, because there's an unwritten law: if you ain't from here, you shouldn't benefit from our resources. This has turned out to be a very bad philosophy, since our young people grow up and, unable to find jobs, move away. It leaves these hills vulnerable to outsiders looking to exploit our natural resources. There are still hundreds of years of coal in these mountains, and a world in desperate need of that kind of energy. The only reason our traditional mines are closed is because the coal can be gotten more cheaply elsewhere.

My husband, though, knows all of this and yet, ever hopeful, listens to Tyler Hutchinson as if the story is brand-new. It's almost a gold-rush situation: we sit here, a little bit like suckers, hoping that the ending will change with the promise and glory proposed by yet another salesman looking to cash in.

There's not even a single car on Main Street. Lew Eisenberg's Lincoln Town Car is parked outside his office, but that's the case most days into the night. He is married to his work because it's too hard to be married to Inez.

In Big Stone Gap, when it snows, folks hit the panic button and stay home. The phone starts ringing. This is my sign that I will spend most of the day delivering pills. Maybe I'll stop by Iva Lou's in Danberry Heights later.

'Mom! I heard Uncle Theodore is coming for Christmas,' says Etta when I talk to her from home a couple days later.

'How do you know?'

'He instant-messages me all the time.'

'I'm glad you stay close.'

'Are you kidding? He's a riot.'

'I'm going to miss you, honey. I'm really dreading the holidays without you here.'

'Oh, it's not so bad. You won't have me to do all the grunt work. Now you'll know how talented I was when it came to hanging lights.'

'I always knew, Etta,' I say, smiling.

'Ma, the holiday isn't such a big deal over here. It's so funny. Christmas is nice, but Easter's the big one.'

'Really?'

'My Italian friends think I'm a kook. They can't believe I'm going to hang lights. It's just not done.'

'Tell me about your friends.'

'Okay. There's Salalena; she's Calabrese and works admissions at the university. She's twenty-one and drives a turquoise Vespa motor scooter. I'm serious. Turquoise. If you saw her, though, you couldn't imagine her driving anything else. She's a pip. Stefano is close to two of his old professors – they've been married, like you and Dad, forever, like twenty years. Her name is Gina and his name is Apollo, like the Greek god.'

'That's cool.'

'Very cool. And then there're the girls I've met at – don't laugh – my sewing class.'

'You're sewing?'

'I just feel like it's in my DNA. I'm named for my grandmother, who was a seamstress – and Grandma Mac was also a good one – so I'm hearing the call.'

'Have you made anything yet?'

'Nope. We're starting with patterns. The teacher is hard-core. We're actually having to draw our own patterns. Sometimes I look at the other girls and think, This is like 1812 – eventually, we do get to use electric sewing machines. But not till much much later.'

'It sounds like fun.'

'It is! How are you, Mom?'

'Well, I'm okay. I have a problem.'

'What is it?'

'I just found out something that's got me upset. Aunt Iva Lou sort of . . . Well, she kept a secret from me.'

'So?'

'It's a big one. She has a daughter.'

'Oh my God.'

'She had her years ago – before she moved to Big Stone Gap – and she gave her up for adoption.'

'When did she tell you?'

'She hasn't yet. The daughter came to see me.

She wanted me to talk to Iva Lou, to convince her to tell her who her father is.'

'Mom, you have to talk to Aunt Iva Lou.'

I feel my eyes burn. 'I can't.'

'Why? Don't be a dork. It's not like she's fifteen and you need to have "the talk." What are you afraid of?'

'I don't know.'

'So you *are* afraid.'

'Maybe I'm scared it will change everything.'

'That's lame. That's not it. It's something else, Ma. You aren't thinking clearly. What does Dad say?'

'To mind my own business.'

'Easy for him to say!'

We laugh. For twenty years, Jack has always said the most obvious, practical thing. His advice is so bland, we usually don't even seek it. He avoids confrontation with such regularity, he's turned it into an art form. I'd call him a fence-sitter, but at the first whiff of a conflict, he doesn't sit, he passes through. He wants no part of it.

'Etta, are you happy over there?' I ask.

'Ma, it's an adventure. I'm always happy. I know that sounds silly, but it's true. I love a great guy, and I'm around my family. I miss you guys, but I had you for nineteen years, and now I have to experience something else. It feels completely natural to me.'

'I understand.'

'Do you?'

'I really do. You're so much more sophisticated than I was, and I guess I was holding you to my marker. That wasn't fair.'

'It's okay.'

'What's the best thing about Stefano?'

'Every night, after dinner, we go for a walk. And we talk about our day, the good stuff and the bad stuff. And when I tell him things, he really listens. I'm sort of learning how to listen from him. He is so focused on me – it's as if my welfare is more important to him than his own. Can you imagine that?'

'I'm so glad.'

'I mean, I don't listen, Ma. He's so thoughtful. I'm hoping it's rubbing off on me. I think we're forever, but even if something terrible would happen and we're not – and I'm not saying that's gonna happen – but if it did, I'm better for having known him.'

'That's how I feel about your dad.'

'I know. He's feeling much better, isn't he?'

'Like new.'

'How was his last PET scan?'

'The artery in his neck is clear. They're keeping an eye on his heart.'

'Did they see something?'

'Not yet. But when you have one blockage, sometimes there's a chance of more.'

'Oh.'

'Don't worry.'

'Yeah, don't worry,' Jack barks into the phone.

'When did you pick up?' I bark back, but I'm teasing.

'When you were talking about potential blockage. You make it sound worse than it is.'

'I thought there was nothing there,' Etta says, worried.

'See there, Ave, you're triggering a chain reaction around the world.'

'I didn't mean to. Sorry, Etta.'

'Believe me, Etta. Your mother worries enough for all three of us. In fact, I'm thinking about putting in an eight-hundred number so people can call in and let your mother worry for folks across the country – she's that good at it.'

'You're hilarious, Jack. Okay, I'm getting off the phone now so you two can talk. I love you, Etta.'

'I love you, Ma.'

'Thank you. And love to Stefano.'

After I hang up, I take the last of the laundry out of the dryer and dump it on the worktable on the sunporch. I begin to fold it. On the windowsill, Shoo the Cat raises his head off his paws, looks at me, and blinks, then curls up and goes back to sleep. I hear Jack laughing from the phone in the living room. Lord knows how long he'll be on the phone with Etta – those two can talk for hours.

The sun is long gone over Cracker's Neck. I turn on the outdoor porch light and watch the woods, as I have done every day since September, when I thought I saw a young man hiking through. Jack doesn't know it, but I go out and walk the woods every afternoon or early evening, looking for what or who, I don't know – just walking. If I told Jack I go into the woods alone, he'd say I was looking for Joe, and then he'd get concerned, and pretty soon he'd call Iva Lou or Father John or somebody to talk some sense into me. So I keep my little hikes to myself.

Every bit of relief I felt when Jack's PET scan results came back good has been replaced by a new dread. Or maybe it's just a new version of an old dread: I feel I'm going to lose someone I love again. I don't know who, exactly, but I remember this feeling before my mother died, and before Joe died, and boy, it was acute right before Spec died. The feeling came back a couple of weeks ago, before Nonna died. Jack can call me a worrier all he wants, but what I'm feeling is beyond worry. It's a knowledge that the moment is slipping away, and I'm not in it. How can I tell Jack this when he's more aware of his own mortality than ever. I can't burden him with my fears. He felt so close to death that he went about making lists. Imagine that! I never make lists. Maybe it's time I started. Maybe that will slow the clock.

The first snow of winter has turned our holler into a fairyland. The treetops look like crystal chandeliers as daggers of ice hang from the branches. The brook in the woods has frozen into ribbons of clear spun sugar, and the sun, now far away in the December sky, is a cold white diamond set in the vast cornflower blue.

I hope we get a good snow when Theodore arrives. Christmas is only a week away.

I pull on my old boots and yank the laces tight. I throw on a knit cap and Jack's barn jacket and head down the hill to the mailbox for the paper. I inhale the pure, clean winter air, almost gulping it down. Is there a more perfect spot on earth than right here, right now? It's so clear. It's a day you can put your hands through.

The paper boy who drops off the Kingsport *Times-News* every morning is very dependable. I open the rusty door on the mailbox and pull out the newspaper. I feel something else in the box. It's a fat business envelope. It's addressed to Jack, but there's no postage on it. In the return address box, it says T. Hutchinson, Bituminous Reserves, Inc.

Jack is flipping pancakes in the kitchen. On a plate, there are two that folded funny. 'I'm practicing,' he explains. 'Company's coming.'

'Theodore loves your cooking. It'll be nice.' I smile and put the paper on the table and give Jack the envelope. 'What's this?'

'I asked Tyler to run some numbers for me.'

'What sorts of numbers?'

'He's pitched out a couple of scenarios for me as consultant.'

'So you're still thinking about it?'

'Yeah.'

'Jack!'

'Okay, how about a little support?'

'Don't make me the bad guy. I'm very proud of how you've made a living all these years – and to be perfectly honest, I'd be ashamed if you hooked up with these people.'

'Ashamed?'

'Ashamed. They're ruining the mountains. People over in Kentucky are devastated. There is no way to reclaim a mountain that's gone forever.'

'They are required to put fill back where they mine. Okay? And if I hook up with them – *if* – I would have a say as to where they did the mountaintop removal—'

'Strip mining.'

'It's not called that anymore.'

'Of course not. It's a red-flag phrase. The people in these hills would beat them back with sticks if they knew what this company was planning.'

'I don't think this company is like the others.'

'Then you are a gullible sitting duck, darling.'

'You know, Ave, I'm not a stupid person.'

'I never said that!'

'You don't listen. You have your ideas, and that's the end of it.'

The pancakes begin to burn, their black edges starting to curl with smoke. Jack lifts the pan off the stove and scrapes the burning batter into the sink. I move to help him. He turns away.

'I'm sorry,' I tell him sincerely.

'Do you ever think that maybe I know what I'm

doing? I'm fifty-four years old, and I collapsed on the job three months ago. I don't have a lot of options for the rest of my working days. I can't do what I used to; I can't lift what I used to.'

'Your strength will come back.'

'You're dreaming. I'm not thirty years old. Maybe in your fantasy mind, I'm as young as the day I murried you, but trust me, I have aged, and I took a hit with this thing. I am not the same man I was.'

Panic races through me. In all the travails in the hospital, and the entire time Jack was mending, he never once admitted that the surgery took a toll on him, or that he had changed in any way. To hear him say these words aloud terrifies me. 'Okay, okay, take the job,' I say quickly.

'That's not what I want to hear you say.'

I raise my voice. 'What, then?'

'How about "Do what's right for you. And what's right for you will be right for us."'

I can't say the words.

Jack continues, 'I was born in this house. The morning I was born, my father cleared the back field so I'd have a place to play. Silly, right? He had a couple of years before I'd use the field, but when I was born, he got right to it. And that mountain over there – Stone Mountain – it was there that I learned to hunt and shoot a gun. It was the first place I camped with Pa. I saw a bobcat up there, and I wanted to shoot it, and my pa told me that there weren't many bobcats left in these hills, so let 'em be. So I did. We ate the berries that grew in those woods. Mama cured us with the herbs she found there. When I had the colic, she made catnip tea that grew wild under the brush. She'd make a poultice from the milk-weed she found growing near the creek, and Pa knew which mushrooms we could eat and which were poisonous. All those things came from these mountains. I would never jeopardize this place. I love it as much as you do. But you seem to think I don't.'

'I know you love these mountains,' I say.

'What is precious to you is just as precious to me,' Jack insists.

'Okay.' I have a way of ending an argument that has always worked in my marriage. I give up; I stop fighting. I pretend to agree, and then we move off the hot topic and on to the business of life.

Men are very delicate instruments. Their egos are like fragile eggshells, and yet physically, they have the brute strength of a bear. When their health is challenged, they recede quickly and quietly into such despair that no one can pull them out of it.

A woman has a whole different way of coping – at least the women I know. We make things pretty when the road gets rocky. We put a new dress on an old body and temporarily fix what ails us with something new: a big ring, a dangling bracelet, anything with a lot of shine. I can go to the third aisle at the Mutual's and turn my hair back to ebony. I can perk myself up with the right lipstick and beat back the fine lines on my face with alpha hydroxy acid. I'm more than happy to rent a cabin in the Revlon land of delusion when I need a lift.

My husband won't. He is wood and nails. He wants facts, answers, and drop-dead ultimatums. Though I like to pass through pain as if it's not really happening, that's not the Jack MacChesney way. He feels everything, and he holds it close. He's a true mountain man.

The next day I load up all my overdue library books in the Jeep. They're just an excuse, really – an excuse to go and see Iva Lou. I have a conflict going on inside me: to do as Fleeta says and ignore it until Iva Lou says something about her daughter, or to follow my gut and open up the conversation. I roll down the hill in reverse, watching our old stone house against the lavender sky. There's a part of me that wants to throw it in drive and go back up the mountain and mind my own business.

I take the road into town slowly; it gives me a chance to think.

Iva Lou and I became closer after Theodore left Big Stone Gap to live his dream in Knoxville as the band director for the University of Tennessee. It was a great job, but he took it for personal as well as professional reasons. It was time for Theodore to begin living a real life, to find himself, to fall in love. That wasn't something he was ever going to do in Big Stone Gap – not with me here, and not with old attitudes about new freedoms as firmly in place as chin straps on the Tuckett twins. So off he went, leaving Iva Lou and me, and we've been close ever since.

I've never had an argument with Iva Lou. We've never had a rift in our friendship; we could always talk about anything. So the silence between us has led us into unfamiliar emotional territory. I very much want to hear Iva Lou's side of things. I pull in to the library parking lot, and instead of parking next to Iva Lou's Miata, I park at the far end of the lot. I've never done this, because there's always a space next to her car. (Iva Lou parks a certain way because she's afraid of getting dinged. As meticulous as she is with her appearance, her car is a close second. It's always washed, buffed, and waxed (thank you, Gilliam's Car Wash). Tonight I park with the public. I need a little distance.

I pull the tote bag out of the backseat and climb the steps to the library. I push the door open and inhale the sweet smell of books. I take my tote to the front desk. Serena Mumpower, the assistant librarian, is working behind the desk.

'Hey, Serena. Iva Lou around?'

'She's in her office.'

'Thanks.'

Serena grunts. She hasn't been friendly since word got out that my daughter married Stefano

Grassi. Serena and Stefano went out on a few dates the summer he came to work in Big Stone Gap, and you would think my son-in-law jilted Serena for Etta. The last thing I need is to get caught up in some stale drama from years ago.

I make my way back to Iva Lou's office. The break room is filled with posters from book campaigns. There's one from the 1970s of Bette Midler in pajamas announcing National Book Week. I knock on Iva Lou's office door.

'Come in,' she says from inside. I open the door and enter. She says, 'Hey, girl. Take a load off. Are you here to fire me from the musical?'

'God, no. You're the best thing in it. Well, you and the dark horse, Ravi Balu. He's really doing a good job as Rolfe.'

'Imagine that.' Iva Lou offers me a seat. She gets up and reaches for a tin of cookies on a shelf. She opens it and offers me some. 'Faith Cox's ginger snaps. She only makes 'em at Christmastime, so I try to make them last.'

I take one as well as a deep breath. 'I've got a problem,' I say nervously.

'Spill.'

'I don't know how to say it.'

'Honey-o, you just tell me. You know I take any morsels about you and Jack Mac to my grave.'

'It's not about him.'

'Who, then?'

'You.'

'Oh, Lord. What have I done?' Iva Lou rolls her

eyes dramatically and heavenward, like Saint Teresa in the alcove of Sacred Heart Church.

'Lovely Carter came to see me.'

The mention of the name causes Iva Lou to snap the tin shut and put it on her desk. I wait for Iva Lou to say something, but she just sits there.

'Why didn't you tell me?' I ask her.

'Tell you what?' Now, Iva Lou is a smart woman, and she knows she's stonewalling. I won't let her.

'That you had a daughter.' I try not to sound accusatory, but I'm hurt, so it comes off as shrill.

Iva Lou rolls her seat away from me. It's a small office, so she has nowhere to go. It reminds me of the time we had a squirrel in the house, and the only way to get it out was to corner it. Iva Lou turns her back to me. It seems like minutes go by. I don't know what to do, whether to stay or go.

'Iva Lou?'

'Yes?'

'Are you going to talk to me?'

Iva Lou turns to me so quickly that I lean back. 'What do you want me to say?'

'I want to understand why you didn't tell me and why . . .'

'Why I'd give my own baby away? Is that what you're concerned about?' Iva Lou asks angrily.

'Hey, I'm not judging you.'

'You most certainly are. You set me up. Trapping me in here like this. It's my place of work. I can't hardly have feelings here, can I?' she whispers.

151

I lower my voice. 'I'm sorry. I should have come to your house. But I didn't know if Lyle knew—'

'Of course he knows!' she thunders.

I'm confused. 'He knows?'

'He's my husband. Of course he knows.' Iva Lou stands and starts shuffling papers.

'Do you want me to go?'

'I think that's a good idea.'

I turn to open the door. My heart is pounding. I can't believe what is happening between us, and at the same time, she is so dismissive of me, it makes me angrier still. Instead of opening the door and leaving, I want to shake her. I feel rage burn through me. I want to hold her accountable. I turn and face her as I stand against the door. 'How dare you.'

'What?'

'How dare you treat me this way? Who do you think you are? I'm not here on some small-town gossip mission. You're my friend, and I found out something – not from you, by the way, from an outsider – that you should have told me.'

'I didn't want to tell you.'

I ignore the comment. I am angry, and I want her to hear why. 'Fleeta knew. Spec knew.'

'Oh, so you didn't get to know, and that's why you're upset with me?'

'Partly. I guess,' I stammer.

'Maybe I didn't think I *could* tell you.'

'What? Why?'

'You have definite ideas about things. There's very little room for human error with you.'

'Maybe I don't look at Lovely Carter like she's a mistake.'

Iva Lou's eyes fill with tears. 'I want you to go.'

If I leave, it will be one of the biggest mistakes of my life. I should stay here and work things through. But it takes two people to solve this kind of problem, and Iva Lou doesn't want to.

'Good night,' I tell her as I go. She doesn't answer. As the door snaps shut, I wait outside for a moment, hoping that she will push it open and say, 'Come on back in here, we need to talk.'

But she doesn't. And I can't.

CHAPTER 8

WILDEAT HOLLER

It seems whenever I drive from Big Stone Gap to Kingsport, I'm in a rush. I'm either late to pick up someone at the airport (today!), or worse, somebody's sick and I'm on my way to Holston Valley Hospital. It's a shame, because the road to Kingsport is plenty scenic, meandering through the Wildcat and out of town toward where Virginia turns into Tennessee. As far as the eye can see, the landscape is a lush patchwork quilt of deep blue farm fields set among wild green pine forests.

I have dreaded Christmas this year. The thought of being alone, just Jack and me without Etta, has been too much to bear. Theodore, who has managed to save the day so many times for me in the past, is landing at Tri-Cities Airport. Boy, do I need him now.

I pull in to the parking lot, jump out of the Jeep, and run into the airport. I see throngs of people coming off the escalator. They haul carry-on bags filled with foil-wrapped Christmas boxes. 'Is this the flight from Atlanta?' I ask a stranger.

'Yep.'

154

I scan the crowd for Theodore. There are no direct flights from New York, so you get your choice of changing planes in Charlotte, Atlanta, or Cincinnati. During the holidays, there are delays everywhere, so you never know if a plane will reroute and throw off the schedule. I don't want to wait another second to see Theodore.

Then I hear that familiar voice behind me. 'Ave!'

'Theodore!' I run to him. 'Sorry I'm late.'

'You're always late, so I went ahead and picked up my bags.'

I throw my arms around him and refuse to let go.

'No one has ever been this happy to see me.'

'Thanks for coming.'

Theodore holds my shoulders and surveys me from head to toe. 'You look good.'

'You look better.' And he does. Theodore is always in excellent shape ('It's the walking in the city'). His hair has a dusting of gray through the red, but it's as thick as the day I met him thirty-some years ago.

'With all I've been through, it's a miracle.' Theodore gives me a small tote and picks up his suitcase. He puts his arm around my shoulder as we push through the crowd and outside to the parking lot.

'What happened?'

'The Radio City show is over. But good news: I'm working on a new musical with a terrific composer. She's amazing. Marcy Gendel, heard of her?'

155

'Nope. Then again, I only know Rodgers and Hammerstein these days. Broadway! You must be thrilled.'

'It sounds glamorous, doesn't it?'

'Isn't it?'

'We're developing it at the Cherry Lane Theatre. A sweet little theater in the Village. Off-Broadway. Until we have the guts to blow it up big and take it to Broadway.' Theodore and I walk to the Jeep.

'Isn't that theater in your neighborhood?'

'Walking distance.' Theodore throws his bags in the back of the Jeep. 'This is just like the old days. You and me and the Medicine Dropper.'

I give the old Jeep a pat. 'I can't give her up. Or maybe I can't stand change.'

'Get used to it. Now is when change starts happening fast and furious. We don't have the luxury of time anymore, Ave.'

We climb into the Jeep. I'm in the driver's seat, Theodore is in the passenger seat. 'You sound like my husband,' I say.

'He got a wake-up call, huh?'

'A big one. Jack thought he wasn't going to make it.'

'How is he now?'

'Much better. You want to drive?'

'Sure.'

Theodore and I get out and exchange seats. He turns the key and backs out of the space. It's so funny; back when I thought he'd be the man for me (can it be twenty years have come and gone?

156

They have!), I always let him drive. It just seemed right. It also gave me a chance to look at him, really look at him, for hours on end. How many evenings we'd go for long drives in the mountains and never run out of things to talk about. I miss those conversations a lot. My husband is many wonderful things, but he's not a yakker. 'What happened with Max?'

'I got tired of his long hours at the restaurant, and he got tired of mine at the theater. We didn't see much of each other, and neither of us was willing to compromise. So here we are.' Theodore adjusts the rearview mirror. 'How about you and Jack?'

'He's obsessed with money lately.'

'Money. That doesn't sound like Jack.'

'He wants to leave me comfortable – whatever that means.'

'Jack's at that age where retirement is ten years away. He wants to put away savings while he can.'

'I guess. But I'm worried about him. He's taking a job as consultant with a mountaintop removal company.'

'Consultant?'

'It's a fancy title for a man who can show outsiders the terrain. They need someone who knows the mountains around Big Stone. And with Jack's mining experience, he's golden. These companies know what they're doing. They find a local guy who's trusted by the community and use him to swing the popular opinion their way. The last thing they want is resistance from the natives.'

'You don't like it?'

'Not one bit.'

'How's Iva Lou?'

'She's cordial at rehearsals, but she doesn't call or come around anymore.' My eyes fill with tears. I wasn't expecting that. 'Sorry.'

'You have to make up with her.'

'I can't.'

'Why?'

'I don't know. I just can't.'

'Are you angry she kept a secret from you?'

'Well, it wasn't much of a secret. Fleeta knew.'

'That makes it worse for you. You thought you were her closest friend.'

'I guess I did.'

'You have to talk to her.'

'It's so weird. I like to think that I can talk to anybody about anything. But lately, it's so hard for me to say what I'm feeling, because I don't *know* what I'm feeling.'

'You're in shock.'

'About what?'

'Oh, let's see: that your daughter's moved abroad; that your husband has been sick; that your friends aren't perfect; that life goes on even when you're terribly disappointed in people. No wonder you don't know what to say; you can't believe what's happening. Well, life goes on. Not much you can do about it.' Theodore smiles.

As we head toward home, we fall into a comfortable silence. I realize how good it feels to have a neutral party to listen and help me sort through my feelings. Theodore knows me as well as anyone. 'You know exactly what's wrong with me.'

'I'm on the outside looking in. It's the best seat in the house when it come to empathy. That's all. By the way, I kept a secret from you for years, and you had it in your heart to forgive me. The same should be true for Iva Lou.'

'Yeah, well, your secret was about you. It didn't involve a third party.'

'True. Still, I think Iva Lou deserves a little slack.' Theodore veers off to take the road through Gate City and into the mountains. 'I can't believe I remember how to get around this part of the world. I guess it's in my bones.'

The story of *The Sound of Music* is simple and perfect for Christmastime. At its center, it's about love and family and overcoming outside forces of evil while learning to sing in harmony. It's set in the late 1930s in Salzburg, Austria. A young nun goes to work as a nanny for a handsome widowed sea captain and his brood of seven children. With her guitar and gumption, she turns the kids from glum to happy, finds herself falling for the Captain, goes back to the convent in horror that she is attracted to a man, then is forced to return to the children by the Mother Superior, who insists she face her demons instead of running away. When she returns, the Captain is engaged to be married to the haughty Baroness Elsa

Schraeder, who ends up getting dropped by the Captain when he realizes he is really in love with the almost-nun. All of this happens on the eve of World War II, with the destruction of the world looming at every turn. Show business also looms, as the kids form a singing act under the nun's direction.

I've tried to keep the production simple, but between Carolyn's costumes and Nellie's casting, I couldn't. I like to think the overly ambitious production is not my fault but due to the egos of my producer and cast run amok. Community theater is an excuse for normal folk to become show people. I watch as plain, simple women put on false eyelashes, bold lipstick, and high heels (even when playing nuns) and become sexpots. Bored husbands put on their costumes and pancake makeup, becoming their version of Cary Grant. Our leading man puts a little too much into the kissing scenes (the script doesn't call for much woo pitching, but our Captain grabs Maria every chance he gets, and she pushes him away every chance she gets).

Our annual musical is the closest most folks in Big Stone Gap get to stardom, and they milk it from the first rehearsal to opening night like the cows at Pet Dairy. Our cast parties are all-night and elaborate, rivaling Truman Capote's infamous Black and White Ball at the Plaza Hotel in New York City back in the 1960s (granted, our parties are held in a smaller venue – the Fox house – but still). After the final curtain, folks dress up, drink up, and then come Sunday morning, fess up. More than one drunken chorus member finds a way to ask for forgiveness for a theatrical indiscretion at the United Methodist Church during testimony (the Methodist version of Catholic confession, except they don't go into a booth, they stand up in front of everyone at the end of the service and admit their sins. It takes a lot of guts!) We can't blame ourselves entirely, though; it's the path of all art. The theater brings out the gypsy in all of us and, evidently, our share of sin.

The Botts family has done a lovely job painting the scenery, a series of trompe l'oeil backdrops that will fly in and out on a pulley system operated by our stage crew. There's a cathedral with an altar for the opening number and a palace on a lake for the Von Trapp family home. The abbey is a black velvet scrim with a gold cross on it (it's slightly creepy, but it works); and for the finale, there's a scrim of an endless blue sky and clouds. Our chorus of nuns turns upstage and flips its veils to reveal green velvet foliage, thus becoming pine trees to conjure the Alps (it was Nellie's idea, and I liked it).

'I need to make an announcement,' says Carolyn, our costumer, coming out from the wings.

'Go right ahead,' I tell her.

Carolyn sighs. 'Lordy Mercy, I know what your mama went through, sewing for all these plays.'

'She loved every minute of it.'

'She was a better woman than me, that's for sure.'

'The floor is yours.' I turn to the cast, assembled in the first three rows of the auditorium in their Act One, Scene 1, costumes. They're giggling and chatting with anticipation. 'Everyone. Please. Listen to Carolyn.'

'Just a reminder about costume etiquette.' Carolyn takes her place, center stage of the Powell Valley High School auditorium, with a set of pinking shears in one hand and an extra nun's wimple in the other. She attempts to straighten her shoulders, but years of bad posture won't let her, so she makes her point with the big scissors. 'I need y'all to be careful. I ain't got time to wash and press these costumes during the run. Therefore. Do not eat or drink in your costumes. And for the love of sweet Jesus, use the makeup hoods before applying the pancake. Iva Lou, please demonstrate.'

Iva Lou stands in the first row and turns to the cast. She pulls a sheer hood over her face.

'Makeup is a killer of fine fabrics. Be careful of smears. I ain't got time to fix them neither.'

'Is that it, Carolyn?' If I let her continue, she'll harangue all night, and we'll never get the Lonely Goatherd puppet show set.

'One more thing. Please, and I'm begging you. Return the costumes to the proper rolling rack in the Glee Club practice room. And mothers of the Von Trapp children, don't allow them damn kids

162

outside in their costumes. I had to dye Gretl's white party dress celery-green on account of the grass stains she got on it when she was allowed to play out back. Remember: it might be a costume to you, but to me, it's about three nights of sweatin' over my sewing machine. I wouldn't piss on your performances by banging a pot during your solo, so give me the same consideration when you wear your costumes.'

'Thank you, Carolyn. Round of applause for our costumer, please.'

The cast applauds. Carolyn is less than galvanized for opening night. She slinks offstage like an old cat.

I begin my pep talk. 'Tonight is our final dress rehearsal in front of a live audience . . .' Just the mention of an audience sends the cast into a chattering fit – they can't contain their enthusiasm. I wait for them to quiet down. Final dress rehearsal is the biggest hurdle for amateur performers. The adrenaline runs high, and my actors don't know what to do with it, so they get silly. The show will stink tonight; there will be mistakes and outright unprofessional behavior. The cast will giggle uncontrollably during dramatic scenes, flub lyrics, and miss entrances. It's not just the young folks either – it's the older ones who, in costume and makeup, get a taste of the stage and want to suck the experience dry and live the dream.

I can relate to how they're enamored of the world of live theater. It's fun to make a play. Each cast becomes a family. Rehearsals give that wonderful feeling of being a lug nut in a well-oiled machine. When you're cast in a play, you belong somewhere, you have a place to be, lines to say, and a personality to project. A drab secretary from the courthouse becomes a singing nun; a coal miner becomes a handsome sea captain. All it takes is a book and music by Rodgers & Hammerstein.

Who doesn't love the applause? No one ever gave me a standing ovation at the Pharmacy, or Nellie at the bank, or Greg in his cubicle at the accounting firm. We'll get it tonight, though, and we'll revel in it. If there's one thing in this world that folks need, it's to feel that they've done a good job. How rare that reinforcement is! Most of the work in this world is thankless: parenting, the drudgery of our daily jobs – we contribute so much that no one sees or acknowledges. But in the theater, when it's good, that gratitude is there, audience to actor. They let us know they like what we do with applause and whistles and standing ovations. You can't beat it.

My cast is grateful for the opportunity to temporarily be in show business. They are proud to be hams. There's something exciting about getting to be somebody else; to put on makeup and sing and dance. It brings out sensuality in a person who, under normal circumstances, might not know she has any. Our community theater is the last place of daring and escape in Big Stone Gap. These annual productions give us a touch of glamour and connect us to the outside world. We figure we are as good as any productions out there. We also believe we have as good a talent pool as the next town, including Hollywood. 'After all, Ava Gardner was from North Carolina. Right over the mountain.' Nellie Goodloe sniffs. (As if *that* will destine my cast for the silver screen.)

I go on, 'I'd like to thank you all for a wonderful rehearsal period. I believe you are ready to give our audience a terrific show. Remember dressing room and backstage etiquette. Keep your chatter backstage to a minimum, and please whisper — there's nothing worse than a scene drowned out by backstage antics. Now, places, everyone, for the abbey. Nellie, when the curtain is closed, please let the invited audience in.'

The stage manager, Sweet Sue Tinsley, corrals the talent up the stairs and into the wings. My old classmate (and Jack's ex-girlfriend) Sweet Sue still has her looks; she's as blond as she was when we were in school. She's trim, a devoted user of aqua eye shadow (Revlon's cornflower hi-glow powder; she buys it at the Pharmacy), but there's a sadness about her now, for the first time in her life. Her husband, Mike, recently left her for a younger woman. Not to worry, though, I understand she's dating a widower from over in Powell Valley. She wasn't about to let the situation get her down.

Theodore sneaks in the side door. 'Ave, where do you want me?'

'Come to the light booth with me.' As we turn to go through the door to the hallway, Theodore is spotted.

'Theodore Tipton!' Louise Camblos screams. 'You're back!' Louise takes off in a sprint toward Theodore, wimple and veil askew as she trips on her billowing skirt. She is followed by her fellow nuns, among them Carol Wilson, Nina Coughlin, Nancy Toney, Dawn Suzette Burnett, Liz Ann Noel, Flo Kelley, Catherine Brennan, Paula Pruitt, Pat Bean, Nita Wilson, Sharon Burns, Dee Emmerson, Ann Hunter, and Mary Susan Giles, who storm the lip of the stage en masse, as if it's Normandy Beach. Linda Church, busy bobby-pinning her wimple, turns and shrieks when she realizes Theodore is in the auditorium. She follows the pack. Louise reaches Theodore first and smothers him in kisses as the others gather round for a turn. If Big Stone Gap has a rock star or ever did, it's definitely Theodore Tipton.

Theodore steps back. 'Now, ladies.'

Tayloe emerges from the stage right wings, wearing her novice costume. 'I'm gonna be a nervous wreck knowin' you're here,' she tells Theodore. She puts her hands on her hips and pushes aside the bangs on her short strawberry-blond Julie Andrews wig.

'Just do your show. Remember, you're actors!' Theodore claps his hands.

Sweet Sue fans her arms to herd the loose nuns to their places in the wings. Once they are all backstage, I holler, 'Let 'em in!' to Nellie, who throws open the entrance doors of the auditorium.

'What happened to Sweet Sue?' Theodore whispers.

'Love gone wrong.'

'Too bad. She's wearing it. She's more beat than sweet.'

The audience take their seats. I excuse myself to go backstage and give the sets one final look. God love her, Sweet Sue is in the wings corralling the Von Trapp children, like show dogs, into single-file rows for their entrance. Friedrich is playing with the stage weights, but I shoot him a look and he stops, taking his place in line behind the others. I go back to the dressing area, which is quiet now that the cast is in position to begin. I wander among the dress bags filled with street clothes, as well as piles of schoolbooks, purses, and other gear.

I poke my head into the small makeup room. Iva Lou sits at the mirror, pressing the narrow glue strips of her false eyelashes to the tips of her eyelids. She can't see me; her eyes are closed. I should go, but I can't. I look at her for what seems like a long time. Finally, she opens her eyes and flutters her new, lustrous black eyelashes. Iva Lou does not age: her heart-shaped face, hot-pink Cupid's-bow lips, and lake-blue eyes are every bit as alluring as the day she drove the Bookmobile to town for the first time. Iva Lou does not wear her pain, suffering, and tragedy; rather, she throws it off like a light overcoat and never looks back. She leans in to the mirror and smiles, liking the effect.

'Have a good show, Iva Lou.'

Startled, she looks at me. 'How long you been standin' there?'

'Just now.'

She stands and smooths the skirt on her costume. 'This has been a lot of fun. Thanks for having me in it,' she says formally.

'You're a great baroness. Have fun!' I chirp. I want to leave on a high note; after all, Iva Lou has a performance to give. But I'm so sad about our friendship. We haven't spoken at all since we argued. I just can't pick up the phone. I'm not sure why.

She smiles and grabs her fur capelet for her entrance.

I weave through the actors in their positions backstage. I give Ravi Balu a pat on the back; Greg Kress gets a Ricola lozenge from my pocket; and various nuns get high fives. As I perform these rituals, I think about Iva Lou. Maybe our friendship is like other kinds of relationships that have a life and then, for whatever reason, end. If that's to be the case, then it's an enormous loss: there's a hole in my life where she lived. Although every day I have a moment when I wish we could reconcile, somehow, as time passes and the distance grows, it seems more improbable that we can work things out. We have a new manner with each other, cordial and polite, much as we behave with strangers. It's too bad. Maybe Iva Lou and I know everything about each other, and we've reached a place where we can no longer be useful to one another as confidantes. It happens. I just never thought it would happen to us.

Iva Lou brushes past me as I give Tayloe some final direction. She doesn't look back at me as she takes her place. Rather, she keeps her eyes steady on the stage.

As I go out the stage door, I meet Theodore in the hallway beside the auditorium. He tells me, 'I'm going to say hello to Iva Lou.'

'No, you won't! It'll cause another nun stampede!'

He agrees, smiling and we walk together up to the light booth in the back of the theater.

'We got us a packed house,' Otto says as he opens a pack of Nabs (cellophane-wrapped peanut-butter crackers). He offers Theodore and me crackers. We politely decline. Chomping on a cracker, Otto gets behind the follow spot. Theodore and I sit on two rolling stools, well under the beam of light from the follow spot.

'Cue the orchestra,' I tell Otto.

Otto takes a red bandanna out of his back pocket and waves it at Virginia Meador, who nods back. Her reading glasses slide down to the tip of her nose. She motions to the musicians to begin, and then she puts her long, tapered fingers on the piano keys. As the orchestra plays the overture, the audience sings along to the familiar tune.

Theodore rolls his eyes. 'Oh, boy, this production is going to be hokey from Muskogee.'

'Welcome home, Theodore.'

The curtain rises on the cathedral set. As the nuns usher in, singing a kyrie, the audience bursts into applause. Only Liz Ann Noel drops character and winks at the audience, causing a titter that spreads through the house. Then it's all business as the nuns sing their lungs out.

Theodore watches intently, as though it's the first play he has ever seen. No matter how grand a Broadway production, or how small a community-theater presentation, he is a student of the lively arts. Theodore is not jaded; he says he learns something new with every show he sees. I wish I could say I do the same.

I scribble notes throughout the first act. Occasionally, Theodore leans over and gives me a tip. *Maria: project more. Captain Von Trapp: watch the ends of your phrases, you're dropping them. Rolfe: a little less prim, give me more emotion.* And so they go.

During the scene at the ball, Carolyn Beech's costumes shine: 1930s drop-waist dresses in jewel tones. Iva Lou is stunning in a floor-length emerald-green sheath and tiara. She slides all over the Captain like a parlor snake, and he loves it.

In most productions, at the conclusion of 'So Long, Farewell,' it's usually Liesl who carries Gretl up to bed. Instead, I had the Captain carry her up so that I could secure a moment between Maria and the Captain on the landing at the top of the stairs. I thought it more effective than leaving him on the floor below with the Baroness.

Theodore and I watch as the Captain carries Gretl to the top of the stairs. The Captain puts her down; she runs up the landing and disappears into her room. As the door closes, the Captain turns back to Maria. He makes a gesture toward her. Maria, in her sweet white eyelet dress, looks down, embarrassed. Then the Captain looks to the hushed audience. He pivots to face the Baroness below and extends his hand as if to say, 'You are the woman for me.' Iva Lou smiles up at him. The smile unglues my poor actor. He pivots, his heel catches on the top step, and he tries to regain his footing but cannot. The pitch of the stairs catches him and thrusts him forward like one of those blow-up birthday-party clowns that's been slugged. He throws his arms up in the air to regain his balance. The audience gasps.

The Captain's body plunges forward. 'Holy shit!' he hollers. He reaches for the banister, but it is too late. He goes down on both knees, leans back on his rear end, and makes like a sled. The only sound we hear in the stunned theater is the whap, whap, whap of his legs as they hit the steps and propel him down to the stage floor. Finally, he hits bottom with a splat.

The paralyzed party guests suddenly come to

life and surround him. Tayloe looks up to us in horror. Blackout and curtain.

'Jesus. That was bad.' Otto turns off the follow spot. 'You'd better go and check him. I think I heard a femur snap.'

The audience chatters nervously. Otto pulls on the house lights. Theodore and I run out of the booth, down the stairs, and around to the hallway through the wings to the stage. Greg, our Captain, is lying on the floor with a nun's wimple under his head for a pillow. There are two perfect seams where the fabric wore away on the front of his trousers as he peeled down the stairs. 'Are you okay, Greg?'

'I think I blew out my knee.'

'Can you walk?'

'I can try.'

Theodore and I help him up. He cannot straighten his right leg. We set Greg back down on the floor.

'We'd better get him up to Lonesome Pine. Doc Rock can check him,' I tell Peanut Rogers, the laid-back head of our stage crew, who is getting an associate arts degree up at Mountain Empire Community College. Peanut, around thirty, is tall and thin, with a head of loose brown curls. He's got the pep of a turtle.

'I'll get the Nova.' Peanut slowly heads for the stage door.

'Wait! My dad's in the audience!' Ravi Balu volunteers.

'Well, run and fetch him. We need a doctor!' Sweet Sue tells him. Ravi heads for the house.

'How was I doing?' Greg asks. His thick pale blue hair is sprayed into a George Jones bouffant. Not a hair moved as he plummeted; it's still a perfectly formed stage helmet. Our captain is a goodlooking man, with a high forehead and a determined chin that leads his profile in a scoop. He oozes strength, even though he's turning peaked under his pancake makeup.

'In the show?' I can't believe he's asking. He must be in tremendous pain.

'Yes, ma'am. In the show. How was I doing?'

'Very well. I thought you were doing great.'

'Me too. I was feeling it. I was finally feeling like the Captain, and then this had to happen. Hubris. That's it. Hubris. I got too big for my pants, and I paid fer it.'

'It was an accident. You're not being punished.'

'You don't think so? I was so tickled when Nellie told me I was gonna be the Captain. This part meant the world to me. I got to come here every night for two months and rehearse. It gave me something to do, something to look forward to. I love to sing and perform. It wears me out down to my bones. I'd go home and fall into bed, so tarred, I could hardly move. I loved being spent like that. Nothing like being in a show. Nothing.'

'We'll get this knee taken care of, and then you'll be back on the boards,' I lie.

'I hope so.'

The nuns push Dr Balu onto the stage, taking his program from him. He kneels next to the Captain. He tears the pant leg to expose the bad knee.

'Goddammit, Doc. Tear *on* the seam! *On* the seam!' Carolyn shouts.

'This is life and death!' Peanut hollers back at Carolyn in a moment of unbridled energy. He pulls her away. 'Screw the pants!'

The Captain's knee has swollen to twice its size, looking like a bowl of Fleeta's cherries jubilee at the Pharmacy.

'Call the Rescue Squad,' Dr Balu instructs us. 'Right away. We need a stretcher. You should not bend this knee, Mr Kress, and you cannot walk on it.'

The next day Fleeta scrapes down the open grill at the Mutual's. Theodore slides onto a stool at the counter while I open the pharmacy.

'What'll it be, Ted?' Fleeta is the only person on earth who can get away with calling Theodore Ted.

'How about biscuits and gravy?'

Fleeta beams. 'Can do.'

'I've traveled the world, Fleets, and nobody makes biscuits and gravy like you.'

'You're darn tootin'. I was trained by the master. Shorty Johnson spent the better part of her life in the kitchen. What with her sons, Roy and Shep, hungry around the clock, she mastered the great Southern dishes, that's for sure.'

SHORTY JOHNSON'S BISCUITS AND GRAVY

Serves 4 (double these recipes for hearty appetites!)

BUTTERMILK BISCUITS
2 cups all-purpose flour*
2 teaspoons baking powder
½ teaspoon baking soda
¾ teaspoon salt
⅓ cup Crisco, chilled
¾ cup buttermilk

COUNTRY SAUSAGE GRAVY
1 pound pork sausage
3 tablespoons flour
2 cups whole milk
Salt and pepper to taste

For biscuits: Preheat oven to 450 degrees. To 2 cups sifted flour, stir in baking powder, soda, and salt; then cut in Crisco until mixture resembles coarse meal. Add buttermilk. Stir lightly until ingredients are moistened. Form dough into a ball and transfer to a lightly floured work surface. Knead about 6 times (too much kneading will make tough biscuits!). Roll to ½-inch thickness. Cut into 2-inch disks with biscuit cutter (or inverted drinking glass). Arrange on a lightly oiled baking sheet so that the biscuits are not touching. Bake 16 minutes or until biscuits have risen and are golden-brown.

For gravy: While biscuits are baking, prepare sausage gravy by browning sausage in a heavy, well-seasoned iron skillet over medium-high heat until cooked through, stirring frequently to break up meat. Using a slotted spoon, transfer browned sausage to a bowl and set aside. Discard all but 3 tablespoons of pan drippings. Return skillet to medium heat. Sprinkle flour into drippings and whisk 2–3 minutes until lightly browned. Whisk in milk. Increase heat to medium-high and stir constantly, 2–3 minutes, or until it begins to bubble and thicken. Return sausage to gravy, reduce heat, and simmer 1–2 minutes, until heated throughout. Season with salt and pepper to taste (use lots of black pepper!).

NOTE: Gravy can be prepared using dripping from fried bacon, chicken, steak, or pork chops too! For those on a budget, you can even make gravy from fried bologna drippings!!!!
* (If using unbleached self-rising flour, omit the powder, soda, and salt.)

I line up three mugs on the counter and pour each of us a cup of coffee.

'So, Ted, what happened with your love affair up in New York?' Fleeta asks earnestly.

'Didn't work out.'

'Let me tell you something. Love is a many-splendored thing until it's over.'

'You got that right, Fleets.'

'Damn shame.' Fleeta stirs the gravy on the stove. I've never had biscuits and gravy in all these years, but it smells so good, I might try it this morning.

'Sure is.'

'Nellie Goodloe came in last night. I've never seen the woman so depressed. Even that damn Christmas sweater she was wearin' looked down in the dumps. Twelve lords a-leapin' looked like they'd rather lie down.' Fleeta sighs. 'What are you gonna do about the show?'

'Well, Reverend Mutter offered us the Methodist Church, so we could perform it as a concert, since our Captain can't walk,' I answer.

'Great idea.' Theodore puts cream in his coffee and stirs. 'We did that with *Godspell* back in the seventies, remember?'

'My *Sound of Music* cast almost tied me to a stake when I suggested it,' I say.

Theodore shrugs. 'Can't blame them. They've worked hard.'

I think aloud: 'We could put him in a wheel-chair!'

'Terrible idea. Nobody would be thinking about the show – they'd be focused on that knee of his.

Ted, why don't you step in?' Fleeta pours the hot gravy over the biscuits. 'Back in the day, you was a thespian. That's Greek for "actor," you know. Hell, you used to tear it up as the Red Fox in the Drama. Plus, you can sing as good as anybody around here. Why don't you just go on and suit up and be the Captain?'

'My acting days are over.'

'Listen here. Many great people are called upon late in life to do an encore. Think about it. Why, Charley Pride is still going strong in Branson; Johnny Mathis surfaces every now and agin in Vegas. Loretta Lynn just made a record. Hell, if they can do it, you can.'

'It's a crazy idea, Fleeta,' Theodore says firmly.

'You're far easier on the eyes than Greg Kress. If there's one thing I hate, it's when I go to a show and the leading man doesn't do it for me. What is the point of going to a show if it don't give you the flutters? When I look at Greg Kress, I don't focus on his face and manly form – I think of accountants, which he is in real life, and then I think of bills, which I hate, and then taxes, which skeers me, and then and there, the entertainment value of the play goes right in the crapper for me. But you, you got the debonair thing. I could look at you for two hours and not tire of it.'

'Thanks, Fleeta.' Theodore enjoys the compliment and straightens his posture on the counter stool.

'Save the day!' I chime in.

Fleeta raps her knuckles on the counter. 'You ought to do it.'

'I came here to rest.'

Fleeta puts her hand on her heart. 'You owe it to the people of Big Stone Gap.'

'I do not!' he protests.

'Sure you do,' I say. 'Think about it. This is where you got your start. And now you're a world-renowned director. You perfected your craft right here. It's time to give back.'

'For Christsakes, it's Christmas, Ted. What's a ding-dang holiday without an act of Christian charity?' Fleeta cracks her knuckles.

Theodore smiles and takes another sip of his coffee. He looks at me. 'You set me up.'

'Sorry. I thought that if the plea came from Fleeta, you might consider helping us out. Well, would you? Please?'

'Don't railroad me,' he says. Fleeta places the hot plate of biscuits and gravy on Theodore's place mat. He puts his napkin in his lap. 'I never make any major decisions on an empty stomach,' he adds.

'Mr MacChesney, please lift your hands over your head.' The nurse demonstrates, and Jack follows her lead. As he sits up straight on the examining table, his legs dangle over the side like those of a boy who's gone fishing on the pier up at the lake. Whenever we come to the doctor, my husband looks so vulnerable, all I want to do is protect him.

'Good. Thank you. The doctor will be in shortly.' The nurse smiles and goes.

Jack sighs. 'I hate these checkups.'

'Me too.' I take his hand. 'But we have to stay on top of it.'

'I did fine on the stress test.'

'I know.'

'And I'm feeling good.'

'We want to keep you that way.'

Dr Smiddy pushes the door open, still giving the nurse instructions about another patient.

Jack extends his hand. 'Thanks for seeing us so close to Christmas.'

Dr Smiddy smiles. 'The holidays can be stressful.' He seems like a giant next to Jack. He checks Jack's blood pressure, the usual stuff. Then he sits down on the stool with the wheels and looks up at us. 'Your PET scan came back.'

'Anything of interest?' Jack tries not to sound nervous.

'Well, your heart looked good – we don't see any further blockages.'

I clap my hands together. 'Great.'

'But now we need to keep an eye on your right lung.'

'What's the matter with it?'

'You're a miner, you know.'

'Don't tell me I have black lung.'

'You show some signs of it, though it is in no way advanced. But we're thinking that maybe the shadow on your lung, along with the blockage in your neck, combined to cause your problem a couple of months back.'

'But black lung won't kill him, will it?'

The way I ask the question makes Jack burst out laughing. 'Easy, Ave.'

'I didn't mean to cut to the chase, or maybe I did. I know that black lung is a chronic condition that can lead to other problems, and I just want to make sure that Jack doesn't show signs of those other diseases,' I say.

Dr Smiddy looks down at the chart. 'Like emphysema.'

'Yes, like that,' I say.

'We don't see a progression. Of course, it's new. We'll keep an eye on it.' He asks Jack, 'Have you had any trouble breathing?'

'Nope.'

'Pain?'

'None.'

'You want to avoid any allergens. I would stop clearing asbestos pipes when you do construction, and you need to stay away from anything involving small particles.'

'My wood shop?'

'Wear a mask.'

'Okay, Doc.'

Dr Smiddy wishes us a merry Christmas and then goes. Jack and I look at each other. We were not expecting to hear this news.

'I have to die of something someday, Ave.'

'Don't talk like that.'

'My daddy lived with black lung for twenty years.'

'I know.'

'And in the end, he had a heart attack and died in his sleep. I'd take that.' Jack jumps off the table and goes behind the screen to dress.

'You're going to be fine,' I tell him. I want to reassure my husband, but saying it aloud helps me believe it too.

In tan lederhosen and a green felt alpine hat, Theodore Tipton strides downstage for the finale of *The Sound of Music*. He removes the hat and launches into 'Climb Every Mountain.' The years fall away from Theodore as he sings. Even I, who know him in real life as well as anyone, see the utter and complete transformation from the man I know into Captain Von Trapp. Theodore is so gifted, you believe him. Yes, he's standing on a stage floor dusted in Ivory Snow soap flakes, and yes, those are fake trees on the backs of the Shawnee Avenue Bridge Club, but it doesn't matter. When he speaks, you listen, and when he sings, you soar. He loves Maria, and their marriage will last forever. As the Von Trapp children encircle him, Tayloe does her best Julie Andrews and looks up at her Theodore with a combination of admiration and lust. (I have to say, as much as Tayloe avoided kissing scenes with Greg Kress, she's thrown herself into them with Theodore.)

The children sing in perfect harmony. Otto, one

hand steady on the follow spot, uses the other to wipe away a tear. The orb of white light quivers a bit, and Otto quickly puts both hands back on the levers. There is not a dry eye in the house. The audience rises to its feet as Otto hits the spotlight to black. The upstage lights silhouette the Von Trapp family. Curtain.

For the curtain call, Virginia Meador and her orchestra launch into a high-spirited rendition of 'How Do You Solve a Problem Like Maria?' As the layered drapery of red velvet pulls away, the cast locks arms upstage, then they walk downstage. They take a group bow, and each of the major characters steps forward to take a separate bow.

Iva Lou gets the most applause as she does a deep curtsy without faltering. For curtain call, she changed into a completely new ensemble not seen in the show. She wears a winter-white floor-length satin slip gown and matching marabou high-heeled slides. (I guess the Baroness will go on to new and greater heights once the Nazis are defeated.)

I get a twinge in my gut as the crowd cheers for her.

The Fox house, the historic landmark home of Big Stone Gap, is a rambling clapboard house with many rooms and a wrap-around porch on a grassy plot right off of Main Street. Whenever people in town need a nice catered dinner or a party, this is where they are likely to end up. This was the home of the famous author John Fox, Jr., who wrote *The Trail of the Lonesome Pine*. His office and study are intact in a sweet little room off the garden. There are a red leather wing chair where he did his reading; a turn-of-the-twentieth-century oak desk with a swivel seat; and his typewriter, a glorious old-fashioned black enamel box with bright white letter keys.

The large kitchen is in the grand old Southern style, with walk-in pantries, a cooling porch, and a fireplace. Many of us have tried to copy the layout in our own houses: it features counter space in a full rectangle around the room. In the center, a long old farm table with benches is perfect for any job that requires an assembly line.

For the closing-night party, Nellie Goodloe has seen to it that the house is decorated in an Austrian theme with a little Christmas thrown in. There are paper edelweiss flowers everywhere, and small votive candles that look like they belong in a Catholic church. Evidently, Patsy Arnold attempted to make Wiener schnitzel for the party, but it didn't turn out too well, so she quickly substituted her famous fried chicken instead.

Theodore grabs my arm as I make my way to the bar. I laugh.

'Do me a favor,' Theodore whispers in my ear. 'When you see me swallowed up in a gaggle of chorus girls, rescue me.'

'You've got a deal.'

'Beth Hagan had such a grip on my forearm, she left a hematoma.'

'Sorry.' I pull Theodore into an alcove between the living room and hallway.

'You offer absolutely no protection between me and the general public. You're a bad date.'

'I always was.'

'Hey, you two.' Jack pokes his head into the alcove. 'They want to give you a toast.'

'Him or me?'

'Both of you. Get on out there.'

Even at this stage in our lives, Theodore and I are still a couple of people pleasers who want everybody to like us. Therefore, we do as we are told and take our places near the mantel. George Polly, the town manager – a dead ringer for young Arnold Palmer in his navy Shetland sweater – raises a glass to us. 'We'd like to thank Ave Maria for a fine production. We'd also like to thank our old friend Theodore Tipton, who rode back into town like Gene Autry and saved our asses by steppin' in for Greg Kress and his blowed-out knee. We thank you, and God speed.'

'Hear, hear!' Greg raises his glass from his wheel-chair.

We clink our glasses. I smile and look out over the cast and their guests. When I turn to look up at Theodore, I catch Iva Lou's face in the antique mirror over the upright piano. She stands on the far side of the room in deep conversation. I turn to see who she's talking to, and I'm stunned when I catch a glimpse of Lovely Carter.

'Have you spoken to Iva Lou?' I ask Theodore.

'A little here and there. It was tough during those crash rehearsals. There wasn't much time to talk.'

'We're like strangers now.' I can't hide my sadness.

'I think you'll have to make the first move.'

'I tried. I went into the dressing room before our first runthrough, and she was cold. I don't know what to do.'

'You're not trying hard enough.'

'You're gonna make this *my* fault?'

'There's something else going on here.'

'I wish you'd tell me.' I'm annoyed with Theodore; he's being indirect. I need him to shoot straight. 'Please.'

'You're angry at her,' he says.

'I am not. I understand how hard it must have been for her in her situation. I have a lot of compassion for her.'

'No, you don't.'

'What do you mean?'

'You don't understand it at all. You've always played it very safe when it came to men. You don't relate to women who fall in love, lose their minds – sometimes more than their minds – then are hurt and disappointed and move on. That's out of your orbit entirely.'

'Oh, I'm unsophisticated?' I sound defensive.

'You used to be. Now you're more of a snob.

You carry around that imperious morality of your dear mother's like a shield.'

'I do not.'

'You don't like anything unsavory.'

'Having a baby out of wedlock is not unsavory.'

'Well, it's not admirable. And you don't like it. Why don't you just admit it?'

Just then Theodore is pulled into the kitchen by Arline Sharpe and Billie Jean Scott, who want to tell him all about their trip to Knoxville to see the national touring company of *Cabaret*.

'Excuse me, Mrs MacChesney?'

I turn. Lovely Carter smiles kindly at me. Her blue eyes have the same intensity as her mother's. I wonder if people look at Etta and see me in her eyes in the same way. 'Hi. How nice of you to come to the party,' I tell her.

Lovely runs her fingers over the beads on her evening bag and takes a breath. 'I saw the show tonight – Iva Lou invited me. You did a great job. It was wonderful. I loved it.'

'It was the best cast we ever had.'

'I wanted to thank you. Whatever you said to Iva Lou made a difference. We're talking. She's going to drive me up to Ohio to meet my birth father.'

'Really?'

'After the holidays. It's a terrible time of year to drive north, but it's been a mild winter, so we shouldn't have any problems. Anyhow, I wanted you to know that you really helped me. I hope someday I can do something to repay you.'

'I didn't do a thing.'

Lovely gives my hand a squeeze and goes to the entrance. She gives Iva Lou and Lyle a hug good-bye, then Lyle helps lva Lou into her coat.

'You aren't leaving?' I say to Iva Lou.

'I'm tarred. And so is Lyle. You stay and have fun!' Iva Lou says with a big smile.

'I remember when you'd stay till the last drop of punch was gone.'

'Not anymore. Tell Theodore to stop by and see us before he heads back up to the big city.'

'I will,' I promise, even though the invitation excludes me.

'Good night.' Iva Lou turns and goes out the door.

I look around the party. Theodore is still in the kitchen with the girls, and Jack is having a deep conversation with Scott Hatcher about some heavy mining equipment. In an instant I am over-whelmed by Iva Lou's dismissive treatment of me, and I run to the bathroom. I bolt the door shut. I sit down on the edge of the claw-footed tub and have a good cry.

The Gap Corporation (our local chamber of commerce of sorts) can't believe the money they made on ticket sales for *The Sound of Music* star-ring Theodore Tipton. Three nights of packed houses, plus a final Sunday matinee, put them in the black. The coffers are full for the coming fiscal year, which means new streetlights, a bigger and better Christmas parade, and new teeter-totters and slides for the kiddie playground at Bullitt Park. Merry Christmas to us!

At first we couldn't figure out where all the people came from. Then we realized that when word got out that Theodore was the Captain, every University of Tennessee fan in the area showed up to support him. His days as band director there are legendary, and they figured this was a way to pay homage to a great visionary. It was wonderful to watch Theodore sign autographs after every performance, as though he were John Raitt from Broadway. The goodwill didn't stop with Theodore; his participation helped our other actors. The Kingsport Renaissance Players, a small theater group, asked Tayloe to play the lead in *The Pajama Game* for their dinner theater. Not bad for a girl in a Julie Andrews wig.

I have much to be grateful for this Christmas Eve as I make the rounds in our house, dimming the lights and checking the fires. The living room is so cozy. I picked up a fresh cranberry wreath at the Kiwanis Club tree sale. It looks festive on the mantel, with our stockings hung below.

There's a full moon over Cracker's Neck Holler that throws a silver veil across the valley. From our front porch, the lights in the far houses tucked up in the hills look like pearls on blue satin. I flip on the Christmas-tree lights. We loaded it with ornaments, down to the paper chain Etta and Joe made when they were little. I try not to cry. After all, my husband tells me to remember what I have, not what I don't have: 'Count who's here, not who's missing.' Good advice, if I could follow it. Is it too much to wish my daughter were home for the holidays? Etta said Christmas wasn't a big deal in Italy; why can't I be a little more Italian this year and put it all in perspective?

'Honey, Theodore's doing the dishes!' Jack shouts from the kitchen. I go back to the kitchen, where Jack is stoking the fire and Theodore is clearing the dishes from the table.

'Stop right there. You're company,' I say.

'Back off. I love scullery duty.' Theodore plunges his hands into the suds. 'Good for the cuticles. That was delicious.' He runs more water in the sink. 'I've never had better fettucini. Jack, you've become an Eye-talian.'

'Live with anybody long enough, and you start looking like them and, eventually, cooking like them.'

'Is that a good thing?' I ask.

My husband smiles at me. 'What do you think?'

'I talked to Etta. She's going to my dad's house for Christmas. They're driving up there today.'

'She's going to have a great holiday,' Jack assures me.

'I don't know how you do it.'

'Do what?'

'How do you accept things? You handle whatever life throws you, and you don't agonize.' I put my arms around my husband.

Theodore interrupts before Jack can answer. 'Let me shed some light on this for you, Mrs MacChesney. May I, Jack?'

'Go right ahead,' Jack tells him.

'First of all, Jack's not Catholic. We invented agony. And secondly, your husband is able to cope with life because he's a man.' Theodore rinses the dishes and looks out on the field. 'A man is a simple creature. He deals with what's in front of him and not what might be.'

'Sometimes all I think about is what might be,' I admit.

'Is it really so bad to know your daughter is happy in another part of the world?' Jack asks.

'When you put it that way . . .'

'She's happy. That's all we want for her.'

Jack and Theodore decide to play poker while I get ready for Midnight Mass. I hear them laughing and talking as I draw a bath upstairs. It really is an okay Christmas; after all, Jack is doing better, and Theodore, my best friend, somehow knew I needed him and showed up to lend his support. I have nothing to complain about.

The steam from the bath fills the room quickly, so I open the window. I lean out and breathe in the cold night air. Jack hung a string of lights on his new bridge in the woods; through the bare branches, I see the soft pink lights twinkling like a bracelet. I study the woods for a while, looking carefully from tree to tree. The wide trunks are covered in frost, and their tangled black arms look like ink scrawls in the white moonlight. I guess I'm looking for someone, or maybe just a clue. Some sign of the morning when I saw the young man. 'I wish you were here, Joe,' I say aloud to the black sky. 'I hope you know I miss you every day.'

I hear the escape drain gurgle on the tub, which tells me it's full. I turn off the water, then light an elegant freesia candle Iva Lou gave me for my last birthday. This may be the final gift I ever receive from her, I think. But then I put the sad thoughts out of my mind. I climb into the tub, and as I sink down into the suds, the cold outside air makes a mist. I feel the warmth all around me. I float in the tub like a rose petal. A few moments pass, and then suddenly, an odd feeling goes through my body. It's the very same feeling I had the night before Joe died. I felt him leaving me.

I climb out of the tub and throw on my robe. I go into our bedroom and find Jack's cell phone and press Etta on direct dial. The phone rings on the other end.

'Hello? Dad?'

'No, honey, it's Mom.'

'Mom, why are you calling?'

'I don't know. I had a feeling.'

'A bad feeling?'

'Yes, I got really scared. Are you okay over there?'

'Mom, we're fine. Isn't Uncle Theodore there?'

'He's playing cards with Dad.'

'Well, don't talk to me. Go and have fun with them,' she says.

I hang up the phone, feeling like a fool. This is so typical of me, to mistake my hunches for something real, to give in to doom when there is none and to panic when I can't control things. Ever since Joe died, I have over-reacted to the slightest waves of intuition. Sometimes I'm right, though. How many times have I replayed my son's death, hoping for a different outcome? I remember kneeling next to Joe's bed in the hospital. Etta was lying next to him on the bed, and Jack knelt on the floor on the other side. We made a canopy over him with our bodies. It was as if we were hiding him so the angels wouldn't find him and take him away. I was watching Joe breathe, and in an instant, everything changed. He was still alive, but it didn't seem like he was there anymore. I sensed him going away before he was gone. My mother radar had always stood me in good stead; now I knew of the doom and could do nothing to stop it. Mothers know the comings and goings of our children on an instinctive level, but this was different, deeper.

After hanging up with Etta, I go back into the bathroom. The hot water and the glorious suds have been sucked down the drain. I must've kicked the stopper out when I went to use the phone. I'm too weary to draw another bath, so I dry off and do my hair.

My husband whistles when I enter the kitchen.

(Anytime I wear a dress and high heels, I get a whistle.)

'Double or nothing,' Theodore says to Jack.

'Is it appropriate to gamble on Christmas Eve?'

'Probably not.' Theodore smiles. 'By the way, I agree with your husband. You look pretty.'

'Thanks. Anyone want to go to Midnight Mass with me?'

'Sure.' Theodore puts down his cards.

'I'll go too, honey.'

While Jack and Theodore get their coats, I turn off the lights and blow out the candles on the mantel. I'm instantly sorry not to have left a light on for Joe.

Midnight Mass is my favorite gathering of the year at Sacred Heart Church. For the most part, Big Stone Gap shuts down around seven P.M., unless there's a sporting event. On Christmas Eve, you would swear that the population picked up and left, it's so quiet. Except for the sound of an occasional decorative bell or the winter wind, there's pure silence. Only the twinkle of the lights, draped and roped throughout our trees and on our windows, reminds us that there are still folks here.

The church is decorated with pots of poinsettias. There's a large tree covered in homemade ornaments inspired by stories in the Bible. There are Noah's Ark, made of Popsicle sticks and the animals made of bits of fabric; the tablets with the commandments on them, made of felt; a calico Star

194

of David; and apples (the kids went heavy on the Old Testament this year).

Theodore, Jack, and I sing along to the pre-mass Christmas carols. I look out the picture window behind the altar and see a light snow beginning to fall outside. We couldn't have planned a better backdrop for our Mass.

We get our share of non-Catholics on Christmas who enjoy the small choir accompanied by fiddles. Fran and Henry Keuling-Stout read the Epistles, and I always like that, because they fill them with meaning. Jack, who never had any interest in converting to Catholicism (and still doesn't), enjoys the celebration. Like me, Theodore remembers Latin masses, and he was an altar boy, so it's old home week for him.

At the end of the service, we say good night to Father Drake.

'Hey, I'm starving. I could use a plate of waffles right about now,' Theodore announces.

'Now?'

'Yeah. I burned off Jack's pasta, begging forgiveness for my sins. I need to refuel.'

'How about the Huddle House?'

'Let's go.'

Jack drives Theodore and me up to the Huddle House, on the outskirts of town. Their neon sign is never turned off, even in day-light. It says: ALWAYS OPEN ALWAYS FRESH. We take a seat in the orange booth and order our wee-hour breakfasts off of the orange menu. There are a few folks in the place, mostly night workers from the prison. Ralph Stanley plays on the radio. The lonely twang of his guitar makes me miss Etta even more.

'Theodore, I wish you'd stay through the New Year,' I say.

'I have to go back after the board meeting at UVA-Wise.'

'Oh, come on. Stay. Bask in the glory of your theatrical success. The folks around here want to make a fuss over you. You sold out *The Sound of Music*.'

'We'll see.' Theodore smiles.

The trip back to Cracker's Neck is quick. As we pass Powell Valley High School, it's hard to believe that twenty years ago, Theodore was the band director. Harder still to believe that Elizabeth Taylor choked on a chicken bone, thus giving Theodore a shot at the big time. He didn't squander it.

I put my head on my husband's shoulder as he drives. Sometimes I feel I've been married all my life. I was the town spinster for so long, but the years before Jack and the children have melted away like honey in hot tea. So much life happened after we married, so many things that I couldn't predict, and now there's more behind me than ahead of me. I'd trade all this wisdom for more time. I would.

We don't talk as Jack takes the turn up the hill to the stone house. I left the tree on – is there any sight more comforting than a Christmas tree in a dark house? It's a glittering heart in a home filled with memories.

I make sure Theodore has extra quilts for the cold night ahead. I climb the stairs to our bedroom to join Jack, who has already burrowed under the covers. I change out of my dress and into my pajamas. It's so cold, I skip to the bed and jump in.

'Did you have to leave the bathroom window open?' Jack grumbles.

'You know I like the night air.'

'You were looking out at the field again, weren't you?'

'Yeah.'

'There's nothing there, Ave.'

'If you say so.'

'It's not good to let your mind play tricks on you.'

'I know.' I feel myself begin to cry. I stop the tears and wipe my eyes on the scalloped edge of my pillowcase. 'I like the lights on your bridge.'

'Pretty, right?'

'Very.'

'Merry Christmas, Jack.'

'Merry Christmas.' My husband rolls over and kisses me good night.

I roll over onto my side. The feather bed is soft, and I burrow in next to Jack for warmth. As he puts his arms around me, the excitement of the day sends me into a deep sleep. I dream.

I'm flying over Cracker's Neck Holler on a dark

night. The sky is full of pale blue stars, and the moon is carnation pink. On the ground, four children lay out a picnic on a crazy floral tablecloth. The wind keeps kicking up the edges. The children fight the wind and do all sorts of things so the tablecloth won't blow away. They stand on it. They sit on it. They gather rocks and try to place them on the hems to anchor it. Nothing works. Overhead, I'm frustrated, wanting to help them, but below, they laugh and play as though it's a game. I try to fly down to help them, but something holds me back. I become tired, trying to fly down to them. Sometimes it seems I almost get my feet to touch the ground and then am pulled away again. I shout to the children, but they do not see me.

Suddenly, a small cyclone made of leafy branches surrounds me, and I am pushed higher and higher in the clouds. I can still see the children, who are now looking up at me with their arms outstretched. They can't reach me. One of the little girls cries, 'Mom! Mom!' I try to descend but can't. It's frustrating. I push and push. 'Mom, Mom!'

I feel Jack's arms around me. I slowly open my eyes as he whispers, 'Ave Maria, wake up. It's Christmas morning. I have a surprise for you.'

I roll over into the soft down comforter and pull it over me. 'I know what you got me for Christmas.'

'How do you know?'

'It's a new hitch for my Jeep. I saw it in the wood shop with a bow on it.'

'I wish you wouldn't snoop.'

'I can't help it. Italian girls spy on their husbands. Generations of my Italian sisters have found it effective as a tool to keep husbands in line. It's in our bones.' I nestle into the pillow. It was a late night; I need my sleep.

'Honey, get up. You'll be happy you did.' Jack stands next to me, holding my bedroom slippers. He pulls the quilt and comforter off of me. 'Merry Christmas.' He smiles. 'Come with me.'

CHAPTER 9

DREAMLAND

I grudingly put on my slippers. Jack takes my hand and leads me to the top of the stairs. 'Surprise!'

'Hello, Ave!' My father stands at the bottom of the stairs with Giacomina.

I practically jump off the landing and into his arms. 'Oh my God! This is much better than a Jeep hitch! *Buon Natale*!'

Papa, dressed for the cold, wears dark brown corduroy pants and a matching cashmere sweater. He manages to look crisp after a long journey. Giacomina looks beautiful in jeans and a pale blue boiled-wool blazer.

I look up at Jack, who grins down at me. 'Jack, you knew!'

'Yep.'

'And you didn't tell me.'

'It would have been a lousy surprise if you knew about it.'

Theodore comes out of his bedroom in his pajamas. 'We had to tell Jack. You know, because of his ticker.'

'Yeah, well, what about mine?' I put my hand

on my chest. My heart is racing with more joy than it can hold.

'Etta wanted to be here – she knew how much it would mean to you – but Stefano's work wouldn't permit it. So she sent us instead. I hope it's not a disappointment.'

'Oh, Papa.' I throw my arms around him.

'How did you get here?' Before he can answer, I hear another voice I recognize.

'Good morning, Ave Maria,'

I turn to the living room. There, standing next to the Christmas tree, is Pete Rutledge.

What woman would not want to find him under her tree? For a second I forget where I am; it's years ago, and I'm standing in a field above Schilpario under an endless blue Italian sky, looking into the eyes of a man who could change my life with a few promises and one of his grins. I didn't take the bait, but there are moments when I remember how close I came, and this is one of them. Pete seems as tall as the tree, and his eyes are as blue as the pine. There are flecks of white in his thick black hair, but not many. He smiles, and I blush.

'Pete?' I clear my throat. 'What the heck . . .'

'Hope you don't mind,' he says almost shyly.

'Mind?' I smooth my hair and yank up the elastic waistband on my flannel pajamas. Pretty. What possessed me to put on these old things last night? I have a new nightgown that would have been perfect for company. 'Of course not. You're family.' I go to him and give him a big hug, keeping it fraternal and short.

'Pete flew us in. On his plane,' Giacomina tells us.

'The company plane.' Pete smiles. 'They came in on Continental from Italy, and I met them at Newark Airport last night. We drove over to Teterboro, flew out, and landed in Wise an hour ago.'

Jack puts his arms around me. 'I told Pete he was welcome to stay as long as he liked.'

'Great. Well, come on, everybody. You need breakfast, right?' Theodore claps his hands.

'And you knew about this too?' I say.

'Of course. Why do you think I dragged you and Jack to the Huddle House last night? It wasn't for the cuisine, I assure you. These folks were due around one A.M., and I was doing a full-tilt vamp. Was I convincing?'

'Very.'

'Except we had a weather delay last night.' Pete extends his hand to Theodore, who shakes it heartily.

'Well, you made it. What a surprise for my best friend,' Theodore says warmly.

'The best.' I cry.

'Now, honey. Stop the tears. If you don't, I'm sending everybody home,' Jack jokes.

'Don't you dare.'

Jack takes Papa, Giacomina, and Pete into the kitchen. I move to follow. Theodore yanks me behind the staircase. 'They didn't tell me Pete was coming,' he whispers. 'I would have ruined the surprise if they'd bothered to tell me *that*.'

'Look at me.' I smooth the front of my pajama top, covered with grinning half-moons, over baggy matching pants. 'I look like a set of sheets from the Goodwill.'

'You look adorable.'

'For Ma Kettle. Oh, who cares? My father is here!'

'How great is this?' Theodore points to the kitchen. He lowers his voice again. 'Ave?'

'What?'

'How about Pete? TBHS.'

'What's that?'

'Too bad he's straight.'

'TBIM.'

'What's that?'

'Too bad I'm married.'

I hear the clang of pots and the clink of dishes downstairs as I dress for Christmas dinner. Fleeta, Otto, and Worley have a system when prepping food, so they threw Theodore and me out of the kitchen in order to do things their way. I don't mind a bit; it gives me more time to put on mascara and fuss over my hair. Having Pete Rutledge around gives a woman incentive to dress her best, put on the jewelry, stand up straight, and refresh her lipstick before it fades away. If Jack wonders why I'm fussing in the beauty department, he certainly doesn't let on.

The phone rings as I spritz my mother's Chanel No. 5 behind my ears. I pick up the receiver. 'Merry Christmas,' I answer.

'Merry Christmas, Ave! It's Pearl.'

'How are you?' What a surprise. The sound of her voice fills me with joy.

'We're moving again. Get this – we're going to New York. Taye got a job at Mount Sinai. We're moving to a town called Garden City on Long Island.'

'Fantastic. But I feel terrible – I never made it to Boston to see you.'

'I'm going to miss it. India loves her friends here.'

'How is she?'

'Growing like a weed. She's going to be five in April. At least she'll start kindergarten in her new school in New York. How are you?'

'Great. My dad and his wife came from Italy for Christmas.'

'How perfect!'

'Pete Rutledge flew them in. Theodore came down too. Wait till he hears you're moving to New York. If you need anything there, I'm sure he'll be happy to help you.'

'I'll be sure to ask.' Pearl's voice breaks.

'Are you okay?'

'I miss Big Stone Gap.'

'Pearl, are you crazy? Your life is so exciting!'

'I don't know. I miss the mountains.'

'They're not going anywhere.'

'I know.'

'Come and visit.'

'Taye's schedule is crazy. It's so hard to plan anything. Look, I don't want to keep you. I just wanted to send our love.'

'We'll see you soon, okay? We'll make a point of it!' I promise her. 'How about the summer? Maybe you could come down for a nice long visit then.'

'Let's try for the summer,' Pearl agrees.

I hang up the phone and feel a pang of sadness. I miss Pearl. I wish there was some way to have everyone I love home for Christmas, but that will never be.

The house is filled with the smell of cinnamon, butter and rum, rolls baking, and Fleeta's dressing, savory herbs and bread crumbs. As I pass the dining room table on my way to the kitchen, I see that she's replaced my Christmas-angel centerpiece with one of her gorgeous cakes on a ceramic pedestal.

LONG WINTER'S NAP CHRISTMAS CAKE

(ONE BITE AND YOU NEED TO LIE DOWN)
Serves 12
COURTESY OF CINDY ASHLEY

1 stick butter, room temperature
½ cup shortening
3 cups sugar
5 eggs

3 cups all-purpose flour, sifted
1 cup milk
1 tablespoon rum flavoring
1 teaspoon vanilla
½ cup green maraschino cherries, quartered
½ cup red maraschino cherries, quartered
1 cup shredded coconut
1 cup black walnuts, chopped

Beat together butter, shortening, and sugar until fluffy; beat, beat, beat!!!!! Add eggs one at a time. Add sifted flour and milk alternately. Add rum flavoring, vanilla, cherries, coconut, and walnuts. Bake at 325 degrees for 1½ hours in a large tube pan. 'The secret of the cake is in the beating!'

'Don't you look fancy.' Fleeta looks up at me as she places pats of butter on the Pyrex dish of whipped sweet potatoes.

'Is that a good thing or a bad thing?'

'If it were bad, I'd keep my mouth shut.'

'I doubt that.'

'This right here is the best fried turkey I ever made,' Fleeta says proudly as she peels the tinfoil off of the thirty-pound bird. 'Fried turkey means Christmas Day to me.'

'I don't think you made enough,' I joke.

'Never fear. I also whiskey-soaked a fresh ham. Whiskey and butter and brown sugar.' Fleeta lifts another tinfoil tent off a roasting pan and inhales the sweet mist. 'Get out of town!' she says with delight. 'Why don't you go on and call the men in? I put out Uncle Lou's cheese log in the living room. Worley couldn't stop eating it, and I didn't want him to ruin his dinner.'

UNCLE LOUIS FISSE'S HOLIDAY CHEESE LOG

Serves 20, if they don't hog it

1 can (2 ounces) black olives, drained and chopped
4 ounces pimento peppers, drained and diced
8 green onions, finely chopped
1 pound butter
8 ounces cream cheese, softened
4 ounces blue cheese, crumbled
1 cup almonds, chopped, or any nut of your choice
Maraschino cherries, for garnish

In a medium bowl, mix olives, pimento peppers, and green onions. Mix butter, cream cheese, and blue cheese, then add olive mixture. Form mixture into a log or ball and then roll on a piece of wax paper. Add nuts to cover the entire log. Garnish with maraschino cherries and serve with buttery crackers.

Theodore comes into the kitchen. 'Where are the matches?'

'On the windowsill,' I tell him.

'I'm lighting the candelabras. At my age, soft lights during dinner are mandatory.'

'You look handsome,' I tell him.

'You had a thing for Theodore. Still do, evidently,' Fleeta says to me as she shoves a serving spoon into the scalloped potatoes.

'Ave Maria and I have been very happy on the Isle of Platonia for years now. The best thing that ever happened to us was Jack Mac.'

'Oh, you two could've made it work. Ave Maria could have swung you to the dark side.'

'Don't think so, Fleets,' Theodore says pleasantly.

Papa comes into the kitchen. 'May we help?'

Fleeta narrows her eyes and surveys my father. 'How old are you, Mario?'

'Seventy-four.'

'Damn Eye-talians. Twenty years come and gone since I first saw ye, and you ain't changed a bit. You people don't age. What is your secret?'

My father whispers in Fleeta's ear. She smiles. 'Hell, me and Otto do that vurry thing every Sunday night right, here in the mountains of Southwest Virginny, but it don't seem to help my wrinkles none. I must be doin it wrong.' Fleeta winks at my father.

I hand her the salad tongs. 'Christmas Day is not the appropriate time for a tutorial.'

Papa and Giacomina help Fleeta carry the platters of holiday fare from the kitchen to the server in the dining room. I look out the window and watch Jack and Pete make their contribution to Christmas. My husband and my old crush, two middle-aged lumberjacks, split logs like a couple of Abe Lincolns. The wheelbarrow is practically full. The competition is pretty mild between them as they chat and go about their chores.

Theodore comes up behind me at the sink. 'Stop spying.'

'Jack still thinks he's twenty. Look at him.' Jack lifts the ax in the air with two hands and guides it square onto a large tree trunk, which shucks in two. 'When Dr Smiddy said he could get back to normal, Jack didn't waste a minute resuming his chores.'

'Pete and Jack. Fantasy and reality,' muses Theodore.

I look around to make sure we're alone in the kitchen. 'Don't say that.'

'It's true, isn't it?'

'I'm very grateful to Pete. He brought Papa and Giacomina home for Christmas.'

'What does he want in return?'

'You're bad!'

Theodore smiles. 'Oh, let's have some fun. Play the vamp for me, please? If I have to look at Fleeta's reindeer sweater throughout dinner, I need something to raise my holiday aesthetic above the mundane. I need a little danger. Some intrigue. A teeny-weeny indiscretion. A kiss under the mistletoe. Come on. You can do it.'

'What's wrong with my sweater?' Fleeta barks from the door. 'It was a gift.'

'You know, Fleeta, you don't have to wear everything you're given.'

'What the hell else am I supposed to do with it?'

'There's a concept at most stores these days. It's called exchange.'

'I don't have time for that nonsense.'

'Fleeta, will you call everyone to the table, please?' I say.

Fleeta goes to call our guests from the living room. I wash my hands, go out on the sunporch, and push the screen door open.

'Boys? Dinner is on,' I call into the backyard.

Jack waves from across the field. Pete picks up the handles of the wheelbarrow and pushes it toward the house. I go into the dining room and help Otto and Worley find their places. Giacomina fusses with the platters on the server while Papa pours the wine. Jack and Pete laugh as they wash up in the kitchen. A few moments later, they join us at the table.

'It looks great, honey.' Jack kisses me.

'You need to plant one on me, Jack, since I did the lion's share of the cooking,' Fleeta complains, and Jack complies, giving her a kiss on the cheek.

Theodore looks around the room. 'Seeing as we're in the Bible Belt, who's going to pray?'

'Sure as hell not you, you're a fallen-away Catholic.' Fleeta puts her unlit cigarette on her bread plate (for later, I suppose).

'*Disaffected* Catholic,' Theodore corrects her. '"Fallen away" means more time in purgatory than I've actually earned.'

'Why don't you let God be the judge?' Fleeta says.

'Can you two hold the philosophical discussion until after dinner?' Jack says, smiling. 'That's coming from a barely there Methodist.'

'I'm an agnostic,' Pete pipes up.

Fleeta sniffs. 'You proud of that?'

'I won't apologize for my religious beliefs – or the Jell-O mold, which I made with Theodore this morning.' Pete looks to Theodore.

'Pete Rutledge may not believe in a Supreme Being, but he knows his way around a tub of Cool Whip.'

Pete bows his head like a preacher. 'Thank you, Theodore.'

'In lieu of an actual prayer, let's give thanks to the things we're grateful for,' I offer.

Theodore raises his hand. 'I'll go first, since I'm full of gratitude.'

'And my eggnog, but that's not to the point.' Jack laughs.

'I'd like to thank my host and hostess for their fine lodging. I am grateful that you two didn't sell this old house and downgrade to the Don Wax apartments in the Southern when Etta moved to

Italy. I'd like to thank Otto and Worley, who didn't pass judgment when I placed the holiday cheese log on the ottoman, too close to the fire, and it melted into a pool of . . . well, cheese. I would also like to thank the Lord for Fleeta's sweater, which reminds all of us that there can never be too many sequins at Christmas.'

Fleeta nods. '"Bedazzle or die" is a motto to live by.'

'I thank you all for being friends and family to us.' Otto puts his arm around Fleeta. 'And I thank God for my wife.'

Worley pipes up. 'I'd like to thank you all for letting me come to dinner without a date. I guess this is as good a time to tell you all that I am no longer with Joy Crabtree.' He shakes his head sadly.

'It weren't your fault that she took off with that Chevro-lette salesman Mike Allen. She needed a new car, and I guess he offered her a little more than that,' Fleeta grunts.

Worley sighs. 'I can't compete with that.'

I aim to get the prayers back on track. 'Thank you for Pete's plane, which brought us all together.' I take Papa's hand.

'Thank you for the break in the snow until we landed,' Pete adds.

'Thank you for the flask of sweet vermouth on the transatlantic flight. It was very soothing during the turbulence.' Giacomina smiles at Papa.

'Thank you, Giacomina, for the pizzelles, which

212

were delicious when the plane food was not. And I would like to thank Pete for the ride here – it was our first on a small plane, and it was perfect. And I'd like to thank my daughter and her husband for their hospitality.' Papa smiles too.

'Well, amen, then.' Jack pats Pete on the back and sends him to the server. The other guests follow suit, forming a line. Fleeta juggles two plates, one for her and one for Otto, who sits at the table with a napkin in his lap and his knife and fork at the ready. (Fleeta's a real wife now, waiting on him hand and foot.) We pile steaming buttery turkey, thinly sliced whiskey-soaked ham, a soufflé of sweet potatoes, the reliable green-bean casserole with bread crumbs, delicate tortellini in pesto, hot scalloped potatoes dripping in cheese, and, yes, Jell-O mold onto Mama's china.

Once we're seated, we lift our glasses and toast the coming year.

Otto clinks glasses with Theodore. 'I hear you're heading to Broadway to do a big show. What's it about?'

'It's about a kid from Scranton who moves to a small town in the South to teach, and finds himself.'

'Your life story.' Fleeta takes a sip of the wine and likes it. 'Sounds like one Theodore Tipton who moved to Big Stone so many years ago. Nothin' wrong with true stories, mind you.'

'That's just the starting point.'

'Where does it go from there?'

'He gets a job, and a famous movie star, Elizabeth Taylor, comes to town and chokes on a chicken bone, and then he gets his big break.'

'You got a part for Burt Reynolds in it?' Worley's eyes narrow.

'Yeah, he could play you!' Otto agrees.

'Nobody like Burt,' Pete chimes in.

'I was in my twenties when I moved here,' Theodore says tersely. Evidently, he thinks Mr Reynolds is slightly long in the tooth to play him now. 'Besides, this is live theater – a play, a *musical*, not the movies.'

Fleeta says, 'What's the difference? It's still a show. And if you're that set on it, Burt could play you as you is today. All the good stuff that happened to you came about when you was older. I'm gonna tell you why you need Burt Reynolds.'

'Please, Fleeta.' Theodore is losing patience.

'Because that's the only way you'll get my ass in the seat to watch your show. I remember when Burt was in them *Smokey and the Bandit* movies. I must've driven over to Kingsport to see them movies twenty times if I went once. In my mind, there was never a finer-looking man that lived. That coal-black hair of his, them dark eyes, and them jeans he used to wear. No wonder Sally Fields fell for him—'

'It's Field. Sally Field,' Theodore corrects her.

'Burt had him a sense of humor too, which usually don't go hand in hand with them kind of good looks. A man that handsome ain't gotta do

214

nothin' but stand there, but Burt, well, he delivered. You had a sense he'd sleep with you—'

'Thank God Father Drake went to the Keuling-Stouts' for dinner,' I interrupt.

'Let me finish,' Fleeta continues. 'It was like when I was a girl and I was in love with Clark Gable. I felt like if I got on a train and went to Hollywood, that if I met him, he might give me a tumble. That's how I feel about Burt. He seemed like he'd give every girl an equal shot to get in his drawers. That's all I'm saying.'

Fleeta eventually gets off the subject of Burt Reynolds and on to local politics. Conversation meanders around and over us like the lazy snowflakes coming down outside the window. The candlelight throws a glow on us that makes the tableau of those I love seem eternal. When I get a twinge about who is missing, I just think of Etta and Stefano laughing at their own Christmas table with friends who love them. I wish Iva Lou and Lyle were with us, but I want her to be happy and comfortable, and that isn't possible with me at this time. I can't help but remember those I've lost through the years: my dear mother; our son, Joe; Jack's mother, Mrs Mac; and the great Spec Mumpower. I resist the sadness and regret that comes with grief. The here and now is good enough. In fact, it's plenty good enough.

There's a loud knock at the front door. I stand up to answer it. Fleeta looks at me, thinking what

215

I'm thinking. It's Iva Lou, and we'll have a Christmas reunion. I run to the front door and open it.

A young man stands in the dusting of snow on the porch. Big wet flakes cling to his navy blue peacoat and nestle in his black hair. My heart begins to race; this is the same person I saw in the woods in September. He has my son Joe's thick eyebrows and deep dimples.

He smiles at me. 'Um, excuse me, ma'am. I didn't mean to skeer you.'

I'm about to speak when Jack comes up behind me and puts his hands on my waist. 'Can we do something for you, son?' Most men around these parts refer to young men as 'son,' but hearing Jack say it to this particular boy brings tears to my eyes.

'I'm Randy Galloway. I'm a student at Berea.'

'In Kentucky?'

'Yes, sir. I've been studying the plants over here on Stone Mountain.'

'On Christmas?' I hear my voice break.

Randy smiles. 'It's just another day to me, ma'am. We're in a bit of a hurry with this study we're doing, so we're working through the holidays until we finish. I'm working on a joint horticulture project with a couple of professors from Mountain Empire. I'm on the team to compile a report on indigenous herbs in the Blue Ridge Mountains. If you don't mind, I need to borrow your phone. My cell phone went dead, and I need my professors to come and pick me up before it gets dark.'

'Do they know you're working on Christmas?'

'Yes, ma'am. We've got a January deadline to file our report. We're working so fast because we're going to Congressman Wampler to stop a bill for mountaintop removal that's about to go through.'

I fling open the door and smile. 'Well, come on in, Randy.' I look at Jack, who rolls his eyes. 'I want to hear all about it.' I show Randy to the phone in the kitchen. I hear Jack explaining our guest's arrival as Randy tells his professor to come and get him.

I interrupt. 'Randy, you might as well eat some dinner before you go. Have them come and get you in an hour.'

'No, really, that's okay.'

'You shouldn't miss Christmas just because you're saving our mountain.'

He smiles again. 'Okay, ma'am.' Randy fills the professor in, then hangs up. I show Randy into the dining room and introduce him around the table.

'My son, Pavis, almost went to Berea College,' says Fleeta. 'Of course, the list of schools Pavis almost went to is as long as my leg. P.S., he finally got his degree on the Internet.'

I make a place for Randy at the table, and he sits. I go into the kitchen for a fresh plate. Jack follows me into the kitchen, leans against the sink, and looks at me.

'He looks so much like Joe.'

'He's the same young man I saw in the woods.' I give Jack a quick kiss on the cheek. 'I'm relieved – I'm not crazy.'

Giacomina and I stand before my linen closet and survey the stack of quilts and blankets. Randy, Fleeta, Otto, and Worley went home with plenty of leftovers in tow. Giacomina holds out her arms, and I give her sheets for their bed. We are full up for the night. Every room is taken. Jack and Theodore are making sure all the fireplaces have plenty of wood and buckets of coal for the long, cold evening ahead.

'Here is my mother-in-law's warmest quilt,' I tell Giacomina. I place a gorgeous Drunkard's Path pattern of greens and yellows on top of the sheets. 'Papa seems awfully quiet.'

'He is having a difficult time. Your grandmother's death made him very sad. Sometimes I find him in tears.'

'They were very close.'

'At first it wasn't good at all.'

'Why?'

'I was an outsider. She thought Mario would never marry, so they had their system. She was kind to me, though. Nonna tried to include me in everything, though it was her hosue, and I respected that. But make no mistake, she was the boss.' Giacomina takes the quilt and sheets into Etta's old room.

I go down the stairs. Laughter is coming from the kitchen. I poke my head in the door. Jack, Theodore, and Pete sit around the old farm table, playing Monopoly. I slip out again, unnoticed, and go into the living room to check on the fire. Papa is sitting in Jack's wingback chair.

'Don't you want to play Monopoly, Papa?' I take the wrought-iron poker from the coal bucket and stab at the fire. The orange sparks turn to black embers as they hit the grate. I throw a few lumps of coal onto the wood, making soft blue flames dance over the coal's orange center.

'They're having too much fun without the old man.'

'Papa, you're not old.' I sit down on the ottoman and face him. 'When did you start feeling this way?'

'The past few months.'

'You're not old, you're grieving.'

'What does that have to do with it?'

'Grief makes you feel ancient. I know. You join the worst club in the world. You stand in line with anyone who ever lost someone they loved, and you mourn with them. There's no diversion from it, no quick way through it, no free pass to acceptance. You just have to live through it. At first that seems impossible. When Mama died, I was only thirty-five, and I thought my life was over. Somehow, though, I didn't fight it; I let myself be sad for a very long time, and after a while, my world opened up. Look at all the things that happened because she left to make room for me to have my own life. It was so hard for me to make that connection – to think that she had to leave in order for me to grow up. I had to make a way, and then you arrived with Nonna and my aunts and cousins. I finally had a whole family to call my own. I began my life with Jack, and we added to the family I had found. It was as if Mama gave me a gift when she died. At the time I would have given every-thing I had to bring her back, and believe me, there are days when I would give everything I own to see her again, but that's impossible. Now I look back and see that there was magic in the timing of Mama's passing. She didn't stop being my mother when she died. She just went to the other side. She's still there, pulling for me. I can feel it. If you let her, I'll bet Nonna will do the same for you.'

'So far, no gifts. I am reminded only that I am next in line.'

'Well, you can't go by your age either. Children die, and some adults live to a hundred.'

Papa reaches over and squeezes my hand. He's thinking about my son but would never say it.

'Anyhow, Papa. There's no list. No order to it.'

'That's true. But when you get to be my age, you think about it.'

'Nonna lived a long life with family she loved

and had a reason to get up in the morning – to serve you and iron your shirts.'

Papa laughs. 'I do miss the way she pressed my collars. Giacomina . . .' He gives a thumbs-down. 'Not so good.'

'I miss Nonna too. I'm so glad we visited before she died.' I'll never again second-guess Etta's decision to marry. I realize it gave me one final visit with Nonna.

'Mama must have known she was dying,' Papa begins. 'She prepared the house and her room. Every stitch of her clothing was washed and pressed. She had a new nightgown and slippers. She ate her breakfast, said she wasn't feeling well, went back to bed, and went to sleep.' Papa reaches into his pocket and gives me a small black velvet pouch. 'She wanted you to have this.'

I gently pull the strings on the pouch. Inside it, I see a hammered gold chain with oval links shimmering against the velvet. I lift the chain out of the bag. A small oval locket dangles from the chain. There is a single small pearl on the face of the locket.

'It was her mother's,' Papa tells me.

'It's beautiful.' I open the locket. Two photographs are framed on either side. A boy with jet-black hair, around a year old, and on the other side a girl, around three, with ringlets and a frown. The frown makes me laugh.

'The girl is Mama, and the boy is her brother, Sergio.'

'I love it, Papa. Thank you.' I give my father a hug and kiss.

'Someday I have to write down the stories she told me.'

'I wish you would. She told me some good ones when I visited. But she couldn't talk about your dad without crying, so I never asked about him. What was he like?'

'Very stern. But also loving. Giuseppe Barbari. He was a serious man, but he would try to give me whatever I wanted. When I was a boy, we played near the water wheel in the center of town. When the water came over the wheel, it would land in a pool and then flow out to the stream. One summer my cousin came to visit. He had a small blue wooden boat – you know, a toy – and we would spend hours playing with it in the water. When my cousin left to go back to Bergamo, he took the boat with him, and I cried and cried. We didn't have much money; everything Papa made went into tending his horses. One day I went with Papa down to Bergamo for supplies, and I went into shop after shop until I found a store that had toys. I brought my papa to the shop, and he looked at the boat. He said it wasn't good enough; he thought it was cheaply made, so he wouldn't buy it for me. I was disappointed. A few weeks later, my father left for work early in the morning. When I came down to breakfast, there was a boat. It wasn't exactly like my cousin's or the one in the shop in Bergamo, but it was a fine replica. On the back of the boat, it said *Mario Barbari* in small black letters. I couldn't believe my luck. My mother told me that Papa made it for me. In those days he worked fourteen hours a day, but he stayed up at night to make me the boat.'

'He wanted you to be happy.'

'More than anything. My mother was the same.'

'I always wanted to ask you something, Papa. Nonna was very principled. She spent more time in church than the priest. When you told her about me, what did she say?'

Papa shakes his fist, just like Nonna used to. 'I was fifty-seven years old, and I was afraid to tell her! I didn't know what she would say. But I knew she had always prayed that I would marry and have children, and when I didn't, she accepted it. She knew I had friends, so she didn't worry that I was lonely; she just wished our family would continue. It's only natural. So I went home after reading your letter. I sat her down and told her the whole story. You know she was a pious woman; she lived her life by a code. I thought she would discourage any contact with you. In her day, an unmarried woman with a child was not virtuous. The woman and the child were marked. It seems silly now, but then a situation like that could ruin a family name. Nonna surprised me; she listened like a judge. She took a few moments to respond, and I thought for sure she would be furious. Instead of reacting with anger, she said, "We will all go with you to America to meet your daughter."

223

She didn't hesitate. When Jack called us and offered us the tickets to come to meet you, she knew it was the right thing to do. It brought her so much joy – to have you in her life, and then your children.'

'It makes me so happy to hear it.'

'She was so pleased Etta married an Italian. Mama felt confident that our family would go on, and at the end, that was the most important thing to her.'

'So Nonna got her dream.' The irony that Etta's teenage wedding was my worst nightmare is not lost on me.

'My mother was completely fulfilled. Which is why I'm sad but not too sad. She lived her life the way she wished.'

I always feel I never have enough time to talk with my father. Maybe that's because I didn't know of him until I was thirty-five – or maybe because the things I want to know, that only he can tell me, are an endless list. 'Papa, would you have married my mother if you knew about me?'

Papa looks off in the middle distance and thinks about the question. 'I was very young. A boy, really. Around the age of Randy. When I look at a boy that young, I wonder.'

'You mean you might *not* have married Mama?' I almost don't want to ask the question. I always think of my parents as star-crossed lovers, with lots of passion and very little choice involved in their love story.

'Her father would have made me! I loved Fiametta, I did. When she left, I wondered if I had done something that made her leave. It turns out that I had, but I didn't know what it was at the time. Of course, it ended up to be you. Does that answer your question?'

'When I think about you and Mama, I think of your story like it's a fairy tale. I imagine myself as a girl in an enchanted Italian village, living in a charming stone house by a clear river, with two parents inside that house who love me. I am one of many children you had together. There are always lots of brothers and sisters in my story. Lots of noise and love and laughter pouring out of every window. I guess we always dream about what we don't have.'

Papa shrugs. 'What else is there to dream about?'

'My, you two are so serious,' Giacomina says from the doorway.

'Oh, we're just talking about the past.'

Giacomina sits down with us. 'Happy stories?'

'Always,' I promise her.

Giacomina gives me a small photo album. 'I almost forgot to give you this. Your daughter made it for you.'

The title, in Etta's handwriting, says *The Newlyweds*. I open the photo album. The first page is a collage of all of our faces from Etta and Stefano's wedding. Each subsequent page is a photograph of Etta and Stefano: their first apartment; Etta's first gnocchi (made with her own hands!); Stefano going off to work; the University of Bergamo campus, where Etta is in school; Papa, Giacomina, and Stefano sitting at the small table in their sweet kitchen; and finally, a beautiful photograph of Etta climbing the mountainside in Schilpario in the snow. She wears a blue tulle skirt and a ski jacket, and her footprints are deep impressions in the white snow.

How I wish those footprints would lead her home to Cracker's Neck Holler.

CHAPTER 10

WISE

I tiptoe through the house, not wanting to wake our company. When I get to the kitchen, I fill the big coffeemaker with cold water. I scoop fresh-ground coffee beans out of the sack into the filter. I take a pinch of cinnamon and sprinkle it on the coffee grounds. I light the fire in the hearth. Then I set the table with cloth napkins and small plates. Jack picked up a large sack of Cab's doughnuts yesterday morning, so we're set for breakfast.

'*Buon giorno,*' my father says as he comes into the kitchen.

'Good morning, Papa.' I give him a big hug. 'Let me get you a cup of coffee.'

Papa sits down at the table. After our talk last night, I feel closer to him. Our relationship grows every time we're together, and when we part and come together again, we pick up where we left off. I wish I lived next door, where I could do things for him every day. For now this visit will have to do.

I put a small pot of milk on the stove to steam it. I take a small ceramic soup bowl and put coffee in the bottom, and as the milk foams, I add it to the bowl. I bring it to him. I pull the sugar bowl off of the shelf. I place the doughnuts on a platter.

Papa takes a bite. 'Cab's doughnuts,' I tell him. 'The most famous doughnut in Wise County.'

'I remember them.' Papa takes a sip of coffee. 'Dinner was so good yesterday. Fleeta is a funny woman.'

'We have a lot of laughs.'

'You have good friends. Do you mind if we go and visit Iva Lou?'

'No.'

'Etta called her to wish her a merry Christmas and told her that we were in town.'

'Oh.'

'If you don't want us to go . . .'

'No, no, Papa. She loves you and Giacomina. Remember our trip with her to Italy?'

'The people of Schilpario still ask for Iva Lou, Iva Lou.'

'She's unforgettable.'

'Jack told me you and Iva Lou were not too friendly anymore.'

'I heard something, and I didn't handle it very well.'

'What happened?'

'It turns out that Iva Lou had a baby before she moved to Big Stone Gap, and gave it up for adoption. But she never told me about it. So I went and asked her if it was true. It turns out she told some people and not me.'

'So your pride was hurt.'

'No, she can have secrets. That's okay. It's just with all we've been through, I really counted on her, on her honesty. I've always told her everything. I guess I was hurt when the trust wasn't mutual.'

'Like Fiametta. Your mother had opportunities to tell you about me and never did. She had to pass away to let you know the truth.'

I lose patience. 'It's not the same thing.'

'It was too hard for your mother to tell you the truth. You see, it didn't have anything to do with you; it had to do with the choices she made in her life. Your mother wasn't happy to leave Schilpario, but she didn't want you to think that it was your fault. So instead of telling you the truth, she kept it from you.'

'When I look back, I know she tried to tell me, but it was too painful for her.'

'Maybe it was too painful for Iva Lou.'

Jack comes into the kitchen. 'Am I interrupting something?'

'Papa is talking about Iva Lou.'

Jack whistles low. 'Sore subject around here.'

'I've tried to reach out to her.' I sound like a pouting child. 'She doesn't want to talk to me.'

'Maybe you need to try harder.' Jack pours himself a cup of coffee.

I give Jack the creamer. 'Don't gang up on me.'

Papa turns to Jack. 'Have you thought about talking to her?'

'You know what happens to a man who gets between two women? It ain't pretty.'

'It's not your affair, anyway,' I say to Jack. 'I would never come between you and a friend.'

'Jack is Iva Lou's friend also, no?' Papa reasons.

'Yes, he is. But this problem is between Iva Lou and me.'

'Good morning.' Pete comes into the kitchen, dressed for his trip home. He takes a mug and fills it with coffee.

'Ave, will you drive Pete to the airport?' Jack asks. 'I was going to take him, but I have a meeting with Tyler and a couple of engineers down in Lee County.'

Pete shrugs. 'If it's any trouble, I could call a cab.'

'I'm happy to take you,' I tell him. 'By the way, there's no car service in Big Stone this time of year. Conley Barker is off between Christmas and New Year's.'

'Isn't this the busiest season for travelers?' Pete wonders.

'Conley plays Joseph in the traveling Nativity that the Church of Christ puts on every year. He's unavailable until the Epiphany,' I explain.

'January sixth,' Jack confirms.

'So it's you and me, Pete.' I pat him on the back.

Pete smiles at me. I don't know why, but I blush. Theodore joins us in the kitchen. It's starting to look like lunch rush at Fleeta's café.

Theodore claps his hands together. 'Morning, all. Okay, okay, which vehicle can I use today?'

'My truck,' Jack volunteers.

'My meeting is this morning. I'm going up to the college to see what kind of trouble I can cause on their board of directors.'

'They need dormitories,' Jack says. 'I read all about it in the *Coalfield Progress*.'

'Construction is not my area of expertise. Ideas, poetry, music, and other arty pursuits are my specialty, in case anyone is wondering.'

Jack smiles. 'I stayed up all night thinking about it.'

'Oh, you.' Theodore gulps down his coffee and goes.

We hear a car horn out front. 'My ride.' Jack gives me a quick kiss and follows Theodore out the door.

'I hate to do this, Ave, but I need to get a move on too.' Pete puts his cup in the sink.

I feel sad at the mention of Pete leaving. I haven't had much time to talk to him. We had a houseful of company. But I don't want him to go. I cover it up nicely, I think: 'No problem. I'll get my purse.' I go upstairs and take my purse off the bureau. I turn to go, think better of it, and head back to the mirror. I take a moment to comb my hair and check my lipstick. I don't linger too long – that would make me feel guilty, as though I want to look good for Pete. I stand sideways and look at my figure. Not bad. My mother was right. Good posture makes all the difference. The shell-pink cashmere sweater Giacomina gave me for Christmas tucks into the jeans perfectly, and the warm color gives my skin a lift. I give my face a final once-over. The right shade of lipstick really melts away the years and gives a girl oomph. Iva Lou told me I was a blue/red years ago, and I've always chosen my shade accordingly. Nothing wrong with going for pretty, I reason. I'm not doing this to impress anyone; I just want to look good for me (this is what I tell myself, anyway). I don't think I'm fooling Jack, though. The obvious sign that we have company of the old-flame variety is that I am dressed and wearing lipstick before breakfast two days in a row. I skip down the steps and go into the kitchen. 'Ready?'

Pete says good-bye to Papa and Giacomina. 'I'll see you in Bergamo,' Pete says, and slings his duffel over his back. He follows me outside to the Jeep.

I toss him the keys. 'Why don't you drive?'

'Sure.' He smiles.

I don't know why, but the way he looks at me, with that gaze of his, well, it unglues me. It's as if he's studying me, not wanting to forget a single detail of my face. 'Follow the signs to Wise. And then the ones to the airport.' My voice breaks. I clear my throat quickly.

I climb into the passenger seat. Pete slides the driver's seat as far back as it will go, to accommodate his long legs. He adjusts the rearview mirror. His strong jaw and straight nose have not softened with time; in fact, his features seem more deliberate. The lines around his eyes are etched from laughter, not disappointment, which for a man is the difference between pleasantly weatherbeaten and dilapidated.

Pete has a sense of humor about himself that comes through in everything he does. He's tall and distinguished without being stodgy. He's a head turner, but he doesn't rely on his looks (he doesn't seem to, anyhow, though I don't think he *minds* it when women notice him). What makes him truly attractive is that he's interested in everything around him. He listens, and that's irresistible.

I look at his sideburns, which are beautifully groomed. I trim the insides of Jack's sideburns into a perfect straight line next to his ears. I notice that Pete's are trimmed into a perfect straight line also. I wonder who does it for him.

When I was a girl, I didn't think older men were attractive, but I do now. Pete's hair, which looks more smoky than black in bright daylight, makes for a striking palette against his clear golden skin. You would want to know this man if you saw him walking down the street. He's compelling and yet attainable. His faded jeans and crisp white shirt give him a youthful edge. I always look at hands and teeth, and he passes both tests with high marks. There are men who fall apart without a woman's care, but Pete is not one of them. He's well groomed without the fussiness. The white shirt makes the bright blue of his eyes stand out like sapphires in the sun. He's beautifully handsome in a classic way, unlike my husband, who is of the rugged variety. I decide that I like both, and at my age, I figure I'm allowed.

As Pete throws the Jeep in reverse and backs down the mountain, I imagine what my life would have been like if I had left Jack and gone with Pete years ago. It's been over ten years, and Pete is still the most compelling Plan B in a life that has stuck to its Plan A with a vengeance. (If anything, I'm good at following a plan!) There wasn't another crush, not another Pete for miles in the landscape of my life. He's it.

There's still that small, secret corner in my heart where I imagine myself the person I would have been without Jack and all that happened as a result of marrying him. I don't grieve in that place, and I don't regret. I'm just living. In my mind's eye, I'm beautiful and full of possibility and hope, and, yes, young. I am adored for all the things my husband and daughter don't really notice. I'm a woman of the world without ties to anyone. I'm free to love whom I please without the banal rigors of everyday life: no chores, no doctor's appointments, and most importantly, no worries. I'm free to seize the world in my fashion. Pete Rutledge also represents that corner to me, which is why I can say I love him. He is the man who made a place there when the bigger part of my heart was already taken.

I'm still attracted to Pete, and unless my radar equipment is totally rusty, I think he is still attracted to me. It bothers me that I like it. Make no mistake, I like it.

'Thank you for bringing Papa and Giacomina home for Christmas,' I say as we drive.

'My pleasure. It was pretty great, wasn't it?'

'The best.'

'When I was in Italy, Etta told me you were having a rough year. Jack's health.'

'Yeah. It's been really hard. I'm worried all the time.' I can't believe I said this out loud. I go around like everything is fine. No one knows I wake up on the hour every night and check to see if Jack's okay. I constantly do the math: if Jack does this, it buys him this many months, which will translate into this many years. I worry about whether there's a blockage somewhere that the PET scan didn't catch or can't catch, or whether there's one forming right now, undetected, that could cause a problem down the line. I've become a numbers girl. I calculate the length of illnesses by going online and reading about black lung and all its stages. I hound the doctor's office for test results until they call me back. I even try to imagine my life if the worst should happen, so I can plan ahead and be prepared – but I get so sick to my stomach that I call off the game.

'Jack's a strong guy,' says Pete. 'I know. I chopped wood with him.'

'I hope his good genes carry him through all of this.'

'You know, men don't do too well with aging.'

'How would you know? You don't age.'

'You're not looking closely. That divorce took a piece out of me. The whole thing was a big mistake.'

'What went wrong?'

'Everything – and not until after the ceremony. It was the strangest thing. I thought it was the right thing to do; I thought Gina was a terrific woman, I liked her son, it all seemed fine. And then we got married, and overnight we changed. I felt trapped, and she felt abandoned.'

'Why do you think that happened?'

'We wanted to do right by each other. We'd been together a long time. It seemed like a natural progression. Beware of natural progressions! We should have sat down and figured out that we were better without a contract. You know, some of the best deals in the world are done on a handshake. That's not a bad idea for some men and women. Marriage can kill a romance.'

'Marriage is hard.'

'I found that out.'

'I don't know what makes it last. Sometimes you stay in because you know that everything changes, including feeling bored or rejected – and if you hang in through those phases, they turn, like the phases of the moon. Contentment creeps back in, and lots of times, it gives way to happiness. You just never know.'

'Yeah, well, there was very little moonlight in my marriage.'

'You know, it's difficult, when you've grown so familiar, to remember to take care of each other the way you did when you were falling in love. I'm good when Jack is sick. I can sort of determine what he needs and give it to him. I don't even have to ask.'

'That's real love. When you don't have to ask.'

'Sometimes. And the rest of the time, you *must* ask: you have to talk, you have to communicate, even when you can't figure out which words to use. That's what I'm not good at. I don't know how to say what I'm feeling.'

'You're doing a pretty good job of it right now.'

'With you.'

'Why do you think that is?'

'I don't have anything to lose.'

'Right, you know you've got me.'

I laugh, because what he's said makes me nervous. 'You're kidding.'

'I'm not kidding. You've got me.'

'What does that mean?'

'It means I see a lot of women – I'm seeing one now, she's very nice – but the truth is, none of them comes close to you.'

'I'm sorry.' And I am. I wish Pete had someone he was crazy about.

Pete laughs. 'That's okay. It's just unrequited love. It happens all the time, and people survive it.'

'I want you to be happy.'

'I am happy.'

'No, I mean, you should have . . .'

'What you have?'

'No, what I have might not be right for you. But you should have love.'

'Why?'

'Because it makes life very sweet. God, that's a lame answer – I don't know why. Maybe you should have love so somebody takes good care of you and you won't get old and be alone.'

'Ah, so love protects you from all of that.'

I say nothing for a few seconds, then, 'I guess it can't.'

'So you see my problem.'

'It's not exactly a problem.'

'Love doesn't fix anything. People give up. People go. It's not an insurance policy against pain.'

'It's a commitment to a life. To a way of life – you guarantee to that person that you will be with them no matter what.'

Pete looks at me. 'You're beautiful. You always were, and you still are.'

'You're crazy. We are in the middle of a very serious conversation where some pretty hefty revelations are occurring, and you're just saying that to throw me off point.'

'You get better, you know that?'

'No, I don't know that at all.' I'm not fishing for compliments, but I don't mind hearing that I'm not an old hag. There are days I'd stand on Shawnee Avenue in Big Stone Gap, waving a twenty-dollar bill for someone, anyone, to tell me

I still look good. There are days even Fleeta won't take the bait.

'Why do you think I go to Italy so much? The women are ageless. There are sexy sixty-five-year-old women there.'

'Married?'

He laughs. 'Some.'

'Not the women too!'

'I have news for you. The men of Italy get a bad rap as lotharios, but the women have their minds on romance just as much.'

'I guess it's in the DNA.'

'Evidently.'

We ride in silence for a while, because I'm afraid of where this conversation might go. My husband hasn't been feeling well, and I don't need guilt on top of all the other disparate feelings of loss and despair that I've been juggling. I don't need to flirt with Pete just to prove I'm not old, and I don't need to flirt with him to keep our secret attraction going. It brightens that corner of my heart like soft lamplight.

'Ave Maria?'

'Yeah?'

'I want you to call me if you ever need me.'

'Of course I will.'

'I'm serious. If you ever need to get to your father quickly, or if there's something I can do for Etta or Jack, will you let me know?'

'That sounds so serious. You're scaring me.'

'I don't mean to. I sold my company, and the

buyer was very generous. I'm under contract as a consultant to them for five years. That's how I have access to the plane.'

'Are you telling me you're rich?'

'Very.'

'Oh my God. Congratulations!'

'When the five years are up, I'm going to go back to school and teach, I think.'

'Great.'

'I love the whole lecture thing.'

'You're so good at it.'

'So I don't want you to hesitate if you need anything. Promise?'

'I promise.'

Pete drives the Jeep up to the terminal at the Lonesome Pine Airport. What a perfect name for a place to say good-bye to loved ones. He gets out and pulls his bag out of the back. I get out to hug him.

'Thank you.' We hold each other closely for a long time. I should not have chemistry with anyone besides my husband, but I do, and here he is. I stand in wonder of all it all for a moment, liking it so much I don't want it to end. Women, no matter how old they are, need to feel desirable, if only because it puts us in a better mood to face the less romantic drudgery of life. As Pete holds me, I feel immortal, as though the end is nowhere in sight. I like this feeling; it means I still have something to offer. A brisk winter wind kicks up, catching the open passenger door. It starts to slam shut and whaps me on the ass. God's revenge for my thoughts and sin, or maybe just a reminder *not* to.

'Jack's going to be fine,' Pete reassures me.

I think it's odd that Pete brings up Jack in this moment, but maybe he uses Jack to keep his feelings for me in check. God knows I do. 'I hope so.'

'Jack asked me something, and I think you should know.'

'What is it?' My mind begins to race. Did I say something at Christmas dinner to Pete that was flirtatious – something that might have made Jack suspicious enough to confront Pete? Did I stay too long at the window, watching them chop wood, deciding whether I married the right guy? Did I fuss with my hair too much on Christmas morning, a tip-off that I wanted to look my best?

Pete looks at me. 'Are you okay?'

'Fine, Fine,' I tell him. 'What did Jack ask you?' I might as well hear the bad news now, I decide.

'Jack said if anything ever happened to him, he wants me to take care of you and Etta. I promised him I would.'

I can't speak. Pete leans down and kisses me quickly on the lips, as if to seal inside me whatever words I might have spoken. He turns and walks into the terminal, waving before he goes out the far set of glass doors to the runway.

I climb back into the Jeep. My hands are shaking so badly, I can hardly turn the key. I can't believe my husband told Pete to look out for me. I hope this doesn't mean Jack knows something about his health that he won't tell me. I begin to cry. The tears come quickly. Months of tears. My heart feels as though it's breaking. I don't want to live in a world without my husband. I have to stop this bad turn of events from happening. I must.

I went to work after I dropped Pete off at the airport, but I don't remember the ride back to Big Stone Gap, what I ate for lunch, or any of the prescriptions I filled today. All I could think about was Jack and what he said to Pete. It threw me into an emotional tailspin. I'd do some work and then sit and panic. I was short with customers and Fleeta (so unlike me). I left a message for Jack on his cell phone, but he hasn't called me back. That's not unusual. Most of the time he doesn't even have it on.

I can't blame my emotional meltdown (let's call it a state of instant anxiety, like a long panic attack) on the Change, the empty nest, or my situation with Iva Lou. I'm afraid of losing Jack, and I don't know how to handle it. I'm also afraid that he doesn't tell me everything because I react so poorly. He doesn't tell me bad news, and I know this for certain because he has never delivered any in the twenty years we've been married. I'm the realist, even though it appears on the surface that he is. He is much better at avoiding confrontation than I am. Well, let's face it, we both avoid confrontation, which may be one reason we're still together. So many arguments dissolved because we simply neglected them. Jack doesn't hold a grudge, and I've learned how not to from him.

Papa called earlier to ask when I'd be home for dinner. I don't know where the time went. Fleeta closed the café an hour ago, and the last customer just left with her insulin.

I lock up the back and then make my rounds through the Pharmacy, shutting off lights and turning on the security alarms. It seems silly to have them – after all, we're on Main Street, and a patrol car goes by regularly – but I was advised we needed them when robberies of pharmacies became regular in this part of the country. We have our share of coal miners on medication for black lung, and a popular painkiller is a drug called OxyContin. Some genius got his hands on it and turned it into a component of a street drug called 'hillbilly heroin.' Eddie Carleton advised me not to carry it, so I don't. I've never had a robbery here, and now that the word is out that I don't carry OxyContin, I doubt I ever will.

I step outside and lock the main entrance. I take a moment to look up and down Main Street. The road is never-ending: you can see its expanse for a few miles, like a path in a storybook to some magic land. To the west, Main Street runs up Poplar Hill and disappears down the other side of the mountain; to the east, it curves in a long, lazy C shape, out to the flats of the Southern section.

Main Street makes Big Stone Gap feel like a pit stop, a place on the way to somewhere and not a final destination. Maybe that's a holdover from the railroad days, when we were a designated stop on the way to the big city of Bristol, Tennessee. Some days, even though I love it, I find it odd that I'm still here. There were so many opportunities over the years to pick up and move somewhere else. I thought I had a sense of adventure, but here I am, deep into middle age, and I've never wandered far from the place I was born. Yes, I've traveled, but I never went away long enough to have my mail forwarded. I always returned home and stayed right here, in the middle.

Not much has changed here since I was a girl – at least not on the surface, in the facade of the buildings that face each other up and down Main Street. Most of them are empty now, and though our locals do everything they can to attract new business back into the abandoned buildings, they haven't had much success. Most folks around here do their shopping over in Kingsport, and then there's the Wal-Mart on the outskirts of town that stocks everything from prom gowns to potato chips. Our old friend Zackie Wakin, who charmed Elizabeth Taylor when she came to town, and owned Zackie's Bargain Store –

Clothes for the Entire Family, passed away a few years back. I often wonder how his business would have fared against the big corporations had he lived. I like to think that he was a visionary, an entrepreneur before his time. His fully loaded shop sold everything from half slips to blenders. Sound familiar? He was Wal-Mart before there was Wal-Mart. Big chains are tough on small towns, though. Once Wal-Mart moved in, it just about discouraged anyone from trying to put a small store back on Main Street. I miss the charm of the old shops. Then again, I still manage one.

Mulligan's Mutual survives somehow. We keep our prices as low as we can, and we count on customer loyalty. Fleeta's café helps. There aren't a lot of places to get a good meal, and Fleeta serves hearty, delicious local cuisine. She's a good baker, so some customers just come for pie and coffee. This chaps Fleeta because she's in the café business to make money – those who come and 'set all day' over an endless cup of coffee annoy her.

The sun slides behind Poplar Hill, the color of an orange Dreamsicle. I treasure the sunsets in winter, because they're the only shot of color we see for months. As I stand here in the cold, I try to remember what summer feels like, and I almost can't. That's mountain life for you. The hills are so vast and everlasting, you can't imagine that one day they'll turn from putty gray to bright green again. When the days are short and dark, it doesn't seem possible.

I play my Italian-language tapes on the way home. I practice as much as I can. I want to speak Italian with Papa and Giacomina, even as they want to practice their English.

The sky is coal black, with a smattering of freckly pink stars that glimmer in the far distance. I park the Jeep next to the house. Fleeta baked a blueberry pie for my company, and I juggle it with my purse and paperwork as I climb the stairs to our front door. I push the door open and hear laughter coming from the kitchen. It's the sweetest sound, the one I miss the most when it's just Jack and me. There has to be a way to make the laughter stay.

'What's for dinner?' I ask as I put the pie on the counter. Papa and Giacomina are busy at the stove.

'Tonight I cook!' Papa announces grandly. He is stirring fresh garlic cloves in butter over low heat, in my largest skillet, until they glisten.

'It smells so good!'

Theodore, in jeans and a sweater, comes into the kitchen. His hair is wet. 'I took a shower. I had to wash away the effects of the halls of academia.'

'Oh no, you didn't like the board of directors?'

'No, I liked them. I loathe academia.'

'For someone who made his living as a teacher for so many years . . .'

'I know, I know. I have no patience for bureaucracy of any kind. Well, let's face it, I don't have patience for anything much anymore, period. I went from crotchety to curmudgeon on my last birthday. In a few more years, I'll be really testy. Look out.'

'What happened at the meeting?'

'I was installed on the board, we voted on some tenure decisions, and then we had lunch.'

'Sounds entirely pleasant.'

'It was. By the way, something really interesting came up, and I thought of you and Jack.'

'I am not directing another musical. I am done with the theater!'

'No, no, it's nothing like that. There's a wonderful playwright named Donald Philip Stoneman who lives in Aberdeen, Scotland, with his wife, Rosalind. She's an actress – a good one, I hear. Anyhow, they're empty-nesters too: three children, two girls and a boy who have moved on with their lives and families. Evidently, the University of Virginia has tried to lure him over to teach, as he's a distinguished man of letters. He's finally said yes, but he wanted to be in the mountains, so instead of the main campus in Charlottesville, he chose Wise, Virginia. This is great news for the theater department. He and his wife are hoping to do a house swap – all they need is someone from around here to agree to six weeks in Aberdeen while they come to Wise so he can direct a production.'

'Scotland.' I sit down, my head swimming. I remember Jack's four-item list, including the mention of Scotland. Jack still doesn't know I saw that list, and I haven't been tempted to ask him about it (it's under some business cards in his sock drawer), but here's an opportunity to make one of his dreams come true. 'When would they want to do the house trade?'

'March and April. Coming up. I hear the countryside there is gorgeous in the spring.'

'What would I do with the Pharmacy?'

Theodore shrugs. 'Eddie Carleton?'

'But Jack is starting a new job. Of course, as far as I'm concerned, Tyler Hutchinson and the Bituminous Reserves, Inc., can wait forever.'

'Does anybody like this company?' Theodore wonders aloud. 'Although I thought Tyler was ingratiating and warm, for an establishment type.'

'He's completely likable. That's the problem. Jack has been lured in.'

'You make it sound like a cult.'

'Jack never would have agreed to any of it if he hadn't gotten sick. He's all about security now. He's scared – and he wants to leave something to Etta and me. It's crazy.'

'In Italy, we don't worry about making money so much. And we certainly don't worry about it after we're dead,' Papa says as he slowly pours heavy cream over the butter and garlic in the skillet.

'We're going with white wine with that butter sauce.' Theodore uncorks a bottle of wine.

'This is my mother's recipe,' Papa explains. 'She

248

called it Pasta Delicato. I'm boiling orecchiette, which means small ears.'

'"Orecchiette" is a pretty word. But I would have preferred not to know I'll be eating ears,' Theodore says.

'It's the shape, Theodore. Just the shape,' I tell him. I look in the pot. Small bits of pasta tumble over one another in the water's rolling boil.

Papa says, 'My mother taught me that when you make a sauce with meat, use a pasta shape where the sauce can settle. Smooth sauce is excellent for long noodles. There was a lot of Fleeta's ham left over, so I diced some up.'

'Big Stone Gap meets Bergamo!' Theodore says. 'How do you know how much to make?'

'We're making two pounds of pasta. So we took two cups of diced ham, and we're sautéing it in the garlic, butter, and cream. The more I stir, the thicker the sauce.'

'Then the peas,' Giacomina reminds him.

'Drop the peas into the boiling water with the pasta before straining it.'

Theodore is taking notes. 'Frozen or from the can?'

'No can. Frozen or fresh peas cook very fast – just a minute in the water. Mama taught us never put vegetables into the hot skillet with the sauce; it makes them mushy. After the pasta is drained, put the orecchiette and peas in the skillet, toss them through the sauce, and then when you serve it, add lots of grated Parmesan cheese on top.

Never put cheese on pasta in the skillet. Always grate it on the dishes. Fresh. Always fresh.'

'Like the Huddle House. Always open. Always fresh,' Theodore says. 'I'll bet they don't have orecchiette at the Huddle House.'

'Giacomina, will you toss the salad?' Papa smiles at her.

Jack comes into the kitchen. 'Oh, boy. Pasta on a cold winter's night. I love it. Ave, can you come out here for a second? Excuse us.'

'Uh-oh,' I hear Theodore say under his breath as I go.

I meet Jack in the hallway. 'Is everything okay?'

'My doctor called me. He wondered if I was feeling all right. Evidently, you spoke with him today?'

'I called him.'

'Why?'

'I was worried.'

'Ave, I'm okay. I wish you'd stop calling Dr Smiddy's office.'

'I'm sorry. I was afraid you weren't telling me something.'

'I never keep anything from you,' Jack reassures me. If that's true, who the hell is Annie on his to-do list? But I can't bring *that* up now.

'Okay.'

'Believe me.'

'I believe you,' I lie. Dr Smiddy was a little short with me on the phone; he was perfectly professional, but he didn't indulge my panic. He gently reassured me and then got off the phone. Fast. 'Come on, honey. Theodore opened some wine.' I take Jack's hand, and we go back into the kitchen.

'Take your seats,' Papa says from the stove. Giacomina puts on oven mitts and lifts the pasta to the sink to drain it. Papa lifts the skillet of creamy sauce off the heat and sets it on a cooled burner. We take our places as Papa pours the pasta into the sauce in the skillet, then tosses the buttery mixture and brings it to the table.

'It doesn't get any better than this.' Jack serves the pasta onto our plates. Papa stands by with the fresh Parmesan and the grater while Giacomina cranks the black pepper onto the pasta.

'Jack, I have something wonderful to ask you,' I say.

'I'm listening,' he answers.

'Wanna go to Scotland?'

A look of recognition crosses my husband's face. Maybe he's thinking of that list he made, or maybe hearing his dream realized aloud gives him a sense of wonder that he hasn't known before. Whatever it is, in seconds, his face fills with such joy that he looks like a ten-year-old boy. Then practical Jack surfaces, and his eyes narrow and the crease between his eyebrows deepens, just like it does when he's thinking something through or working on a difficult piece of molding in his wood shop. 'How are we gonna do that?'

'I have a plan.' I reach across the table and hold his hand. 'Courtesy of Mr Tipton here.'

'I'm at the bottom of every good idea, and I don't want anybody here to forget it,' Theodore says.

We laugh as Theodore pours the wine. Scotland in the springtime just might work.

'I'm doing chicken and dumplings for the lunch special!' Fleeta hollers from the café.

It's my favorite dish. Fleeta must be up to something. 'Are you sucking up for a reason?'

'Maybe.' Fleeta peels a paper place mat off a stack and puts it on the counter. She continues down the line, setting out a place mat for every stool. Then, working in reverse, she plunks down the silverware. 'And don't call your daddy and them. I already did. They'll be here shortly. Ain't nothin' better than dumplings when it's cold out. They stick to your insides like glue. This here is a dish that sustains.'

'What do you want?' I tease.

'I was thinking of expanding the café hours and doing dinners on weekends.'

'Here?'

'Yeah. What the hell, there's no place to eat out that's close. Ever since Stringer's went under . . .'

Stringer's was a delicious all-you-can-eat restaurant on the other side of town. Unfortunately, folks took the term to mean all-you-can-eat-all-week, and the place went under because more food walked out than customers walked in.

'I think it's too much work for you,' I say.

'Well, I thought about that. I was thinking I might hire some help.'

'We don't have a lot of extra money to do that, Fleets.'

'I know. But I'd do the cooking, and I'd just hire some kids to help with the serving and cleanup and prep. You know, like we did back when Pearl come to work for us.'

Fleeta adjusts the place mats on the counter. It's so funny that she's bringing up Pearl, because years ago she tried to dissuade me from hiring her. It appears that Fleeta Mullins Olinger has grown a heart of wisdom in the past twenty years. 'I can't believe what I'm hearing. You want to be a mentor?'

'I didn't say that. This ain't an act of charity, but I figger kids around here need jobs while they's in school, and we might as well get back to that.'

'Then I think it's a good idea,' I tell her. Fleeta's chest puffs out as though she's suddenly a major player on the stock exchange. There is no greater thrill for a boss than to see an employee implement a dream in the workplace. Fleeta is happy.

I throw myself into my work, taking pleasure in the knowledge that Papa, Giacomina, and Theodore extended their visit for a few extra days. It feels decadent to have them here for so long, and I'm savoring every moment.

I'm plowing through my e-mails quickly when

an instant message pops up from Etta. *Ma, sending e-mail with attachment. xoxoo E.*

I wait for a few seconds, and sure enough, an e-mail appears from her. *Tell me what you think of this. xoxoxo E.* I open the attachment. It's a sketch of a kitchen. At the bottom of the page, it says *E. Grassi*. I have to think twice before I remember that's my Etta's new name, Mrs Grassi. I look over the drawing: she took her small kitchen and redesigned it, turning it into something functional and lovely.

Most of Etta's childhood hobbies have become an area of expertise in her adulthood. She's passionate about architecture, making her own drawings and renderings. How perfect for her to major in it! When she was a girl, she drew a map of the world on an enormous sheet of paper, marking where she had been and where she wanted to go. She studied the stars over Cracker's Neck Holler through the seasons, and made a map of the constellations. Etta has always had a world-view. I'm not sure where it came from, as she was born in a holler and grew up in the very place her father and I were raised. I had those dreams too, and that same longing, but I let books and the worlds within them fulfill that wanderlust. My daughter looks for experience in the world itself, instead of keeping her passions bottled up inside. One of my goals was to raise her to listen to her own voice, and boy, she's done it – sometimes not to my liking. I wouldn't change a thing about her, though; she's a box of surprises, usually delightful ones.

'Let's go, Ave Maria,' Theodore says from the door of the Pharmacy. 'Fleeta, save me some of that banana pudding of yours. I don't think I've gained enough weight since I got here.'

'Can do, Ted.'

MUTUAL PHARMACY BANANA PUDDING

Makes six servings

½ cup all-purpose flour
1 pinch salt
3 eggs (or fi cup egg substitute)
2½ cups milk (may use skim)
1 14-ounce can sweetened condensed milk
1 tablespoon vanilla extract
3 medium bananas, thinly sliced
36 vanilla wafers
Whipped topping (for garnish)

In a medium saucepan, combine flour and salt; gradually whisk in eggs and both kinds of milk. Cook over medium heat, whisking constantly, for 8 to 10 minutes or until pudding becomes thick and bubbly. Remove from heat and whisk in vanilla. Cool. Arrange one third of banana slices in the bottom of a two-quart dish; top with one third of the pudding mixture and 12 wafers. Repeat layers twice, arranging last 12 wafers around edge of dish. Dollop with whipped topping. Cover and chill.

I grab my purse and coat and follow him out the door. We climb into the Jeep. Theodore backs out of the parking lot. 'I thought we'd take a run over to Kingsport for some shopping.'

'Sounds like fun.'

'I miss our spelunking.' Theodore steps on the gas, and we barrel out of Big Stone. 'Now I go to Bergdorf's and sift through vintage china instead of rock formations in the sand caves.'

'I haven't been in Cudjo's Cave since you left town.'

'I feel bad that I left you without a spelunking partner.'

'Don't. We had a lot of fun, and now we have a lot of happy memories.'

'It was great, wasn't it? Iva Lou and you and me.' Theodore looks at me, then judges from my expression and puts his gaze back on the road.

'Yep.'

'So what happened with you two?'

'I don't know, exactly. We had words at her office one day, about her daughter. I didn't think I said anything wrong – the truth is, I didn't know what to say. And now I guess I'll never know.'

'Don't close the door on her. She's the closest thing you have to family here, besides Jack.'

'I know. But she doesn't want to be friends anymore. She's made that clear.'

'I can't believe you're giving up on this so easily.'

'Maybe I'm just too old to fight.'

'I'm older than you, and I'm still fighting.'

'You're different, Theodore. You'll always be a fighter.'

'That's a cop-out. What's the real reason you won't talk to her?'

'Maybe I don't want to trouble her with my feelings or something. I don't know.'

'You're not happy without her in your life.'

'Do you think so?'

'I looked at you on Christmas Day, when we were having dinner. You looked like something important was missing. Like you'd lost your best friend.'

'One of them. I still have you.'

'What if things changed with Iva Lou?'

'Well, they always do, don't they?'

'I mean changed as in maybe you could work through whatever it is that's bothering you two.'

'That would be up to her.'

Instead of taking the turn for the Fort Henry Mall in Kingsport, Theodore follows the signs to Johnson City. 'Where do you want to shop in Johnson City?'

'Fleeta said there were lots of new stores.'

Theodore pulls in to the parking lot at the Stir Fry Café, a quiet Asian restaurant outside Johnson City.

'Are you hungry?' I ask him.

'Yep.'

We get out of the Jeep and go into the restaurant. Theodore looks around the empty room, with set tables and booths, low lighting and paneled walls. Water flows over an indoor fountain past a green marble Buddha, who smiles at us. 'Follow me, Ave.' Theodore leads me to a booth in the back of restaurant. Someone awaits us there.

'Iva Lou, here she is,' says Theodore quietly.

Iva Lou sits in a booth, perfectly coiffed in a shoulder-length bob, and her typical weekend wear, a black polyester running suit with a white turtleneck and matching sneakers. She looks up at me. 'I thought,' she says, 'well, we thought that we might have lunch. Just the two of us.'

I turn to Theodore, a million thoughts running through my head. I focus on the logistical one, since that's the least challenging. 'What will you do?' I ask him.

'I'm going to Fort Henry Mall to see a movie. I won't be back. Iva Lou will drive you home.' Theodore bows his head and goes.

If I could kill Theodore with my bare hands, I would – how dare he do this? But my manners are too good to make a scene. I stand like an ice block and watch him go out the door.

'Well, set down.' Iva Lou motions for me to sit across from her. 'How was your Christmas?'

'Good. Fleeta and Otto and Worley came. And Pete Rutledge brought my family over.'

'Pete. How's old Pete?'

'Older. But every bit as scrumptious.'

'I figgered. Some men age like rat poison. A box of that stuff can be a hundred years old and it still works.'

I laugh. 'You're right about that.'

We sit in silence. I am so happy when the waitress comes with menus, to give me something to do. I study the menu like it's the Magna Carta and I'm an Oxford historian.

'The shrimp stir fry is good,' Iva Lou says nervously.

'Is that what you're having?' I ask her.

'Uh-huh.'

'Well, then, that's what I'll have.' I put the menu down. I may stink at confrontation, but perhaps the fact that Iva Lou agreed to this means she wants to talk. You never know with her. She might be doing this just because Theodore asked her to. Iva Lou could never say no to my daughter, either.

'How was your Christmas?' I ask.

'Amazing. I met my grandkids – Lovely brought them over. Brandy is fourteen, she's a looker. Emma is eleven, she's a clown. Penny is seven, and she's a spoiled brat.' Iva Lou fishes in her purse and hands me the pictures. The photo album says *Number One Grandma*, which I find odd, because she just met these kids. 'Emma picked out the album.'

'Oh.'

Iva Lou laughs. 'I think it ought to say *Brand-New Grandma* or *Newly Found Mamaw*. Though the idea of actually being a grandma makes me physically ill. Lyle says I'll get over it, and I'm starting to.'

'They're beautiful kids,' I tell her.

'It's funny. They resemble me a little, don't they?'

'Penny is a dead ringer for you.'

'That's what I think!'

'Well, why not? It's in the genes,' I tell her. 'I'm happy for you. This is really wonderful.'

'It's a goddamn shock is what it is. I love her already – my daughter. Lovely. What a name for a daughter of mine, right?'

'It's perfect.'

'I think so. I mean, I've spent my whole life working at bein' lovely. Of course, I've also worked at other things that might not have been appropriate names for a Baptist girl growing up in Kentucky.'

I laugh. I'm amazed that even with the big freeze that happened between the two of us, we can sit here and chat like nothing terrible happened. This is one of the things I always valued about Iva Lou. She had a way of making the worst things seem fleeting. 'Don't get yourself all bollixed up,' she'd say. 'Tumult is bad for the complexion' was another of her favorites. She could draw me out like no one else. Iva Lou would get me talking, and soon I'd be unburdened of whatever the trauma of the day was.

At that moment I make a decision. I'm going to tell her what she means to me. What have I got to lose?

'I've missed you for a lot of reasons, Iva Lou, but mostly because you always put my life in perspective. I could always count on you to be honest with me. Which is why, I guess, I was so hurt by your reaction to me at the library.'

'Well . . .' She sits up straight and breathes in so deeply, I think she might sing an aria, except she just exhales. 'I was hellfire mad at you. And I didn't know what to say. I felt like you were angry at me for giving up my baby when she was born.'

'What?' I'm stunned.

'Yes, you *were* angry at me. In all the years, and all the things I done – you know my conquests and my reputation and my approach to full living via the delicious gift of men in my life, including my engagement and marriage – I never once felt anything but understanding coming from you. But when you came to see me about my daughter that day, you judged me. Now, God knows, I'm not a particularly good Christian, so I sure as hell don't care if you think I've done something to keep my ass out of heaven. But what broke my heart – and trust me, it broke – was that you looked at me like "How could you? How could you give up your own baby?" And I couldn't take that, Ave Maria.'

'I'm sorry. I wasn't thinking that. I really wasn't.'

'Well, that's why I'm here. I wanted to give you a chance to explain, and maybe, hopefully, you'd give me a chance to explain why I did what I did so many years ago.'

261

'I'd like to hear that.' I lean back in the booth. I feel under attack, but I don't want to respond in anger. Instead, I listen.

'I was twenty-five years old . . .'

I've never once heard Iva Lou allude to having an age at all, at any point in her life – I think she likes to create the illusion that times does not apply to her. So this in itself is a revelation. She continues.

'I was raised in a strict home; you know that. And I had the one brother – his name was Cortland – who joined the army and went to Korea and never came home.'

'His picture's in your living room.'

'That's him. Well, when he died over there, I was devastated. And it was right around then that I met a man named Tommy Miklos. He was Greek.'

'From Greece?'

'No, his parents were – he was born here. Anyhow, I fell madly in love with him, and I got pregnant. I went to him and told him what had happened, and he said he had to talk to his parents. So he went to them, and they told him that he couldn't marry me. They had somebody in mind for him, and it didn't matter whether or not I was having a baby, they were goin' through with their original plan for him.' She pauses to collect herself, as if the memory still hurts.

'He came to me, and he cried and told me that he couldn't marry me. I offered to talk to his parents. We even planned to run away together, but he couldn't bear the thought of going against them.'

She takes another of her deep, deep breaths. 'So I went to the doctor and asked for his help, and he told me about this place where Catholic girls went when they were in my situation. I didn't know a single Catholic until I went there, but I always liked 'em on account of the fact that they took me in, no questions asked. It was far enough away so nobody'd know. I told my mama I was going to school to become a librarian, and I left. What was ironic was that when I got to the Sacred Heart Home, they got me some classes in library science that would help me later on. So it wasn't a total lie I told my mother.'

'You must have been terrified.'

Iva Lou starts to cry. 'I couldn't hardly leave my mama. But she didn't have much, and I couldn't ask her to take a baby on, and there wasn't a way for me to do it alone. I tried for nine months to figure out a way to do it – see, at the Sacred Heart Home, you didn't have to decide until the end if you were gonna keep the baby or give it up for adoption. But I couldn't. Not and give her a decent life. I didn't know a single girl who kept her baby.'

I think of my children and can't imagine having to make that sacrifice. 'It's horrible.'

'After I had Lovely and signed her away, I went home to Mama, and for a few months I worked in the county library there. But I needed a fresh start, so I started looking through the *Library Journal* for jobs, which is how I came to these parts. I took over the Bookmobile route from James Varner, 'cause he went off to study poetry and run another library.'

'I remember him well.'

'One day, almost a year and a half after I started the route, I was in the Bookmobile up in Norton. And this blue Cutlass Supreme pulls up. And out of the car comes Tommy Miklos. He was as handsome as a summer day. He came on the Bookmobile and asked if he could see me. Now, this was double-edged for me. I still loved him, but I also hated him for what his choices had forced me to do.

'Anyway, I agreed to talk to him. So he met me after my shift – I'll never forget it, because he said he made dinner reservations at the Wise Inn. I wondered what the hell he could say that would make me agree to have dinner with him, so I made him tell me on the spot instead of going to the restaurant. He said, "I can't live without you, and I want you back. I'm not going to murry whatever her name is over in Greece, I realize now that I want you."'

Iva Lou's face looks shattered. 'Well, I have to tell you, I was never so angry then or since. I told him that he would never know what it did to me to give away my daughter and that I had no further interest in him or his family. He cried a bit, and then he left. We didn't make it to the Wise Inn, needless to say. And I never saw him again, until a few days after Christmas, this year, when I drove up to Ohio with Lovely.'

'Lovely told me you were going to see him.'

'At first I wanted no part of it, but now I'm glad we went.'

'What happened?'

'Well, Tommy's a widower. I doubt he'd of seen us if his wife were still alive. He has three children of his own. When I walked in with Lovely, he could hardly take it. I guess it hit him hard what he had done. It was funny, I didn't shed a tear. Through all of this, I've wept and wept, but when I saw him, I wasn't even tempted to cry. Not one tear.'

'What did he say?'

'He told Lovely that he abandoned me. That he forced me to make a terrible decision, and that if she was going to hate anybody, to please hate him because it was all his fault. He then told her the thing I think she longed to hear most. He said, 'I loved your mother.' See, no matter where you go or what you do, a child needs to know that. They need to know that you brought 'em into this world with the best intentions, that you came together for a divine purpose, no matter how misguided the results might be. That's all anybody needs, really, to know they're wanted. What I tried to say to Lovely was that she was wanted by me and the parents I gave her to. I trusted them. I read their application letters, and then a nun – Sister Julia,

I don't think I'll ever forget her – came in and told me that if it was her baby, she would not hesitate. She would trust the Rosshirt family.

'Life is not doled out by chance. I know that sounds crazy, coming from a woman who accidentally got pregnant, but it's true. You don't have a choice about when a child comes into the world or when they go – I don't care how much science they fool with. Nope, there's destiny involved. There is purpose in all of it, and Lovely needed to know that as crazy as this was, it was her story. She needed to stop looking at her origins like a mistake, to own them like they're her glory.'

'And did she?'

'The three of us, awkward as it was, left it on a very friendly note. Lovely told Tommy that she didn't want anything from him, she just needed to know the truth. She showed him pictures of her parents; her husband, Sam Carter; and her daughters. Tommy seemed relieved that she had a happy life and that she had turned out well.

'Now, that there is my cross. I can't claim what must be the most satisfying knowledge in the world, which is to know that you gave someone life and then all the things they needed to grow into a good person. I'll never know what it would have been to make my daughter a home, to give her a place in this world, and then, once she was grown and confident, to set her free to have her own life. I knew when I gave her up that I was giving her up to a world of chance and uncertainty.

What I couldn't know was whether I did the right thing. Was it the right decision for her? That part of it haunted me. I know for sure she was raised in love by good people, and that's more than most folks get, even from their own parents. All I can do now is be her friend.'

'You're great at that,' I say.

Iva Lou starts to cry. 'I'll never know if I would have been a good mother. After I had her, I swore I'd never have another baby or get murried, which is why I was so drunk the day Lyle and me got hitched. I couldn't believe I was going back on my word to myself. But at that point, children were out of the question, so I only went back on half of my promise.'

'You did the right thing in giving her up. It was the only thing you could do.'

Iva Lou dries her tears. 'I don't know. If it was right, why did Lovely come lookin' for me?'

'She wanted to know you. I know what that feels like. It's hard to live with pieces missing from the story of your life. It's almost unbearable. And then when you get the pieces, you have to sort it all out.'

Iva Lou nods. 'So, that's the story of Lovely,' she says, and looks down at her hands.

We sit in silence for a moment, until I confess quietly, 'I did judge you.' Iva Lou looks at me, and for the first time in months, I see the old fire in my friend. Nothing pleases her more than honesty. I go on, 'I hope you can find it in your heart to

267

forgive me. I couldn't believe that someone I was so close to and relied upon could keep such an important event in her life a secret from me.'

'There was never a good time to tell you, Ave Maria.'

'I understand that now. You couldn't have told me when I was a spinster, because it might have driven me farther back into the cave of fear I was living in. And when Etta was born, I was so happy, you wouldn't have ruined it for me, because that's the kind of person you are. And then when my son died, you couldn't tell me, because you probably thought my loss was worse than yours – at least you could think of your baby in a good home with loving parents. And let's face it, since Joe, I judge anybody who gets a choice in life when I didn't get to choose the fate of my son. But what I know now' – my voice breaks, and the tears come – 'is that you're a better mother than me because you knew what your daughter needed, and you let her go when you most wanted to keep her.'

'It was a different time then. I can't hardly even explain it. Nowadays it's all changed; hell, the world spins differently. I grew up believing that a child needed a mother and a father. Now I've seen every incarnation of family life, and I know that there are many ways to do it. But at the time, in Hazard, Kentucky, I was trapped by the way the world was. I was alone. I couldn't take on the world.'

'Does Lovely understand that?'

'She tries. But you know something – I've learned this in my life and in my job – everybody has a hole in them that can't be filled. It might be better when you can give it a name, but everybody's got one. Hers – Lovely's – was me. Me and Lovely talked about it on the ride back from Ohio. I'd rather been her hero, or her teacher, or her everyday mother, but what I got is where we are now. And I think the world, and the way things are now, helped her find me. Families are put together every which way these days, so she felt comfortable enough to come looking for me. She didn't feel alone when she was looking; there are lots of people in the same boat. And I guess I wanted to be found, because when I signed her away, I checked the box that said *unseal with adoptee's consent*. I don't know another girl in the Sacred Heart Home who did that. They all wanted to put it behind them. But I wanted my girl to know if she ever needed me, she'd just have to look.'

'And now she found you.'

'Thank God. I remember when you and Fleeta came to over to the hospital after I got my double mastectomy. You came in the room, and you were upset because I was crying. I guess y'all thought, Well, it finally dawned on ole Iva Lou that she could be takin' a dirt nap with this cancer. But I wasn't crying about dying, or losing my party horns, or even the pain of it, which was substantial – I paid for every sin I ever committed with the pain of that surgery, I promise you that. I

269

wasn't crying about me. No, I was crying because I thought if I did die then, I'd never meet my daughter. But I felt that it was Lovely's place to find me. If I went searching for her, she may not have wanted that. So I had a dilemma.'

'What did you do?'

'I let it set. I trusted that if it was going to happen, it would. I didn't force it.' Iva Lou reaches out and pats my hand. 'The same way with you. I wasn't going to bother you.'

'I wish you would have.'

'I wasn't ready,' replies my dearest friend.

'I guess I wasn't either,' I say truthfully.

Iva Lou and I eat our lunch and talk about general things – books, local news, Lyle's back problem, and Jack's heart. We're both a little wary, and why wouldn't we be, after this patch of winter between us? But we're still who we are. We catch up as though years have passed, even though it's been only a few months.

I've learned so much from Iva Lou in our long friendship, but I never thought that she'd be the person to teach me forgiveness. I have a hard time forgiving myself. Once again, she shows me how by her example. I hope we are blessed with the gift of time so I can return the favor.

How did she do it? How did she let go of her daughter and trust that one day Lovely would find her? Iva Lou loved her only child so much that she gave her the best life she could without expecting anything in return. I can't say I've ever done that. I certainly did not do that with my children. The expectation was always that I knew best for them, and by God, they were going to listen, because my love was the stamp of approval. How ridiculous that seems in light of everything I've learned from Iva Lou. No wonder I was angry with her; I was angry with myself. I wasn't judging her, I was judging me. I hold everyone I love so closely, it's a miracle they can breathe. I've held on to the memory of my son so doggedly, it's a wonder that I made it through the second half of my life. I clung to Etta with such force, I'm lucky she didn't leave for Italy sooner.

Iva Lou knew her love for her daughter was true and that there were no expectations. She didn't want a thing from Lovely. Iva Lou trusted in the purity of that mother love so deeply, she knew Lovely would find her someday. I was always afraid my love wasn't strong enough to bind my children to me. I had to grip them tightly in every way and never let go. That was not good for them or for me. Even death itself did not loosen the bond I had with Joe. Up until a few weeks ago, I was still looking for him, half expecting him to return, as though his death had been a terrible mistake, a mix-up that could be rectified by the strength of my own will. I held my dying son in my arms, and even that wasn't enough. The proof of my love was was in my forever longing. Love would not change, grow, or end. I made this child, and by God, he was not going to leave me.

When I got on the plane to go to Etta's wedding last fall, I planned to talk her out of getting married and into my way of thinking. I was going to bring her to her senses, so she would cancel the wedding and come home, go to college, and follow my plan for her. Luckily, when I saw her in Schilpario, I knew that she wasn't pulling a stunt or manufacturing an act of defiance to break from me; rather, she was following the path of her heart. She really loves Stefano, and I knew it when she was a girl. I dismissed that as a schoolgirl crush because I didn't want it to be true. No daughter of mine was going to marry young and live in a foreign country with an ocean between us. How wrong I was to judge my daughter. Thank God I didn't ruin her wedding day with my own agenda. The truth is, my heart wasn't open to my own child. But now it is. This is the great miracle of my long winter. I am beginning to let go, and as I do, just like Iva Lou, I trust that peace will come.

CHAPTER 11

HUFF ROCK

My husband rolls over and wakes me with a kiss. 'Good morning.'

'Did I oversleep?'

'No, it's early. But I know you wanted to spend some time with your dad before we drive everybody over to the airport.'

I sit up in bed. I look out the window to where the sun glows pink at sunrise. 'I haven't slept like that in forever.'

'I'm glad you made up with Iva Lou. Now the tossing and turning is over.'

'Was it that bad?'

My husband nods.

'Never underestimate the healing power of a clean slate,' I say. It's true that I feel rested for the first time in months.

'It was only a matter of time.' Jack leans back on the pillow. 'Maybe life can get back to normal.'

'Normal? Don't you know who you're married to?' Jack, Theodore, and I wave to Papa and Giacomina as they board the commuter for Charlotte, where they can catch a connecting flight to Newark and then home to Italy. I don't cry. I really feel that I'm learning not to hold on so tightly to those I love. It makes the good-bye temporary.

'Come on, let's grab lunch before my flight,' says Theodore.

'Let's go to the Cracker Barrel,' Jack suggests.

'Good idea.' Theodore gives Jack a pat on the back. 'I want to get my cholesterol nice and elevated before I return to New York.'

'Then order the chicken-fried steak.'

'I'm an addict!' Theodore shrieks. 'If they took a picture of my arteries right now, they'd look like concrete pipes filled with goo. I ate Fleeta's cooking every chance I got. I know for a fact that between the ham biscuits, the gravy, the dumplings, and that banana pudding, I consumed a tub of lard.'

The hostess at the Cracker Barrel who leads us to our table is a long-legged, lanky Southern girl around sixty. Her blond hair is swept up into a fountain with clips, and her nail tips have tiny diamond accents. Her cinch belt seems to cut off her circulation, but she's going for sexy even though she's bordering on matron. She doesn't wear a wedding ring. Iva Lou always said that a woman who works in a restaurant is most likely to find a husband, regardless of her age. 'Men like to eat,' Iva Lou said. 'Forget the fancy clothes and perfume, and just feed 'em.'

I take Jack's hand as he reads the menu. Every chance I get, I touch him. I read an article that said a man's blood pressure decreases when his wife holds his hand.

'Okay, here's the file from the Stonemans in Aberdeen.'Theodore gives me an envelope. 'Here's their e-mail, address, and phone. I sent them your information. It looks like a pretty simple exchange. They have a cat named Charles, so they won't mind watching after Shoo.'

'Good.'

'They live right outside the city of Aberdeen. You can use their car, and they'll need the use of one of yours. There's only one tricky thing.'

'What's that?'

'They have a garden. It's a serious garden. They grow their own vegetables. Spring is when they do a lot of prep work on the garden, and since they won't be there . . .'

'I'll take care of it,' Jack promises. 'I'd love to. I haven't had a garden for years – it'll be fun.'

'And what else are you going to do over there?' jokes Theodore.

Jack beams. 'Are you kidding? I've got a list!'

It makes me happy to see Jack looking forward to something. I haven't seen this kind of pep in him since he coached Etta's ninth-grade basketball team. You would have thought he was John Wooden, the way he strategized their plays.

He's methodical about planning for his absence. He made sure that Mousey and the boys have enough help with their construction company. Tyler Hutchinson said he'd hold Jack's consultant position open until our return. Eddie Carleton is going to cover for me at the Pharmacy, so except for a learning curve about Aberdeen and Scottish history, we are good to go when springtime comes. It's the power of something to look forward to: it changes the colors of the world from drab to gorgeous.

Jack and I are having a little trouble adjusting to the quiet after our full house at Christmas, but with Scotland to look forward to, we don't give our post-holiday blues much thought.

After putting the last of the ornament boxes back in the attic, Jack is off with Tyler Hutchinson up to Huff Rock. I put on my coat and boots and hat and head for the woods. I promised Jack I'd take the pink lights off his bridge, and I'm finally getting around to it. It's the last remaining sign in Cracker's Neck Holler that Christmas was here.

My feet crunch on the frozen ground as I make my way into the woods. The bright sun fills the forest with streamers of golden light. The gulley that will become a stream, come spring, looks like a black velvet ribbon following the curves of the hill and disappearing into the trees.

I'm lost in thought when I hear the sound of footsteps. I turn to look, but I don't see anyone behind me. I can see our field from this point in the path, but our stone house is almost gone from view. I continue toward the bridge. I've taken two steps when I hear a voice in the woods to my left.

'Hey, Mrs Mac.'

I turn. 'Randy! You're back.' I must be too happy to see him, because he smiles but takes a step back, as if to say, 'Whoa, lady. Calm down.'

'I needed a sample of pokeberries. And you've got 'em in your woods.'

'Go right ahead.'

Randy kneels down and pulls a pokeberry root out of the ground.

'No berries this time of year. Sorry,' I tell him.

'Not a problem. The berries are poisonous. We use them to make red ink.'

'Really?'

'The roots are what's most valuable, though. You dry them and make tea out of them. Some swear it cures arthritis. We got a grant to do a study,' Randy says proudly.

'There's gold in these mountains.'

'Of a type. They're loaded with medicinal herbs. You know: wild greens. Woolly lamb's ear. Catnip. Dandelion. That sort of thing. These mountains have been called a Native American medicine chest, and it's not too far from the truth.'

'I studied about it in school, though not much and not for long, because pharmacology is really about synthetic drugs now.'

'Yeah, but synthetics are modeled on the real thing. You need the original to copy it in a lab.' Randy seals the bagful of poke root. 'I'm almost done with the project at Berea. I'm going to miss this mountain. Did you know if you went into these woods and kept walking west that it's thirty miles of pure mountain forest?'

'I knew it was miles and miles.'

'It's never been surveyed properly, though.'

'How do you know?'

'I've had to spend a good bit of time making maps. There weren't any.'

'If you grew up around here . . .'

'Yeah. But I didn't. I came into this cold.'

'Have you had lunch?'

'No, ma'am.'

'Why don't you come to the house and I'll fix you some? I'm expecting Jack later. I'd like you to tell him some of the things you've learned about this forest.' I have an agenda, obviously.

'I'd like to, ma'am. But I have a lot of work to do yet.'

'Everybody needs to eat lunch.'

He smiles. 'I guess that's true.'

'I just have to take the lights off my husband's footbridge over the creek.'

'I saw that. Did he make it himself?'

'Yep. Anything my husband makes has to last a minimum of a hundred years. That's his motto and his goal.'

'Ain't many around like him anymore.'

'Not many,' I agree.

Randy follows me to the bridge. I don't feel wary with him: after years of trusting my gut and relying on the Ancient Art of Chinese Face-Reading, I can see that Randy is a thoughtful person and a kind one (the curve of his lips tells me that). It's selfish, I know, but having him with me, it's as though Joe is here; if Joe had lived, he'd be this age. I'm desperate to know, or just to have a window into, what that might have been like.

I gently pull the lights off the railing of the bridge, rolling them around my hand and under my elbow, as Jack taught me (I learned how to wrap cable that way when I helped him with the Kiwanis Christmas-tree sale one year). On our way back to the house, Randy stops to record some moss he finds at the base of the old Scotch broom trees near the fence line. He takes out his notebook, jots down a few descriptions, then photographs the moss. His notebook is almost full. He closes it.

'How did you end up at Berea College?' I ask.

He shrugs. 'It's free.'

'For everybody who attends, right? Not just scholarship students?'

'Yep. My dad didn't want to pay for college, and I didn't want to go ROTC. Most of my friends did that. But I'm not the military type – I'm not real good at following orders.'

'Neither am I.'

Shoo the Cat meets us at the screen door on the sunporch. She eyes Randy up and down and then decides he's okay. Old Shoo rubs up against his calf, and Randy picks her up. 'I didn't know you had a cat.'

'She hides on holidays. She's not a fan of crowds.'

'She's an old one.' Randy pets her gently.

'Twenty-two. I can't believe it.'

'I heard of a cat living until twenty-eight once.'

'No way!'

'Yes, ma'am. If they're happy, they last almost forever.'

'Like people.'

Randy laughs. 'I guess some.'

I pull a tray of lasagna out of the refrigerator and put it in the oven. I set the table for three, and I offer Randy a drink, which he accepts. I pour glasses of iced tea for both of us.

'Tell me about your family,' I say.

'My mom died when I was five years old.'

'Oh, no. That's terrible.'

'My dad remarried – a nice woman. Her name is Cynthia, and she had three kids of her own.'

'Do you get along with them?'

Randy shrugs. 'I'm so much older than they are. Really, it's not about me liking them, it's about staying out of their way.'

'I understand.' I take a sip of tea. 'How did your mom die?'

'She died in a car accident. I was in the car at the time.'

'Do you remember it?'

'Sometimes I think I do. But I'm not sure. There was a picture of the car in the newspaper; it was crumpled like a beer can. The headline said, "Boy Survives." I always resented that. It should have said, "Mother Dies."'

'How old was your mom?'

'She was born in 1944.'

'Like me!'

'Wow. She'd be your age now, then.'

'How old are you?'

'Eighteen.'

'My son would have been eighteen on his next birthday.'

We look away from each other, almost afraid of the similarities.

'What happened to him? Your son?' he asks.

'He died of cancer. Leukemia.'

'How old was he?'

'Only four years old.'

'Wow, that's so sad.'

'Last September,' I tell him, 'when I saw you in the woods, I thought you might be him.'

'Why?'

'I don't know. I guess it's because on some level, I like to pretend it was all a mistake. I can imagine that somehow, somewhere, my son survived and he's finding his way back home.'

'Were you with him when he died?'

I nod.

'Then you know he really did die.'

'Yes. My little fantasy doesn't make any sense. But to tell you the truth, none of it has ever made any sense to me. I still wake up and can't believe he's gone. So I guess I imagine things to cope. I even thought you might be an angel, coming to take someone away again.'

'That's wild.'

'Pretty crazy, right?'

Randy taps his pencil on the table. 'So you don't get over it?'

'I don't think so.'

'Like my mom. I always wonder if I ever will.'

We sit in silence awhile. I check the clock; Jack should be home by now. In a way, I'm glad he's late. It gives me a chance to ask Randy more questions. It's not often I talk with kids my Joe's age. When I see his old classmates in the Pharmacy or around town, it's always a little awkward – I guess they can see the sadness in me. I try to be upbeat, but it doesn't work.

'Do you have a girlfriend?' I ask Randy.

He smiles. 'Her name is Tawny.'

'She must be pretty.'

'How do you know?'

'Tawny's a pretty girl's name.'

'You're right about that. She's got black hair and brown eyes. A lot of people say we look alike, but I don't see it. As soon as I graduate, we'll get murried. I really want to get murried.'

'Why?'

'I love her.'

'Besides loving her, why would you get married so young?'

'Well, the way I see it, you never know how much time you got. You might think you got a lot, but I don't believe you can count on that. I think you sort of have to do things that you want to do, because maybe the chance won't come around again. You don't think I ought to get murried, though?'

'It seems to me that you like what you're studying. Maybe you can think about getting an advanced degree. The kids who stay in these parts after they've gotten an education really matter. They give back. That's important.'

'I guess so. But I can do that and get murried. Do you have any other children?' he asks.

It's funny. I'd removed all the silly pictures of Etta from the refrigerator door when I was trying not to dwell so much on her absence. I surely meant to put them back, but I haven't yet. There are formal pictures in the living room, in polished silver frames, but none in the kitchen, the true center of our home. I'll have to work on that, I think. I jump up. 'Yes, I have a daughter, Etta. She just got married in Italy a few months ago.' I go to the living room, fetch a wedding picture with all of us in it, and return to the kitchen. 'Here she is.' I hand him the picture.

'She sure is pretty. She don't look very old.'
'Nineteen, almost twenty.'
'Is that why you're against young marriage?'
'Partly.' I smile. 'I just think it's a good idea to wait. You can be more certain of your feelings if you grow up a little more and have a few more life experiences. Then again, I'm starting to realize that this may be the right thing for her and that I need to trust her judgment.'

'Ave? I'm home,' Jack hollers from the front of the house.

'Back here, honey.'

'I hope you don't mind, I brought company . . .' Jack walks into the kitchen, Tyler right behind him.

'Of course not. I have company too.'

Jack smiles. 'Randy, you back to cause more trouble?'

'Yes, sir, I hope so.'

Randy stands and extends his hand to Tyler. 'Hi, I'm Randy Galloway.'

'Randy goes to Berea. Studies horticulture,' I explain.

'That's interesting. You gonna be a botanist?' Tyler wants to know.

'I hope so. That is, if there's any woods left by the time I graduate.'

I intervene, saying, 'Randy, you have to be careful what you say. Tyler is one of the owners of the Bituminous Reserves, Inc. They mine coal using mountaintop removal.'

'Wow,' Randy responds. 'I never met management before. You guys are the enemy we fight every morning when we go out into the forest to document the herbs.'

Tyler laughs awkwardly. 'I don't like to be called the enemy.'

'Why do you do it?' Randy asks earnestly.

'I'm a businessman.'

'There has to be a better answer than that,' Randy says.

'Now, Randy,' I say.

Tyler puts up his hand. 'That's okay, Ave Maria. Randy, tell me, what would you do if you were me?'

'Well, I sure wouldn't wreck the terrain of a mountain range that is thousands of years old, just for a few years of coal. I'd capitalize on nature's riches in a way that would sustain it. I'd come up with a business plan to do what I'm doing on a larger scale. Why shouldn't the herbs needed to make medicine come from our forests? Most pharmaceutical companies go down to the rain forest in the Southern Hemisphere, but we got a lot of herbs right here.'

'Some folks have tried that. It's not as easy as it sounds,' Tyler tells him in a tone so reassuring, I see why Jack has been won over. Tyler Hutchinson is soothing and in control at the same time. A good salesman.

Randy's not buying, though. 'It seems to me, if you don't value the land and what it produces, it just lays the world open to be destroyed.'

'Coal is made in the earth,' Tyler says.

'Yes, and we need the coal. I'm not saying that we don't. But why would we ruin nature for short-term energy? It doesn't make any sense. We need these forests too – they're a treasure, really. Even if they exist just to make oxygen. That's a huge thing. We've got to trust nature to know something that maybe humanity doesn't.'

'I appreciate your point of view, Randy,' says Tyler, gracious on the surface.

I look at Jack, hoping he caught how dismissive Tyler has been with Randy, but Jack is busy cutting squares into the pan of lasagna he pulled from the oven. Sometimes I'd like to hit Jack over the head with a brick to wake him up.

'Jack, can you handle lunch from here? I have to get to work,' I say. 'Randy, it was nice to get to know you a bit better. Do you think you can find your way back when you're done with lunch?'

'Oh, easy, ma'am. I parked at the high school. I'll just hike down.'

'Or Jack can take you.'

Randy stands and shakes my hand. 'Thank you for your hospitality.'

'You're entirely welcome.'

As Jack and Tyler resume their conversation, I motion with a jab to Randy to stick it to Tyler. He smiles and gives me the thumbs-up.

I began my e-mail exchange with Rosalind Stoneman of Aberdeen as though I were communicating with someone who spoke a foreign language instead of just being from a foreign country. We quickly adapted to each other's use of the English language. Her sense of humor comes through her idioms (my favorite so far: she and he husband are like 'chalk and cheese' – in other words, total opposites), and I hope she gets mine (saying 'bless your heart' can mean 'drop dead' in these parts).

We have lots of questions for each other, but

somehow, on top of both of our lists is what kind of clothes to bring for our husbands. I pictured an erudite, dashing playwright in Donald, but his wife assured me that he is more the farmer type. Her only sartorial advice for me was to bring wellies and lots of warm sweaters. She and Donald love their drafty old house, but we might not be used to it. (Wait till she has her first night in Cracker's Neck. I'll remind Jack to leave lots of firewood!)

I have always loved being a pharmacist, and yet it's never been hard for me to take time away from my job. While it's interesting to study medicine and to keep current with all the latest pharmaceuticals, that part of my profession is the least compelling to me. I love serving the customers, hearing their stories, and, hopefully, making them feel a little better. I still enjoy going into customers' homes when I make deliveries because I'm fascinated by how people choose to live.

For example, when I deliver out in the Valley to Susan Gibson, I notice that her furniture and knick-knacks have not varied in forty years. The house is always as neat as a pin, but not one detail has changed. She has a pale green ceramic frog that sits on the windowsill, and it has sat there, in the same spot, since I was a girl. I used to go on delivery runs with Fred Mulligan – I guess he liked the company, though he never said much to me. I'd spend a lot of time reading in the car, unless he invited me to go inside. I knew that when we delivered to Miss Gibson, we were near the end of the route. Sometimes Fred would have me run the delivery to the door without him. I had favorite customers, and they made me feel special. Whenever I delivered to Mrs Little on West Second Street, she'd have two Nilla wafers and a glass of milk waiting for me.

Time has helped mellow my memories of Fred Mulligan. I even call him Dad, occasionally, when I refer to him. For a long time, I called him Fred Mulligan, as detached as you can get. I've now known my own papa, Mario, for almost as long as I knew Fred. I wish I could have foretold, when I was a girl, how my story would play out. It would have given me great comfort to know that, eventually, my heart would be filled by the love of a true father. I wasn't able to have it with Fred. Maybe, had I been a boy, things would have been different. There is no harder work in the world than trying to get someone to like you, and this was my eternal mission with Fred. Though he knew I wanted him to like me, it was the one thing he withheld.

It wasn't all awful, but as with all childhood sadness carried forward, the past puts a veil over adulthood, a dull achy feeling of guilt, sometimes outright melancholy and sometimes shame for unnamed feelings. The combination of these emotions and juggling them always left me tired. They interfere with the now, which is why I stopped the habit of going back and blaming myself for things that can't be changed. And while I don't forget events altogether, the details have become murky, some disappearing altogether (hallelujah). That's one of the comforts of getting older: the sharp edges wear away, and one is left with a practical view of things. Emotions are for the present; don't squander them on past hurts that are a waste of time. I learned that from Mario, who showed me how to start over again.

But without Fred Mulligan's influence, I wouldn't have survived small-town life. He's the one who showed me by example that things are not always what they seem. He showed me on the old delivery route that even when a home and the family inside seemed perfect, you could always count on the fact that there was a lot going on behind closed doors – plenty of secrets, mysteries, and reinvented histories. 'Every family is its own country,' he'd say. Fred Mulligan was right.

I pull in to Glencoe Cemetery, past the fountain – dry in winter – and up to the hillside where my mother and dad are buried. I get out of the Jeep and climb the hill. There's a small bouquet of posies on Mama's grave that I did not leave. I remove the Christmas wreaths from the headstones. I pick up the posies and see that on one of the long, thin satin ribbons, *M.B.* is printed in ink. My papa left these for my mother.

I can't express how much I miss my mother. Time hasn't helped one bit with this loss. I have tremendous guilt, though I know it's not quite rational, that I couldn't do more to save her life. Sometimes I replay her illness over in my mind and imagine whisking her off to a fancy hospital somewhere in a faraway city where they had the cure. In that fantasy, she is still with me. What a dream!

I think of all the things we didn't do, the trip we were to take to Italy but never did. Why didn't I make her go? I backed down too easily. I let her go back into her cocoon for no good reason. I should have fought her on that – then, at least, she would have seen her sisters before she died. She would have been able to go home one more time. I understand, just a little, that I was her home, and as long as I stayed close, she was happy. But, like all daughters, I wanted more for her. Alas, I wasn't able to deliver it.

I make the sign of the cross and say a prayer.

I take the two dried-out wreaths over to the garbage can by the fence. There's a new grave, with large arrangements of pink, yellow, white, and red flowers thrown haphazardly over the freshly dug dirt. It looks like a big beat-up birthday cake, with the bright ribbons and foil tribute letters whipping in the wind. I don't remember Fleeta telling me of a recent death. The grave is in the Horton plot. Good family, the Hortons.

I walk back to my mother and father's grave, and as I go back down the hill, I stop at the Goins family plot. The Goins family had, as two of its members, the prettiest girls in town, Cathy and

Gail, though they've since grown up and moved away. Recently, one of their relatives died, and everybody told me that I had to come up and see the headstone, because I wouldn't believe it. I look down, and now I know what all the fuss is about. It says:

Goins Goins Gone

I laugh loud. Wait until Jack sees this – it's his kind of humor. It takes a big person to laugh at death, and an even bigger one to laugh after death.

CHAPTER 12

ABERDEEN

'Now, look here,' Iva Lou says as she takes the curves of the road to Tri-Cities Airport with too much firepower to suit me. 'I like a tartan plaid with navy blue, kelly green, yeller, and black. I got me a beret with a kelly-green grosgrain ribbon, and I want my kilt to pick up that hint.'

'You got it.' I turn and look at my husband in the backseat. 'Jack, you'll help me remember, won't you?'

'Yep.'

'I always wanted a genu-ine kilt from Scotland,' says Iva Lou. 'You are the first folks I ever knew that went.'

'Isn't that odd, when practically everybody who lives here is of Scottish descent?'

'And Irish. Don't forget that.'

'Granted, it took me thirty-six years to get to Italy, but it was always a goal,' I say.

'Honey-o, look at me. I'm Scots-Irish, and I went to It-lee instead. 'Course, I felt I already knew about my own roots. I wanted to experience the historical elements of Italy.'

'You mean the men,' Jack pipes up.

'Them too. Everybody knows my ideal man, in theory, is Mario Lanza. Even Lyle knows it. Mario Lanza with the singing – and without the drinkin'. I can't stand a tosser; a man who can't hold his liquor ruins a nice night out. And you know I like my nights out.'

'You have your standards,' I say.

'Yes, ma'am.'

Iva Lou and I have made a real effort to get our friendship back on track. We started slowly – to resume our old routine quickly would have felt phony. Sometimes she stops by for lunch, or we run up to the Mexican restaurant at the Wal-Mart plaza for dinner. She and I go to Garden Club together. Last week we went to a computer seminar at Mountain Empire Community College, where we were like two kids, whispering and giggling during class. We never refer to our estrangement; this is her choice, and I take my cues from Iva Lou: 'What's past is passed.'

'I was telling Lovely my theories about men and drinkin' the other night. One of her friends has a husband who's a little too enamored of Captain Morgan rum. I told her to put her foot down now, before the problem gits so bad she has to put 911 on the speed dial.'

It's so funny – a year ago, I had never heard of Lovely Carter, and now she's a part of our world, as though she has always been here. Iva Lou shares that their relationship is nowhere near perfect – that things come up all the time for Lovely, emotionally speaking, and Iva Lou has to deal with them. Just lately, Lovely has allowed her girls to stay overnight at the trailer. The girls begged and begged, and finally, Lovely let them. Well, the girls had a ball, and now they come over much more often. 'Me and Lovely are friends,' Iva Lou told me, 'and if it gets to be more than that, if we start feeling like family to each other, then that'll be fine too.'

Jack taps me on the shoulder. 'Did you remember my work boots?'

'Do what?'

'My work boots. Did you pack them?'

'Do what?'

'Stop it, Ave.'

Iva Lou, Jack, and I laugh. 'Do what?' is Big Stone Gap speak for 'What did you ask me?' It was one of the local expressions I shared in an e-mail with Rosalind Stoneman. She didn't get it, and I told her, 'Don't worry. You'll get the hang of it once you're in the holler.'

'I did pack your work boots, honey.'

'Thank you.'

'You're a good wife.' Iva Lou adjusts the rearview mirror. 'You'd be a better one if you taught your husband to pack his own damn boots.'

'Too late for that,' I tell her.

Just then Iva Lou skids to a stop in front of the airport terminal. Jack jumps out and starts unloading bags from the trunk.

'Thank you for driving us over,' I say, giving Iva Lou a hug.

'Have the time of yer life.' Iva Lou smiles. 'Take lots of pictures. And if you see any Wades or Makinses over there, you just tell 'em we said hi-dee.'

I laugh. 'Will do.'

Jack puts the bags on the sidewalk and comes around the car. He gives Iva Lou a hug too. 'Glad you two girls worked things out,' he says.

'Listen here, Jack Mac. I either had to make up with her or kill her, and I know you need her, so I opted for Plan A.'

He grins. 'I appreciate it.'

We wave as Iva Lou drives off, then take our bags inside and check in. 'I'm going to get some magazines,' I tell Jack.

The gift shop at Tri-Cities Airport is stocked with local delicacies as well as newspapers, magazines, and Nabs. You can buy a small crate of apple butter, quilted oven mitts, or soy candles made in local kitchens by local craftsmen.

'Avuh Marie?'

I look to the cash register. 'Sweet Sue, what are you doing here?'

'I moved to Kingsport. The divorce came final, and I needed a change.' Sweet Sue reaches up and tightens her ponytail, hoisted high in a rubber band on her head. She wears white pants, a white blouse, and a forest-green apron with a patch that says RUNWAY GIFT SHOPPE.

Every divorcée from Big Stone Gap eventually winds up in Kingsport. It's where you go when you're ready to start writing anew on your clean slate. It's our version of relocating to the other side of the moon when we need space from the gossip, custody battles, and pressures that arise from love gone wrong. Big Stone Gap can shrink to the size of a dime when you're the talk of the town. Better to shove off to sprawling Kingsport when the going gets tough.

I haven't seen Sweet Sue since the cast party for *The Sound of Music;* I've been busy, and evidently, so has she. 'How are you doing?' I ask.

'Well, Avuh, let me just say this. I never thought I'd be this old and on the market again. I figgered Mike and me were till death do us part. Of course, for me, the death part never meant murder, but I got so mad at him, I didn't rule out any possibility. He cheated on me, you know.'

'No, I didn't,' I lie.

'On . . . me! Can you believe it?'

'Not really.' It's amazing to me that Sweet Sue, at our age, still believes she's a viable, hot number. Wasn't being homecoming queen, Key Club Sweetheart, Miss Powell Valley, and third runnerup in the Miss Wise County beauty pageant, back when we were young, enough for her?

'When he cheated, well, that's when I left. I'll put up with a lot – and trust me, I did – but I ain't gonna be second fiddle to nobody.'

'I heard you bounced back after Mike. Weren't you dating Greg Mullins from out in the valley?'

'Oh God, A-vuh, he was about a hundred years old.'

'I thought he was seventy.'

'His shoes might have been seventy, but the rest of him was a hundred. No, next time I belly up to the bar, I want me a younger man. They're not so set in their ways, you know.'

'I've heard that. Well, good for you.'

'Ave?' Jack stands in the entrance of the gift shop.

I turn and motion to him to come in. 'Sweet Sue has relocated to Kingsport.'

'Hi, Jack.' Sweet Sue waves at him, ruffling her fingers.

'Hi, Sue.'

My husband stands in the entrance as though there are invisible lasers across the doorway that might fry him if he sets foot in the gift shop. God bless him, whenever he runs into his old girl-friends, it's like he's trying to swim upstream fully clothed in a shallow creek. 'Honey, we need to hurry,' he tells me.

'I'll be right there.' I grab a couple of maga-zines. Sweet Sue rings them up.

'You hang on to him,' she says quietly.

'I'll do that.'

I meet Jack in the main area of the terminal. 'You were rude to her,' I tell him as we go through security.

'I have a wife.'

'I know that.' Sometimes I think Jack's medication makes him loopy.

Jack shakes his head. 'She's a flirt.'

'Still?'

'Uh-huh. She left a message on my cell phone at Christmas. Needed someone to come over and do a little maintenance work on her house before she sold it in the divorce. Said she needed my "expertise." Well, I wanted no part of it.'

I can't believe what I'm hearing. 'I was nice to her!'

'You don't have anything to worry about, darling,' my husband promises me.

When I made our reservations, I chose to fly to Glasgow International Airport via JFK in New York. I chose it for two very important reasons: a cross-country train ride from Glasgow to Aberdeen would allow us to enjoy more of the Scottish countryside, and I wanted to see Pearl Grimes Bakagese on our layover at JFK. Her new house in Garden City is a quick drive from the airport, and she offered to meet us for the hour or two between flights.

When we get off the plane, Pearl waves from behind security. 'Ave Maria!'

I wave back. Tears come to my eyes as I remember when she was a girl and how hard her life was. She used her intelligence and drive to build a better life for herself and her mother.

Better? How about an excellent life? It's rich and full. Pearl is educated, working, and now a wife and mother. She has come a long way from Insko Holler.

'Welcome to New York!' Pearl gives me a hug, and then Jack embraces her. 'You look great, Jack.'

'So do you, honey.'

Pearl is trim, in a navy blue suit. She wears sneakers and socks with the suit. 'Ignore the shoes,' she tells us. 'It's a New York thing. All the working girls, me included, carry pumps in a sack.'

'You have to do a lot of walking.'

'Yep. It's not like back home, in and out of the car all day. I hardly ever see a car. I take a train in to the city to work, and so does Taye.' Pearl puts her arm around me as we walk inside the terminal. 'Mama sends her love to you. She's watching India.'

'Give her my love! I can't believe India's five years old.'

'Neither can I. We're working on number two now.'

'Good for you.'

'I don't know how we can top her, though.'

'You don't think you will, but each child is so different.' Pearl remembers Joe, and I know what she's thinking. 'Don't worry. Everything will be fine!' I tell her.

'I worry about everything.'

'That's motherhood. I wish I could tell you that you'll worry less as time goes on, but I'd be lying.'

We catch up on all her news, and then Pearl

wants to hear about home, so I pull some pictures from Christmas out of my purse.

'Someday I want to come home,' Pearl says as she looks at a picture of Cracker's Neck Holler covered in snow. 'We've been lucky. We've seen a lot of the world. But I miss those mountains.'

I slept most of the flight over, while Jack stayed awake, too excited to sleep. He pored over his travel book and finished the novel by Ian Rankin (star of Scottish fiction) that he started reading back home. I know Jack loves our trips to Italy and considers it his second home, but the truth is, his own true homeland is Scotland.

It's dark when we land in Glasgow. We pick up our bags and take a taxi to One Devonshire Gardens. It's hard to see much as we speed through the hills in the dark. A dense fog covers the city, a mysterious gray mist that reminds me of the old Miss Marple movies they used to show at the Trail Theatre back home. Miss Marple was a doddering old detective who cracked cases with common sense, putting clues together in her rocking chair by the hearth. Very British.

One Devonshire Gardens is a hotel in a series of connected Victorian town houses. When we enter the main lobby, the building reminds me of a stately home, with its crown moldings, flagstone floors, and portrait gallery (some of the paintings must be ten feet tall). The grand staircase that leads to the second floor is made of cherrywood inlaid on walnut. Jack can't resist and goes to the carvings on the banister to feel the grooves of the wood. He is beyond impressed with the craftsmanship.

The furniture, a combination of eighteenth-century hunting lodge and Victorian, is covered in ocher, deep brown, and beige velvets and faded navy blue matelassé. There are small tea tables situated by the windows, overlooking a garden in the back. An enormous ornate mirror hangs over the deep fireplace. The mantel is decorated with a series of small hunting lamps, all lit.

'This is fancy,' observes my husband.

'The Stonemans' recommendation,' I tell him.

We check in and are escorted to our room. As the valet explains the features of the hotel, I have to listen closely. The Scottish accent takes some getting used to – it's lovely, but they speak at a clip. We are fascinated, though, because there are similarities between the accent here and our mountain one. Jack and I unpack very little. We are exhausted from the flight and plan on getting right to sleep. I put my husband's Dopp kit in the bathroom. When I return to the room, he is standing at the window, looking at the sky. 'What is it?' I ask him.

'Come here. There's a hole in the fog.'

I look up at the sky. The clouds seem to have been ripped apart at the seams to let the moon shine through. It glitters like a whiskey diamond. 'A golden moon.'

'I've never seen one.' Jack smiles and puts his arms around me. 'Thank you.'

'For what?'

'For making this happen. I never thought it would.'

'Hey, that's what I'm here for. I'm supposed to help you make your dreams come true.'

'What about you?'

'I have my dream.'

'You do?'

'I have you.'

We climb into bed, and it wouldn't matter if it were a park bench: I'm in the arms of my husband, and we're in a place he's dreamed of since he was a boy. There is nothing more satisfying than reading about a place in storybooks and then one day making the leap from those pages and into real life, every detail as vivid as it lived in our imaginations. This trip will be more than a tonic for Jack; it will be a new start, and boy, does he deserve one.

Rosalind Stoneman had told us the most scenic way to get from Glasgow to Aberdeen was by train. She explained that she and her husband would be able to meet us at the station before showing us their house and departing themselves. They'll be stopping in London to visit their children before heading on to the U.S.

Early the next morning, Jack and I climb aboard, hoisting our bags onto the metal shelves overhead.

We sit across from each other with a small table between us. The train is beautifully appointed, with deep brown leather seats, polished wood panels, and a patterned sisal rug on the floor. The windows slide open (just like they do in the movies!). As the train pulls out of the city, we look ahead and see a castle on the hill in the distance, and it's as though we're traveling back in time. Its majestic granite walls seem a border unto themselves. The dormers and peaks jut up into the sky like daggers. The slits in the stone have rows of tiny bars. 'Look, Jack, no windows.'

'Would have been a bad idea to let the enemy see in.'

As we head out to the countryside, we sweep past farms, nestled in the rolling hills like jewels. A flock of sheep gathers by a stream flowing down into a gulley and beyond. Their white coats stand out against the soft palette of spring.

Winter is slowly making its exit, and the fields are sprouting pale green, not yet the lush emerald color that Rosalind promised will come. But it's the sky that enchants us. The mountains back home make the sky overhead seem small, doled out in portions where the peaks let light in, but here the sky seems a broad and limitless canvas. It's stippled with swirls of soft peach, and over the hills, we see a hem of ruby red on the horizon, with streaks of lavender against white clouds on the field of bright blue. The explosion of color overhead plays against the taupe tones on the ground, like rubies, opals, and emeralds set in copper.

When the train reaches the North Sea, it runs along the cliffs of the coast, giving us a perfect view of the water. There's a dramatic drop from our perch down to the beach. The shoreline appears ancient, its edges scribbled along the water's edge. The sand itself is rocky, jutted with shards of black stone on brown sand. In the middle distance, the gun-metal-blue sea pitches a fishing boat to and fro on milky waves. The moors are covered in tall brown grass, with hints of beige where the heather will grow soon, and I can't help but think of *Wuthering Heights*.

Jack points. 'Look, seals!'

There, on a series of flat rock formations by the water's edge, two seals are draped, dipping their fins into the water. There aren't many of us in the train car, but we all crowd the windows to watch them. We are startled when the door between the cars flies open, and in comes a concession cart, its shiny aluminum sides a sharp contrast to the muted decor.

The server's name is Iris (so says her name tag). 'Tea?' she asks. Jack and I each ask for a cup, and she gives us several packages of shortbread to eat with it.

'Are you American?' she asks.

'Yes, we are.'

'Scottish descent?'

'Yes, ma'am,' Jack says proudly. 'I am.'

'Where are you going?'

'To Aberdeen.'

'You must go to the Cairngorms. It's what I hope heaven looks like. Oh, the pinewoods. You've never seen anything like it.'

'We won't miss it.'

After she goes, Jack adds the park to the list of things he wants to do. I take the notebook and look at his list. 'We only have six weeks, honey.'

'Don't worry. I'll pack it all in.'

I know Rosalind immediately when the train pulls in to Aberdeen. She waves to us from the platform. She is small and trim, with bright red hair that tumbles out of her scarf in a ponytail. She's around my age, but she has that forever-youthful quality that only theater people possess (Theodore is another example). Her face is quite beautiful, with a small, upturned nose and a wide, warm smile. There's a hint of dusty pink rouge on her cheeks, which makes her blue eyes pop.

'Welcome!' she says, extending her hand. 'Donald stayed home; forgive him. He is a slow packer. We'll be on our way once we show you about the house.'

Jack loads our bags into the back of the van, It's a beat-up old Volkswagen, painted bright orange with white accents. It has a stick shift – I hope Jack can manage it from the driver's seat on the right side of the car. As we wind through Aberdeen, Rosalind chatters, telling us of her favorite restaurants and museums. There is nothing cramped or citylike about this place; it has breathing room. There is definitely plenty of antiquity among the modern. His Majesty's Theatre opened in 1906. It's named after King Edward VII and sits next to a sleek shopping mall; gardens, with the first crocus peeking through the brown dirt, are planted next to parking garages. I know I'm going to love it in this place: I can feel the possibilities as we drive through. From the front passenger seat, I look back at Jack, who is taking it all in.

I explain to Rosalind what she can expect in Cracker's Neck Holler. It's hard to believe, but she's as excited to visit our home as we are hers. 'This is Spencer Drive, and we're at 145. Here we are.' Rosalind makes a quick right turn in to their driveway. 'We've known the neighbors a hundred years; Arthur Kerr is our close friend. He's next door at 147. He's handy when anything goes wrong with the plumbing, and he's an excellent bridge player. If you don't know how to play, I'm sure he'd love to teach you. His wife died a year ago, so he visits a lot. I hope you don't mind company.'

'Not at all,' I tell her. With drop-in visitors, Aberdeen is sounding an awful lot like Big Stone Gap.

The house is situated on a winding street that seems to go on forever. There is no sidewalk, just a walkway lining either side of the white gravel street. The house is adorable. It's stone, with dark green wooden shutters, a front door that has wrought-iron details (including a scooped handle where the doorknob goes), and a gingerbread window filled with rose-colored stained glass straight out of a Hans Christian Andersen story.

The front yard is wide and deep. There are several flower beds carved into the grass, with a rickrack of bricks defining the borders. There are two circular gardens and a long rectangle bed in front of the porch.

'Oh, these are the gardens?' I ask Rosalind.

'These are just wild beds.' Rosalind points to a mess of leaves that look like tangled lumps of green yarn without their blooms. She smiles. 'The sun and rain are all they need. The real garden is out at the back.'

I look at Jack, who winks at me. 'I'll take care of it,' he whispers. Okay, put gardening at the top of the list.

Donald Philip Stoneman greets us at the door, dressed for travel. I went online and ordered a few of his plays to read before meeting him; he's a beautiful writer. The multiscene family dramas feel like a little of Chekhov and a lot of Samuel Beckett. Donald is a modern playwright, but he looks old-school. I laughed when I read the last line of his impressive theatrical bio: *D. P. Stoneman still has all his teeth.*

'Mr Stoneman, I'm a fan of your work,' I tell him sincerely.

'Thank you, dear.' His green eyes crinkle shut when he smiles. He's lanky, with a shock of white hair, a bulbous nose, and a nice grin. He appears to be about ten years older than his wife. He extends his hand. 'It's a pleasure to welcome you to Stone House.'

'That's funny. We call our home "stone house" too.'

'Well, then, it is all fated, isn't it?'

Donald and Rosalind take us on a tour of the house. 'Say hello to Sir Charles Randolph Wright.' Donald points to a black-and-white cat who appears to be about the same age as our Shoo. Sir Charles is absolutely bored at the sight of us.

Rosalind laughs. 'Mr Personality.'

The living is done on one main floor; the second floor is accessible by a ladder, and it's strictly for storage. There is a large, comfortable living room at the front of the house, with a fireplace open on both sides. To the right of the fireplace is a short hallway that leads to two bedrooms. The guest room is simply adorned, with two twin beds and a floor lamp and straight-backed chair between them. The master bedroom is a bit more ornate, with a double bed, a large bureau, and an easy chair for reading in the corner. The one bathroom is off the master bedroom, and it's almost the size of the bedroom. It has a claw-footed tub and a bench. The commode is behind a screen covered in an ivy-print wallpaper.

We make our way back to the living room. On the other side of the fireplace is the kitchen, a well-appointed room with a wooden table set for four in the center.

The loveliest element of the house is a glass conservatory on the back. There is another table and set of chairs here (for all that bridge playing, I suppose). Plants grow lushly in their pots, set neatly against the glass. 'This is our herbarium.' Donald chuckles. 'I encourage you to use the herbs when you cook. They are identified with markers. See?' He shows us the handprinted stakes in the dirt. 'I am partial to rosemary. When you bake chicken, just pull some of these leaves and sauté them in butter, then dress your bird,' he advises. 'Delicious.'

'Donald, hurry along. We'll be late for our train,' Rosalind reminds him.

We follow Donald out the conservatory door to the backyard. It isn't a yard; every inch is marked and planted. There is a small path around the outer edge to walk, but the expanse is pure garden.

'This is the vegetable garden. If I do my job this time of year, the vegetables last all summer, and what we cannot consume, we put up for the winter. Don't be shy; there are plenty of yams, onions, and potatoes down in the basement. If you don't mind, as the weather warms, there are some seeds to plant, and if you'd be so kind, I would like you to get a head start on my lettuce. This is an organic garden.' He points next door. 'Old Arthur has a garden too. If you have any questions, he can help you. We make our own batch of compost, and we alternate-plant to keep the soil rich. He can explain all of that.'

'I'll take good care of it,' Jack promises.

We walk Rosalind and Donald to the front porch and help them put their bags in the taxi. 'Have a wonderful time in Big Stone Gap,' we tell them. We wave until they disappear down the lane. I turn to Jack. 'What do you think?'

'I'm going to build a fire.'

I put my arms around him. 'I think I love it.'

There is nothing like a new setting to revive an old marriage. Jack and I get up early every morning and take long walks, strolls, really, where we stop and look at architecture and gardens as though the city of Aberdeen were a feast prepared just for the two of us. We talk about everything. Jack is much more loquacious than he is at home, what with work and general exhaustion. It's not that we ignore each other there, but we're so familiar with each other's rhythms. This is the perfect spot to reinvent how we treat each other. It's reconnecting us. We sample the local cuisine: Jack falls in love with haggis (not me), and I fall in love with proper tea at four in the afternoon.

There is a familiar rap on the front door. 'Come on in, Arthur!' I call out.

Arthur Kerr is a handsome eighty-year-old who moves as though he's fifty. His girlfriend, Edith Emerald Turner, is a Scottish beauty of sixty who runs the local painting club where they met. Arthur has already become a regular visitor here.

310

'Where's Jack?' he asks me.

'He's at the university library. He thinks he's close to finding his family's roots.'

'Everyone in America is Scottish, eh?'

'Lots.'

'I've always wanted to be Italian.'

'Why?'

'It's warm there, and the food is good.'

'Two excellent reasons.'

'And there's a third: the women. I don't have to tell you about them.'

'Arthur, are you flirting with me?'

'At my age? I hope so.'

'I accept your kind aspersions,' I say. I pour the hot water from the kettle into the teapot. I arrange some delicate butter cookies from the local bakery on a small plate, and on another, four small sandwiches made with fontina cheese, cucumber, and white bread. I put these on a tray with our plates, cups, and two linen napkins. 'Come on, Arthur, let's go to the conservatory.' Arthur pulls out my chair at the table. I sit. He sits across from me.

'Jack and I took a ride up the coast to the fishing villages. We stopped at Cullen.'

'Delightful.'

'I love the colors of the houses on the sea – pumpkin and turquoise and bright lilac. Why do they paint them such vivid colors?'

'To be seen. It's a style called paintworks. The paint is treated with different elements to make it stronger; it actually coats the house against the weather. Some folks put finely ground sand in their paint, while others texture it with a resin that makes it so thick you almost have to wallpaper it on. It's quite ingenious, really, and practical.'

'It's so quiet on the coast. It's undiscovered, isn't it?'

'It never gets too warm up there, so the thundering herds stay away. Aberdeen is a busy place because of the university – it always has been. Of course, the university is five hundred years old. Everyone knows someone who attended sometime in their family history. Have you visited the grounds?'

'No, but Jack keeps telling me I have to go.'

'You must.'

'I got an e-mail from Rosalind. They're having a wonderful time. Last week they went to a Baptist tent revival. I couldn't believe it.'

'They are good travelers. They do a lot of it. She danced with a folk troupe in Russia when they visited Saint Petersburg. Old Roz will try anything.'

'How long have they been married?'

'Thirty-five years.'

'Wow.'

'All their lives, really. It hasn't always been easy for them.'

'The theater life is tough – and I've only been involved on the amateur level.'

'Their professional lives have gone quite nicely. It's the home life that's been difficult – or, I should say, was difficult.'

'What happened?'

'They had a daughter, Elspeth. She died when she was at university in London,' he says sadly.

'No.'

'She was eighteen years old. It was a car accident. I wish you would have known Donald before it happened. His hair was the color of coal, and his spine was as straight as a plank. The loss aged him considerably.'

'I know all about it.'

'Rosalind told you?'

'No, but Jack and I lost a son. Our Joe was just a little boy.'

'Awful.'

'What can you do, Arthur? Nothing at all. You have to let life play out the way it's going to, and hope that those you love are somehow spared the painful parts.' I pour myself another cup of tea. 'What's *your* sadness?'

Arthur sits back in his chair, his spine straightening as though he's been insulted. 'What do you mean?'

'Terribly American of me, isn't it? To just blurt it out.'

'It's a bit off-putting.'

'Yeah, well, that's a Yankee for you. Though we're not called Yankees where we're from. Yankees are ferriners from the north. Because I'm Italian, I'm considered a ferriner.'

'Who married a local.'

'Right.'

Arthur takes a deep breath. 'I'd rather not answer your question, Ave Maria.'

'That's a blunt answer to my blunt question.'

He smiles. 'Right.'

Jack holds my hand as he leads me into the main quad of the University of Aberdeen, where he's arranged for us to have a private tour of the grounds and building. The interior court is the site of the Crown Tower, which is an actual sculpted crown of sandstone, suspended in the air by six ribbons of white stone. The edges of the stone are mottled from the weather but otherwise sturdy. Sunlight pours through the open vaulting, throwing shadows onto the courtyard.

Jack tells me, 'This was built in 1500. It was preserved during a squabble with the barons of the Mearns, who came at night and stole the bell. The principal armed the student body with weapons to protect the crown, which is why it's still here. I'll show you the library where I've been doing my research.'

Jack leads me into the library – modern by local standards, it was built around 1700. The oak panels and some of the tables and chairs are original. In every corner, students work on their laptop computers. It's a crazy sight to see: antiquity and modernity moving in harmony.

'Hello, Jack.' A beautiful blond woman in her twenties greets Jack. Her blue eyes and champagne-colored hair crackle against the dark paneled walls.

It's as if someone opened a window and a yellow butterfly flew in.

'Paige, this is my wife, Ave Maria.'

She extends her hand. 'I'm Paige Toon. I'm in charge of genealogy research here.'

'So you've been helping my husband.'

'I am giving it a try.' She smiles. 'Ave Maria. What an interesting name. Did you know the University of Aberdeen was originally called Saint Mary's College?'

'I didn't know that. With my name, I fit right in.'

'Brilliant!' she says. 'Follow me.'

I let her take the lead and whisper to Jack, 'Now I see why you spend so much time at the library.'

'With all the reading, I need to rest my eyes once in a while,' he says, and gives me a teasing wink and a quick kiss.

Paige leads us into a research room and closes the door. 'I thought it would be fun to tell you what we've found in our hall of records.'

'Let me guess. Jack descends from a clan of thugs and deviants.'

'Close. They were educators.'

'Really?'

'Are you surprised?' Paige asks.

'Jack's family were all laborers in the States,' I explain, then turn to him. 'Were there any teachers in your family?'

'Not that I know of,' he says.

'Here's the MacChesney tartan.' Paige shows us

a picture of a swatch in the book. It's a red and yellow plaid with a black repeat weave.

'But it says McGuiness.'

'Somewhere between here and there, McGuiness became MacChesney.'

'Does that happen a lot?'

'More than you know. I often think your processors at Ellis Island must have been hard of hearing. It's not a common name – and as far as I can tell, your people did not emigrate from Ireland. We found McGuinesses in Surrey, which is fairly close to London. That also happens. You have to be hardy and persistent to stay in the north. The summers are cool, and the winters are frigid.'

I say, 'So that's why people are so obsessed with their gardens. Signs of spring and life and color. You need them after a long winter.'

'Right. I rather like the winters, though – I love to build fires and ski. It all depends upon your point of view, I suppose.'

We follow Paige to Mitchell Hall, where graduation is held. It was built in 1895. 'This is a baby building,' she says.

I laugh. 'In America, this would be ancient.'

Paige takes us on a tour of the meeting hall, where Queen Elizabeth herself delivered an address to the Scottish Parliament. I take a picture of Jack at the podium where she spoke. Paige shows us the Cruickshank Botanic Garden, which make the Stonemans' conservatory look like a countertop terrarium. 'This garden was founded with pure organic ideals in mind. Since we live on an island, essentially – the UK, that is – we have a sense of the preciousness of every bit of land. It's different from having limitless space, like you do in the States. We have to respect every leaf on every tree. There's only so much to go round.'

'We have some organic farming in the United States,' I say.

'It's all we have here,' she says.

Students mill about between classes, looking very much of their moment, but there is a hushed reverence here that can only come from five hundred years of scholarship.

A few days later, Arthur and Jack are shoring up the irrigation ditches in the garden. Arthur shows Jack how to make the pits in the earth with a long, thin metal pipe. I watch through the conservatory as Jack perfects the technique, with Arthur supervising. My husband is down on his knees, and when he has to attack another patch of ground, he springs up to standing. He looks as young as he did in high school, and I'm not exaggerating. This trip has added years to his life.

It's only now that I can see the rut we were in back home. We had stopped dreaming, Jack and I, and begun settling into the terrible place called 'for all sakes and purposes: practically old.' Arthur is eighty, and yet he stays mentally agile by playing cards and reading; he paints to soothe his soul, and he works the garden to give himself a sense that he is responsible for his own survival.

'Gentlemen, dinner is served,' I announce from the garden gate.

'We'll be right there, honey.'

Jack hasn't had a man to look up to, to learn from, since his father died so many years ago. He revels in his friendship with Arthur. They do things together each day. Jack even went to the art institute to watercolor with him. I don't know what they talk about, but I've never seen Jack so chatty. It's as if he's found his oracle.

For supper, I made roasted chicken with rosemary butter, per Donald Stoneman's instructions. I slow-roasted root vegetables, plentiful in the basement bin, with olive oil in the fireplace oven. It took me a few tries to get the hang of it – I burned plenty of yams and red beets – but now I'm a pro, making certain to heat the oven with a roaring flame for a good bit before I put in the iron skillet. All the things I've learned from living in this wonderful old house will be forgotten once I return home, but it's been great fun to experience them and live as the Scots do.

I've learned about my husband, living here for the past month. I see a lot of his behavior in his fellow Scots. They have great enthusiasm when it's called for, but most of the time, they are introspective. They are also, like the mountain folk back home, extremely wary of outsiders. This probably is a result of generations of war, in which they were called upon to constantly defend their homes against mighty oppressors looking to control the mysterious sea that lies east and north.

You always feel the water around you here. So much of travel and movement is predicated on the fog and rain, which roll in abundantly during the spring. Jack has yet to water the garden – he doesn't have to, since the morning rains give it a good dose. He has also learned to work the garden at the end of the day, at Arthur's suggestion. 'The earth is more open to manipulation then,' Arthur told us. 'The earth is like us; it needs sun and water and, most importantly, rest. We have to nourish it.'

With the beauty we live in back home, you'd think I would really appreciate the land and all it has to offer. I thought I did – but it took coming to Scotland for me to realize that we really borrow the space we inhabit on earth. Arthur and the Stonemans never use chemicals in their gardens, and they have every gizmo known to man to keep the crows out. Some they make themselves – my favorite is the 'tree of small mirrors.' It looks like a funky Christmas tree at the far end of the garden. It seems to be effective.

It's a way of life worth pursuing. I haven't bought a potato or a beet or a carrot since we arrived five weeks ago, and we've barely made a dent on the supply of vegetables in the basement. It's amazing how well a family can live on one garden.

★　　★　　★

I've left most of the planning of day trips to Jack, who has become an expert on where to go and how to get there. We try to go most places by train, because it gives us time to savor the landscape. One of the great surprises of this trip is the reminder of how much I love spending time with my husband. He's a lot of fun, and I forget that when we're back home living a real life without shortbread, castles, and whiskey.

'Today we're going to Edinburgh,' Jack announces on the train platform.

'Great.'

'We'll train it, have lunch, you can stop at that pottery shop—'

'Emma Bridgewater!'

'Right, and then we'll tour the castle.'

'Jack, how many castles have we been in?'

'Are you counting?' Jack puts his arms around me.

'I think it's a hundred in four weeks.'

'You're exaggerating. It's ninety-nine. I can't help it. I love them. I can't get enough of the stonework and the moats, and hearing stories of the knights and their crusades.'

A train pulls into the station, braking slowly, wheezing and whistling until it comes to a full stop. I move to climb aboard.

'Not yet.' Jack pulls me back and holds my hand.

I watch as some passengers disembark. As they chat on cell phones, I imagine a time when there weren't phones of any sort and the only way to send a message was to get on a train and deliver it yourself, in person.

'Mom!'

No matter where I am in the world, whenever I hear someone yell 'Mom,' I always think it's for me. I look off into the middle distance across the rows of train tracks and think about my children, which always fills me with a sense of purpose. I feel a small place in history when I picture them.

'Mom!'

I look up and see Etta waving to me from a window with both arms. I think it's a dream until Jack scoops me up by the waist and leads me to the place where Etta and Stefano step off the train. They're really here! My heart is racing, I can't believe it.

I wanted to make this trip about Jack, and I've only recently, when we're lying in bed, asked if we could sneak down to Italy to see our daughter when we're done here in Scotland. Jack made it seem as though we should get home; after all, we've been away for six weeks. 'Let's go to Italy another time,' he said diplomatically. Now I realize he was setting me up for this wonderful surprise.

I take Etta in my arms. No matter how old my daughter becomes, she's still my little girl with the map of the world on the wall of her bedroom in Cracker's Neck. I hold her closely, giving her a hundred kisses. As I embrace her, she feels different to me. 'Etta?'

Etta smiles and unbuttons her coat. There is no

mistaking the change. 'Ma, we're going to have a baby.'

Jack whoops and does a full spin, like Joel McCrea in *Song of Missouri*. I pull my daughter close, tears forming in my eyes. 'Congratulations, honey.' Jack takes Etta in his arms as I embrace Stefano. I look at my husband. I will never forget the look on his face when his highest dream came true. He's going to be a grandfather.

'How far along are you?' I ask.

'Four months. I had an inkling when we called at Christmas, but I didn't want to say anything until I was sure. It was so hard to talk on the phone without telling you.'

'How are you feeling?'

'Good in the afternoon. The mornings are rough.'

'They were for me too. Keep a box of crackers on your nightstand and eat one before you get out of bed.'

'I will, Mama.' Etta's smile is so real, and so dear, I begin to cry. I imagined this moment far into the future, maybe ten years from now. I could not be happier. I will commence worrying later, when the news has had time to settle. I put my arm around her as we walk. I turn and look back at Jack. 'Are we going to Edinburgh?'

'Not today, honey. That was a ruse to get you here.'

The length of Etta's and my footsteps is the same, just as mine was with my mother's. A parent waits to see the moment when her child is truly happy, and I'm watching the moment unfold as Etta chatters about her doctor and her plans for the birth of the baby.

Outside the train station, Etta stops and looks around Aberdeen. There was a misty rain this morning that turned the light gray granite to black. The buildings of the city look like dominoes in the overcast light. 'Ma, did you think of Jane Eyre all the way up on the train?'

'And Cathy in *Wuthering Heights*.'

'And the Bennet sisters! I could see Elizabeth Bennet walking the fields outside of London. Are you and Dad having fun? Don't answer that. You look fantastic.'

'Thanks, honey.'

'No, really, you and Dad look young. Younger.'

'We'll take it.'

'I love to see you happy, Ma.'

How funny it is to hear that when, since the day Etta was born, all I have prayed for is *her* happiness. I realize now that a happy mother may very well make a joyful child. I remember how much I wanted my mother to smile, to live, to enjoy life. But there was always some obstacle, something that prevented her from having an ease about living. It had a lot to do with the circumstances of her life, but what I didn't realize then was how little control she had over her own fate. I used to look at my mother and think she was so beautiful that she shouldn't ever be sad. Now

I know that her external beauty was a happy accident, and her destiny, a road of hardship and
pain, had one bright spot: me. If only Etta knew
how much I want her dreams to come true, but
there is no way to say it that she would ever
believe. I have a feeling she will find out the
moment she holds her own baby in her arms.
She'll know it then.

Jack waited until Etta and Stefano arrived to make
the trip to the MacChesney family home in
Pennan. As we all wait in the car, Jack comes out
of the Stoneman house with a pillow and blanket.

'Ma, you have to talk to Dad. He won't stop
fussing.'

'Get used to it. That's how he was when I was
pregnant.'

Jack gets into the car and turns to give Stefano
the pillow and blankets. The Stonemans'
Volkswagen is not very big to begin with, and with
the additional pillow and blanket, we are officially
cramped.

'Dad, are we really going to meet your relatives?'

'Paige from the university called them, and they
said they would be happy to have us for tea.'

'It's just so weird. I mean, nobody in all our
years in Cracker's Neck Holler ever knocked on
the door to say, "Hey, y'all, we're cousins!"'

'That might be true. Evidently, over here, it's a
different story. Happens to folks all the time,' Jack
promises.

'Just remember, you're not a MacChesney, you're a McGuiness,' I remind Etta.

As we weave through the cliffs and coves of the Highlands, with a sea of the palest green on one side and the emerald hills on the other, I feel at home. We've been here long enough now that the narrow, clean country roads seem familiar, and I can feel within the space of a few seconds when it will rain, with drops coming out of seemingly nowhere.

Jack drives confidently amid the cliffs; these roads without guardrails remind us of our own mountains.

'Look!' I point to an open field surrounded by dark green hills. An enormous sheet of gray rain moves on the horizon like a glassy curtain toward the field, while overhead, the sun blazes brightly. In the distance, the black-and-white cows, like checkered marble against the green, move away from the rain. In a few moments, the rain has disappeared entirely, and the valley is bathed in white light. This is the mysticism of Scotland, the play of light and dark against the richest blues and greens.

We see the sign for Pennan and make the turn. The road narrows into town. We pass the harbor where fishing boats are docked, their nets lying flat over the side, drying in the sun. The cottages that line the shore are painted bright white.

'We're looking for Violet Cottage,' says Jack.

'The name sounds like a beautiful woman,' Stefano comments.

Jack pulls up in front of a single-story fisherman's cottage connected on either side to identical cottages. The front door is made of wood, with glass-brick accents. It's quaint and charming, like a doll-house.

Jack helps Etta out of the back of the car, while Stefano opens my door for me. I look to the house, where I see a shock of white hair disappear behind a lace curtain. Moments later, a white-haired woman appears in the doorway. 'McGuiness's from America?' she barks. I take Jack's hand and look at him. He is as white as the old woman's hair. 'She could be your mother's twin,' I whisper.

Mrs Fiona McGuiness is petite and slim, like Jack's mother. But it's the face, round with high cheekbones and bright green eyes like buttons, that makes this cousin a dead ringer for Mrs Mac. Her manner, abrupt and direct, is just like that of Jack's mother.

'Well, get on with it. Come in,' she says.

Jack can hardly speak, so I introduce the family. Thank God Fiona likes Italians; Stefano immediately begins to talk about the construction of the old house. The decoration is spare and plain. A sturdy rocker by the fireplace seems the most used; a sofa covered in a cheery yellow chintz does not. There is a stack of photo albums on the kitchen table: evidently, Paige's call spurred Fiona to dig out some family history to share with us.

'I never knew any Americans,' she says, her eyes narrowing. 'You seem all right.'

'Well, we try,' I joke. She stares at me as though I should try harder.

'Tea?' She pivots and goes into the kitchen. We look at each other, not wanting to whisper but desperate to share what we're thinking. I have a feeling this visit will be short and sweet.

Fiona waves from the kitchen. 'Well, come in, will you?'

We enter the kitchen, and she motions for Etta, Jack, and Stefano to sit on a long bench behind the table. They file in like students on the first day of school. I take a seat on the stool at the end of the table, leaving a wooden chair with arms and a needlepoint seat for the Mistress of the House.

'Miss Toon said your name changed between Pennan and America,' Fiona says.

'Yes, ma'am, it did,' Jack says quietly.

'Speak up, will you?' she barks.

'Yes, ma'am,' he says loudly.

'MacChesney sounds soft – now, McGuiness, that's a name!' She smiles for the first time.

I leap in, trying to bridge the awkwardness. 'Paige tells us that we're related through your great-grandmother on your mother's side. She had two sons: one came to America, and my father-in-law was his only son.'

'So I understand,' she says flatly.

'My husband and I are a little taken aback . . .'

Fiona looks at Jack, wondering why he isn't speaking for himself.

'You look like my mother.' Jack's voice breaks.

Fiona knits her brow. 'Where is she?'

'She passed away twenty years ago,' Jack explains. 'Now, I know that we are related on my father's side, so it would be impossible for you and my mother to be relatives, but the resemblance is really something.'

'Was your mother Scottish?'

'As far as we know, ma'am.'

Fiona seems annoyed. 'And what was her family name?'

'Cleary,' Jack answers.

Fiona throws her hands in the air. 'I have Clearys on my mother's side! Mind you, it's a common name, so perhaps she and I are not related at all. But we could be!' She raps her hand on the table.

'Are you alone here?' Etta asks.

'I never married. This is my father's house. My sisters live in Shropshire and Glasgow, far enough apart to avoid too much contact. When we do meet, it's here, so they might count the teaspoons they didn't get when my dear mother died.'

Fiona gets up and pours boiling water into the bone-china teapot covered in deep purple pansies. She floats an old-fashioned tea-leaf cup in the water. A delicious-smelling mist rises from the pot. The cups and saucers are mismatched but adorable. The spoons (evidently a huge hunk of the family treasure) are silver and buffed to a high polish. She adds small, square, pressed linen napkins to the tray, then lifts it to the table and smacks my hand when I try to help. Everything in the cottage is old but beautifully cared for and full of charm. 'The teacakes are in the window.' She points. I get up and find the oblong china plate filled with dainty cookies and shortbread slices. She takes a pot of jam and a bowl of butter from the counter and places it on the table.

I take a bite of shortbread; it almost dissolves in my mouth. 'Did you make the shortbread, Fiona?'

'Yes.'

'May I have the recipe?'

'No,' she says definitively. 'I don't share recipes. It's a bore.'

Etta and I look at each other and try not to laugh.

'What was the McGuiness family trade?' Jack asks politely.

'The men worked in the granite quarry. My father was in charge of the explosives. Very dangerous work – many nights my mother cried, afraid he wouldn't come home.'

'Just like my mother when my pa worked hoot owl.'

'The night shift,' I explain.

'There was a time when men worked in the quarries around the clock. There was so much building going on that the quarries could not keep up with the demand. Every home in the northeast of Scotland was either built with granite or had elements of granite used in the design, and most of the schools and public buildings were built with it. The miners couldn't work fast enough.' Fiona shakes her head. 'And that kind of production comes at a cost.'

'Coal mining is dangerous too,' I tell her.

'Of course it is. It's treacherous work. My father was injured several times, though never enough to count him out entirely. Since we were all girls, we never worked in the quarry, but we would visit him there and swim in the loch made from the pitting. As frightening as the actual work seemed to us, when described by my father, there was also something brave and daring about it. We rather liked the stories of daring.'

'Did you ever want to go to America?' Stefano asks.

'I would have liked to. But I am too old now. I'm seventy-eight, and it's time to act like it.'

'So you've done some traveling?' Etta asks.

'Greece and Spain. I loved both trips very much. Whenever a Scot decides to leave these hills, he ventures toward the sun.'

'Makes sense, with all the rain you get.'

Fiona smiles. 'Isn't it dreadful sometimes?' She finally seems to be warming up to us.

'But it makes everything so lush,' Etta says.

'Yes, indeed.' Fiona looks at Etta. 'You're having a baby?'

'Yes, how did you know?'

'I would never ask a woman that question if I wasn't sure.'

'How can you tell? I thought I was showing only if you knew me.'

'It's an old technique. It's a look in the eyes.'

'Wow.' Etta is impressed.

'You're having a son.'

'I am?'

'A boy.'

'How do you know that?'

'From the way he' – she points to Stefano – 'looks at you.'

I find myself speaking without really knowing why. 'We had a son, and he died when he was just a boy.' Somehow, I guess I am in the presence of a mystic, and whenever I feel that someone has insight into the next world and the mysteries of this one, I am compelled to talk about our son.

'Children who die always come back.'

'How do you know?'

Fiona smiles. 'Look at your daughter.'

'But that's . . . that's . . . *her* baby.'

'If you say so.' Fiona pours cream into her cup and stirs.

Jack and I lie in bed, unable to sleep. Our visit with Fiona McGuiness was not what we had been expecting. I guess we thought she'd be a sweet old lady with a thick accent and some lovely old tales of the North Sea. Instead, we found a prickly pear of a woman with a streak of impatience that put the fear of God in us.

The ride home from Pennan to Aberdeen was a

331

quiet one. I think we were all stunned by the things she said, but more than that, by her direct manner. Fiona seemed to be of another time, with spiritual skills that I have never come across before in anyone else. The Ancient Art of Chinese Face-Reading, which has been one of my most stead-fast belief systems, pales in comparison to the definitive nature of the way Fiona reads people. She can be abrasive, but as they say around here, she's spot-on.

'Have you got my reading glasses?' Jack asks, picking up another Ian Rankin novel from the nightstand.

'They're in my purse.' I get up from the bed and go to the dresser. I pull Jack's glasses out of a side pocket. When I do, a piece of paper slips out and falls to the floor. I pick it up and smile.

'What's that?'

'Fiona's shortbread recipe.'

FIONA McGUINESS'S SHORTBREAD

For your use only: memorize and destroy
Makes 14 biscuits

¾ *cup flour*
¼ *cup rice flour*
½ *teaspoon salt*
¼ *cup super-fine sugar*
½ *cup butter*

In a bowl, mix flour, rice flour, salt, and sugar, then add butter and stir until the dough holds together. Form the dough into a ball and knead well on a floured flat surface. With a rolling pin, roll out the kneaded dough, then cut into round shapes with a cutter. For decoration, make slight indents around the edge of each biscuit using your thumb. Place on baking trays and bake at 350 degrees for 40 minutes or until slightly golden at the edges.

'You're kidding. She gave it to you?'

I give Jack his glasses and climb back into bed. 'She must've liked you.'

'I wouldn't go that far.'

There's a knock on the bedroom door. Etta peeks in. 'May I come in?'

'Sure, sure.' I sit up in bed and make a space near my feet for Etta to lie down. Jack sits up and gives Etta a pillow to rest on.

'That was some trip. Daddy, you come from interesting people.'

Jack smiles. 'I do indeed.'

'I can't believe it's a boy,' Etta says. 'Stefano didn't want to know the sex of the baby.'

'She could be wrong,' Jack says.

'I doubt it. I don't think she's wrong about anything. She's like a Scottish weathervane, picking up vibes and spitting them back out at you like they're real. I think she's totally authentic. Stefano thought she was a nut.'

'She's a mystic,' I tell her.

'Does she really look like Grandma Mac?'

'Exactly,' Jack promises her. 'She was like my mother alive again.'

'Are you okay?' I take Jack's hand. After all, we'd had a such a gentle visit in old Scotland until we came across Fiona. She was like one of those cold winds that cuts across the North Sea and stings you.

Jack shrugs. 'I don't know what to make of her.'

'Well, I'm glad I'm having a boy,' Etta says.

'Why?'

'I want my brother back.' Etta leans back on the bed, resting her head on a pillow. 'I didn't have enough time with Joe. Sometimes I forget things about him, and I don't want to. I guess I'm scared.'

'What are you scared of?'

'I don't know.' Etta turns and faces me. 'After what happened to Joe, I don't take anything for granted.'

'Dear God,' I say aloud.

'What?' Jack looks worried.

'Etta is five months pregnant, and the worry wheel that God puts in all mothers has already started to turn.'

'You just need to have about ten kids, Etta,' Jack says. 'Then you'll find your worry divides down to nothing.'

I kick my husband under the covers. Jack doesn't

get it – he thinks that taking care of babies is simple and raising children is easy. He never minded a moment of the drudgery of parenthood. He loved to bathe the babies, feed them, get down on the floor and wrestle with them. When they were small, I was in a constant state of exhaustion, while he seemed to be in a state of bliss. He felt enhanced around his children, not dragged down by the responsibility. And oh, how daring he was with them. Etta could climb a tree so young; at five years old, she'd go way high in the pear tree in the back woods. Jack taught her how to shimmy down the trunk if she felt herself falling. Joe was smaller, but Jack would let him loose in the field to roll in the mud and meet the bugs and caterpillars face-to-face. I wanted the children on blankets when they were on the grass, but Jack thought they should be exposed to nature, to 'texture,' he called it. It made me nuts. And here he is, planning nine children beyond the one Etta is carrying. 'Increase, multiply, and stay at it' should be his motto.

'Jack, don't push your mountain agenda, please,' I say. 'Our daughter is a little more worldly than we were. And she's going to finish her degree.'

'You'll never take Cracker's Neck out of Daddy.'

'You got that right,' Jack says proudly.

'Don't listen to your father. I didn't want to tell you this, but he's nuts.'

'Who do you think drove me to the edge?' Jack nudges me.

I climb out of the bed and go to my suitcase in

the closet. I pull out a small package I brought to give Etta when I was hoping we'd tack a quick trip to Italy on the end of our Scottish sojourn. It contains some things I saved for her. I thought I would give them to her later, but with the way our year has gone, I take nothing and no one for granted. Time used to be my friend, and now it's a skittish acquaintance at best. I want Etta to know what she means to me *now*, instead of waiting until I die; I want to see her enjoy the things that have meant something to me. 'These are my mother's pearls.' I pull the delicate strand of tiny pink pearls out of the box.

'I can't take these. You still wear them.'

'You dad has given me lots of pretty things. These pearls are one of the few things my mother had that she treasured. She wore them every day, even when she did her chores. She said that the worst thing for pearls was to leave them in a drawer. That's why they're so lustrous. They never spent any time in hiding. So wear them every day, like she did.'

'I will.'

I put the strand of pearls around Etta's neck, remembering how many times I helped her with a button, a zipper, or a clasp – maybe a thousand times, maybe a million, and how I wish I had those same opportunities all over again. How I miss taking care of her!

'This next thing is something you played with when you were little, and I always had to take it away and put it on a shelf because you would leave parts of it all over the house.' I give Etta my mother's sewing kit, a mottled tin box filled with bobbins of bright thread, shiny gold needles, a silver thimble shaped like a hat, and a small pair of gold trimming scissors with the rosebud design on the handles worn away from use. There's also a pincushion made of red felt, in the shape of a tomato, with green felt leaves as an accent. There are a few jeweled buttons and a wire threader.

'Finally, it's mine!' Etta holds the tin box close. 'Ma, I've wanted this sewing box all of my life!'

'I knew the day would come when you'd be old enough to take care of it.'

'Thank you.' Etta kisses me on the cheek.

'And there's one more thing.' I give my daughter a first-edition copy of *The Trail of the Lonesome Pine*. The jacket is a painting of young June Tolliver leaning against the trunk of a tree, looking up into the branches. Her expression is winsome and wistful, like that of any mountain girl hoping for love. The forest surrounding her reminds me of our woods in Cracker's Neck Holler.

'Whenever I get homesick, I'll take this book out and look at it,' Etta says.

'Someday you'll pass it down to your children.'

Jack lets out a yahoo. 'You said children. See, you're coming around to my way of thinking already. There's joy in numbers!'

It's our last night in Aberdeen, and we're going out with a bang. Arthur has made roasted duck, and Jack whipped up a pesto-and-asparagus pasta that fills the Stoneman house with a buttery scent, the perfect send-off after a glorious stay.

Arthur sets the roasting pan on the stove. Stefano, Etta, and Jack are outside, giving a final tweak and nightly watering to the garden. The Stonemans will return to the first leaves of lettuce pushing up through the black earth. With Arthur's help, Jack has done a great job maintaining their garden. I hope they will be pleased.

The traditional Celtic gardens in the front yard burst forth during the last week of our stay, just as Rosalind predicted. A crazy mix of blue jonquils, sweet-scented narcissi and fragrant snowdrops nestle among the odd eager bluebells pushing their faces to the sun. Lemon-yellow daffodils, with their reedy stems, and a clutter of hot-pink cabbage roses rest against a backdrop of crimson and mauve rhododendrons. The effect is an explosion of color that looks like a mop of curling ribbon. I can't wait to plant my own garden back in Cracker's Neck Holler. What was I thinking, leaving the front lawn plain, with a green carpet of Zoysia grass? Just looking out at the mix of colors lifts my spirits.

'I'm going to miss you, Ave Maria,' Arthur says quietly. He looks older to me now, sitting alone at the end of the kitchen table. He becomes robust whenever he goes out back to help Jack in the garden.

I give him a hug. 'I'll miss you too, Arthur.'

'You asked me something when you first arrived,

and I thought you were a little bold – bordering on rude, really.'

'What did I say?'

'You asked me what my pain was.'

'I did? I'm very sorry. You know, when I got here, I didn't take time to understand the way you folks process your feelings – I barged right in with my own brand of on-the-sleeve emotions. It wasn't right. I hope you forgive me.'

'I don't want to forgive you.'

'Excuse me?'

'No, I want to tell you.'

'You do?'

Arthur pulls out the chair next to him, so I sit. I look out through the solarium and see Etta and Stefano at the far end of the garden. Jack is busy tying up some vines.

'I was married once,' he begins.

'You were?'

'There were four sisters in Aberdeen, the McGrath girls. There were Imogen, Esme, Eleanor, and Amelia. I was in love with Esme. She was a robust redhead with enormous brown eyes, not unlike yours. She had a spirit about her. She wasn't considered the prettiest or the smartest, but she had the best sense of humor.'

'That's the talent of middle children.'

'Quite right. I was besotted with her. I was drafted into the British navy, as were all my contemporaries straight out of university – we were required to give up our studies and enlist. Esme was bereft, and on an impulse, we married the night before I was to ship out to the Pacific theater, where we were joining the Americans. Esme was to go to the country with her sisters to wait out the war.

'I sent dozens of letters to the country, but they were all returned. I assumed that it was impossible to have my letters delivered because it was wartime, and I didn't think much of it.

'Eventually, I heard from Esme in a letter with an English postmark. She hadn't been able to stand staying home and waiting; she'd wanted to do something, so she enlisted as an army nurse. She was sent to London, where she worked in a hospital.

'Our correspondence began in earnest then. She wrote marvelous letters to me, full of stories she heard in the hospital, and all of them spilling forth with such enthusiasm for the cause. In one letter, she named our children: a girl would be Lily, and a son, Arthur. That one was the last letter I received from her.'

'Oh, no . . .'

'I had been shipped out on leave, planning to surprise her in London. The night before my arrival, her hospital was hit in an air raid while Esme was on duty. She died instantly, along with most of the doctors, nurses, and patients.'

'I'm so sorry,' I say. What a terribly sad story!

'I tell you this long story not so you'll pity me but to answer your original question. Believe it or not, I had to think about what my pain was. You see, I feel I'm a lucky man. I survived the war,

340

and I live in a comfortable home, and I had a wonderful career, so I didn't think about Esme in terms of my own suffering. I always thought of all *she* missed by dying so young.'

'That's very Scottish.'

'It is, isn't it?'

'Did you ever fall in love again?'

'Several times, thank you.'

I smile. 'Good for you.'

'But I never married again. I never longed for children either. You see, any children I would have had would have been Esme's. After all, I felt I already knew them: Lily and Arthur. She saw them in her mind's eye – in her heart, I suppose – and that made them very real to me. So I never had a desire to create a family beyond them. Does that make sense?'

'Absolutely.'

Jack, Etta, and Stefano come into the house. 'Muddy shoes off, please!' I tell them. 'Wash up. Arthur made duck.'

ARTHUR KERR'S ROAST DUCK

Makes enough for ten people

2 pounds bacon
2-pound duck
Honey

Spread strips of bacon over the breast of the duck and tie them in place. Roast for one hour at 400 degrees, basting the duck occasionally with the drippings. Remove bacon from duck and raise the heat to 425–500 and cook for another 20–30 minutes until the duck is brown on top. Drizzle honey over the top of the duck five minutes before serving.

'Yum!' Etta says as she lathers up at the sink. Then Jack and Stefano wash their hands.

'Arthur, sit and relax. Jack, do the honors, please.' I hand my husband a carving knife and pull the covers off the hot platters on the table. Stefano pours the wine.

'What a way to spend our last night in Aberdeen!' Jack says.

Sir Charles, the cat who could not have cared less that we were visiting, shows up at the edge of the table. 'It's the duck,' Arthur says.

'He never took to us, this old cat.'

'Sometimes we're just too old to bother to make new friends. I'm almost there.' Arthur smiles. 'You got here under the wire.'

'I'm glad we missed the cutoff.'

'I am too.' Arthur raises his glass. 'To my friends.'

'To you, Arthur!'

'And to Fiona McGuiness!' Etta beams.

'To Fiona!' we practically sing.

As we begin to eat, I think how lucky we are to

be part of a wonderful extended family who shows us how to live. I thought the Italians, with their gusto and warmth, invented fine living. And now I see that in the Scottish Highlands, where the winds off the sea blow bitter cold, that shelter can always be found in the loving hearts of friends.

EPILOGUE

HOME

Though our hearts are breaking a bit to leave Aberdeen, we must get back to our lives in Big Stone Gap. I can coast on the good graces of Eddie Carleton and Fleeta Olinger only so long; it's time to get home and back to work.

We land in late afternoon in Bristol, Tennessee. Fleeta and Otto pick us up at the airport. Life has gone on as usual. Fleeta has racked up six weeks of complaints to share with me. If it's not problems with stoves in the café, it's Eddie Carleton's strict adherence to an open/close schedule or the lousy distributors who stiffed her on a crate of Crisco. It's always something. Fleeta music, we call it: the song of the discontented. And I have to admit I missed it.

Spring has come to our mountains. As we drive home through the hills, the redbuds are full of their pale pink velvet blossoms, purple crocuses are pushing up through the bright green grass, and the dogwoods – my favorite – are loaded with blossoms the color of ballet slippers.

When we take the turn up Cracker's Neck Road,

the yellow daffodils tip their heads to us as we pass. The tulips I planted alongside the porch reach up to the steps with their purple and white blossoms. The peonies and azaleas in the side yard are bursting with magenta blooms. The mountains took their magical spring turn while we were gone.

Fleeta and Otto help us with our bags. Shoo the Cat meets us at the front door. She purrs and rubs up against my legs. I flip on the lights and go back to the kitchen. There's a box of mail from the past week, and a crate of wine on the table with a note of thanks. I can't help laughing: we left the exact same gift on their kitchen table in Aberdeen.

I throw open the windows and let the fresh night air into the old stone house. Jack comes to the sink and puts his arms around me. 'Strange to be home, isn't it?'

'Yeah. But I missed it.'

'Me too.'

We look out to the woods, barren when we left, the oak, the elm, and the birch now bursting with yellow buds that look like beads on branches nestled in green taffeta leaves. Jack takes our bags upstairs. I go into the fridge. There's a note from Iva Lou:

Rolls for breakfast, jam and butter from my aunt's down in Lee County. Call me.
I.L.W.M.

I put on my nightgown. I brush my teeth and wash my face. I missed this old sink and tub. I climb into bed with my husband. He's reading another Ian Rankin novel. I'm afraid he's hooked.

I pick up a magazine and read. After a few moments, he puts down his book and wraps his arms around me.

'Ave?'

'Uh-huh?'

'What are you reading?'

'Father Rausch's opus on mountaintop removal in the *Glenmary Challenge* magazine.'

'How romantic.'

'It's romantic when our mountains are left to their natural grandeur.'

'You're a liberal.'

'Uh-huh.'

'Didn't know you were a liberal.'

'Well, now you do. How long we been married?'

'Almost twenty-one years.'

'Is that a deal breaker?'

'I don't think so.'

'Smart man.'

'Ave, I'm going to quit the coal company.'

'You are? What changed your mind?'

'Arthur.'

'What did he say?'

'He told me that if you get to live long enough, if you make it to eighty, you realize that the only priceless gift you can leave behind is that you did more good than harm to the world you lived in.

That's why he still has a garden; he thinks his corner of the world still matters.'

'And it does.'

'There's a lot I can do with my time. I want to feel good about what I'm doing.'

'Good.' I go back to my magazine, smiling. I'm smug. I finally got through to him.

Jack takes the article out of my hands and throws it off the side of the bed.

'Hey, I was reading.'

'Don't want you reading.'

My husband kisses me. Like a lover, not a husband. I like it. Still. 'Jack?'

'Yeah?'

'I have a question.'

'Sure.'

'Who's Annie?'

Jack is surprised, then he smiles. 'Why do you ask?'

'You wrote her name down when you thought you were dying.'

'I did, huh?'

'Yes, you did. It's on a list you wrote on a scrap of paper in the hospital. It's under your business cards in the sock drawer.'

'It is?'

'Yeah.'

'So you read the list.'

'I apologize. I didn't mean to snoop. It was with your personal effects when they took you into surgery.'

'Okay, you get a pass. But I don't read your mail, nor would I read any lists, or a diary if you kept one.'

'I know, I know. I'm terrible.' I reach back and adjust my pillow before I settle back into Jack's arms for more of that kissing. He rolls on top of me. 'So, who's Annie?'

'That's a real romance killer, to bring up the name of another woman when I'm trying to make love to my wife.'

'Imagine how I feel.'

'I'm trying.'

I take his hands off of my behind. 'Well, who is she?'

'Can't I have a secret?'

'You can have all the secrets you want. Just not that one.'

'I see.'

'This one *is* a deal breaker.' I hold my ground. After all, I've gone this far.

Jack rolls off of me and onto his back. He looks at the ceiling. My heart begins to beat faster and then faster still. I'm losing him again. I ask too many questions. The man was kissing me like the first time, and I ruined it. Is a good marriage about the things we don't say? Why do I have to know everything about everything? Will I ever learn to leave well enough alone, to let the little things go? Who cares about Annie, anyhow? He didn't marry her, he married me. Isn't he allowed to have a girl he thinks about from time to time without compromising our relationship? After all, I never talk about Pete Rutledge. He's my little escape-valve fantasy when I need one; why shouldn't my husband have one too?

'Annie was a great beauty,' he begins.

'I figured.' I feel my heart sinking. I'm kicking myself for not leaving well enough alone.

Jack takes my hand. I'm not sure I want him to. 'You really want to know?'

I nod that I do, but now I'm not so sure. I don't need to approve of this Annie in his fantasy harem. It's enough agitation to run into Karen Bell from time to time. It's like finding a rat in your bathtub – I don't know if it's her intentions for my husband that scare me or her year-round tan, but whatever it is, I get rattled whenever I see her.

'Annie was my golden retriever when I was ten years old. She got sick and had to be put down one weekend when we were visiting family. She was buried down in Pennington at my aunt's farm. I had a stone made for her grave. But it always bothered me that she wasn't buried in Cracker's Neck Holler. So one of the things I always meant to do was move her up here. She used to run in the woods out back and go exploring up in the hills with me for hours. We'd get lost in there, collecting bugs and mushrooms and things. Since I didn't have any brothers or sisters, she was sort of the world to me. I still think about her. May sound funny, but losing her, such a good dog, well, it was like losing a member of my family.'

I don't know what to say, so I don't say anything.

'That was Annie.'

'I'm sorry.' I begin to cry.

'You didn't even know her.' Jack rips a tissue out of the holder on the nightstand and hands it to me. Then he holds me close.

'I'm not crying about Annie.'

'Then what?'

'If we both stay healthy and we get more time – you know, as husband and wife – will we use the time to keep learning things about each other? Or will we use the time just trying to get along and keep the peace?'

'Does it matter? Does it have to be one or the other?'

'I think so.'

'I don't. You just have to live, Ave, and let life unfold. Say what you mean. You can't always think about what you've lost, or what you don't have, or what you didn't get. Because when you do that, you're missing out on the now. I'm here with you tonight, but I can't know if I'll be here tomorrow or a year from now – or if you will be. I don't care how many plans you make, you can't know anything for sure either. We shouldn't let a day go by when we don't stop and think about what we are to each other and how the best part of that is the part that changes. That's the mystery. And that's the part of people that's divine. Accepting the unknown and trusting it.'

'How do you know this?'

Jack smiles. 'Because I almost lost everything. And I thought about what I'd be if you didn't love me.'

'And what were you?'

'I wouldn't have ever known real joy or real sadness. I was angry at you for bringing sadness sometimes, and that's just human. It wasn't your fault, but when things went terribly wrong, I looked around to blame somebody. It didn't mean I loved you less – it meant that we had something to learn together, and if we just hung on, we'd get through it.

'The joy – that's easy. You gave me children, and when I needed it most, you took care of me. No woman ever took care of a man the way you've taken care of me – except maybe the way my mama took care of my pa. I waited so long to get married because I wasn't sure that even existed. And here you are. You did not disappoint.

'Those are the two things you brought to my life, and I had two angels to represent them: Etta was joy, and Joe – Joe was the sadness. And both of them, for as long as we had them here, made me a better man. Not a small thing.'

Sometimes, for a man of very few words, my husband chooses the exact right ones. As he kisses me again, I remember Scotland, how I felt when Etta told us about the baby, and picture my husband as a ten-year-old boy with Annie at his side as he explored the creeks, roads, and back woods of this mountain. As for the bridge, Jack needed to build it, if only to know the deep river that runs through Cracker's Neck Holler. May it never end.